recogniti

Earlyworks Press Fiction

www.earlyworkspress.co.uk

recognition

Copyright Information

Printed in Great Britain by the
MPG Books Group, Bodmin and King's Lynn

ISBN 978-1-906451-22-6

Published by Earlyworks Press
Creative Media Centre,
45 Robertson St, Hastings,
Sussex TN34 1HL

www.earlyworkspress.co.uk

Editor's Note

Judging a good quality writing competition is always a complex affair. The stories in this collection were all shortlisted in the 2009 Earlyworks Press short story competition, and five of them spent a fair amount of time in the number one slot. The shortlist, intended to be 20 stories, spent over a week with 25 stories on it. We got it down to 20, then one was pulled for technical reasons - and then we invited two other irresistible stories back in.

The result is a collection of 21 stories which I feel are winners, each in their own way. To pick out a few – I loved 'Lucky Links'. It's such a complex weaving which manages to shine a light on a number of topical issues without falling back on preaching. 'Miniature Beacons in the Purple Dusk' gets to grips with an extremely difficult narrative form and succeeds triumphantly, painting pictures that do not fade from the mind. 'White Snow Like Santa Marta' invites the reader into its characters' world so effectively that I wanted it to be the first chapter of a novel. 'Recognition' (which gave us our title) is one of several stories which do useful work by discussing mental health issues or psychological predicaments which occur far more commonly than they are understood. Several other stories are simply excellent examples of enjoyable yarn-spinning.

Our final choice to head the anthology, 'The Intercessor', took first place partly because it epitomised a theme that was becoming apparent through the collection - perhaps it is a part of the zeitgeist - the notion that a certain common saying should be turned on its head. Believing is seeing; evidence is one thing but what people make of what they perceive is what counts. recognition – may it come soon to these authors, and may its readers enjoy the book as much as I did.

Kay Green January 2010

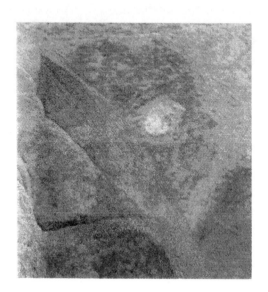

Contents

The Intercessor

by David Frankel

Light entered the room through square windows high in the wall. The thick glass was yellowed by the dirt of ages. The brief warmth of the sun moved around coarse rock walls as another day prepared to pass in silence. Unlooked for, the door of the ossuary opened. Rare currents of air flooded into the room. Air that had once carried the smell of wood fires and decaying rubbish from the streets beyond now brought petrol and fast food to mix with the smell of damp earth and the faded aromas of incense and burnt wax. Drifts of dust caught in the sudden draught disappeared into the oblique shadows beyond the reach of the light from the windows.

The boy who entered left the door standing open behind him, hard white light as brash as the noise of the squealing hinges blasted into the space. As his eyes adjusted he stared about him recalling the scene from his childhood when he had accompanied his mother. The room seemed smaller than he remembered it from the days when he had stood in his best church clothes watching her attend their family's guardian. The boy's mother was one of the last to follow the tradition of her ancestors. Once a year she would make the journey to clean the skull of the family's guardian and place flowers beside it. This year, for the first time, she had been unable to make the trip and the boy had been sent.

Lifetimes ago only the rich of the town could afford to pay churches to pray for their souls. Unable to meet the cost of lying beneath earth warmed by the sun in the church yards above, the town's poor dug the caves to house their dead. When epidemics struck the town the chambers had been expanded and the tunnels filled with the new dead, their bones and skulls stacked neatly in great piles on shelves and in alcoves, peasants and gentlefolk together. As time passed and the poor souls to whom the skulls had belonged were forgotten the townspeople came to revere them as they did the skulls of the saints housed in the churches' reliquaries. Families adopted the skulls and prayed for them to act as intermediaries, polishing them, placing them in boxes and decorating them. It had been tradition that families attended them on religious festivals. They would clean them as they sat and told the skulls of

1

their hopes and fears. Placing their hands on the domed foreheads of the skulls, the families would ask for protection or for a blessing to be bestowed on them by their anonymous saint.

As the decades had passed fewer families had returned to look after the skulls. Photographs or mementos of the skulls' caretakers, themselves long dead, were placed in the boxes with their guardian angels.

Following his mother's instructions, he placed one of her ribbons and a small photograph amongst a clutter of valueless keepsakes that surrounded the skull in its box; pitiful objects left by previous generations of family members, aging reminders of lives that had been swept away before the boy was even born. He tipped long dead flowers from a squat vase that sat before the box. Opening the small bag he had carried with him, he took out a small bottle of water and a bunch of highly perfumed flowers, placed them clumsily into the vase and topped up the water. The small brightly coloured petals contrasted with the contents of similar vases that lined the shelves and ledges, long since decayed to grey stalks.

Looking around the chamber it was possible to see which of the skulls had been watched over by the town's rich, housed in decorated carved wooden caskets with elaborate candle holders, and which had been clung to in desperation by the town's poor, some in simple card boxes, others partly wrapped in paper with the remains of a meagre candle before them. He noticed how the skulls that had the poorest decoration had the more highly polished foreheads where they had been touched and asked for help in a time of desperation. Like the rest of his generation the boy had no time for such beliefs but he had promised his mother that he would perform this task for her. He did not believe in the old superstitions but against all his reason he sheltered an inherited respect for the lesser saint that his superstitious ancestors had adopted. As he carried out his task he began to speak to the skull as his mother had done when he was a child.

'Hello old one. I expect you don't remember me. I have not been to visit you for a long time.' He paused before adding, 'I'm sorry.' He paused as he ran a cloth over the cranium, removing the gathered grime. 'My mother sent me. She is too ill to visit you any more.' The thought of his mother's illness silenced him for a while. More to

2

himself than his supposed companion he added, 'She will need your help more than ever soon.'

A thin sheen of dust washed down the face of a plaster Madonna kneeling in prayer in an alcove, and far away, carried through the dust on a breeze and unperceived by the boy, another voice spoke. 'Why do you drag me back again? Of course I remember you. You are the idiot boy who used to come with his mother and stand fidgeting in the doorway.' Had the boy been able to hear, he would have realised that the voice was not that of a man as he had been told since childhood, but that of an old woman. Nor was the voice that of a benevolent guardian. 'So now she sends you does she, Idiot? Another generation to keep me here long after the others like me have gone. I can remember hearing their voices while I dreamt of my past, but they aren't here any more and even my dreams are fading, but still I am kept here. You pray to me as I prayed to others in my lifetime, and no good came of that I can tell you. At least you aren't here asking for help with the lottery like your useless father. That's something I suppose. I can see fear in you, but it isn't the fear that you had when you came here as a boy and you were terrified of the piles of old bones and the skulls staring back at you.'

He walked around the chamber, occasionally reaching out and touching one of the many cruciforms set on carved stone shelves around the walls or tracing the pooled remains of long extinguished candles in the alcoves. Parallel tool marks on the walls showed the million chisel strokes that had carved out this cave and others like it. The poor labourers that had created the rooms had been amongst the first occupants. Surrounded by the long dead, the silence drew out the feelings that preoccupied him. He began to speak again in order to break the silence and in the gloom of the ossuary even the sound of his own voice was welcome. 'I remember how mother used to tell you news of the town, and things that were troubling her. I wonder if she really believed in you. I guess she believes now because she is afraid. I am afraid for her. I know everyone has to die and it is natural for parents to die before their children, but I am afraid for myself too. Everything will change.' The boy spoke quickly and quietly, believing he spoke only to himself and half embarrassed in case somebody should overhear him. 'You know that after my mother I will be the only member of the family left here. I am in love with someone. Maybe you could give me some man-to-man advice while I am here. I am sure you are a man of great experience.' He paused suddenly as though waiting for a reply, but there was only silence and he laughed to himself. 'She is beautiful and clever but my friends don't like her so much because her parents are rich, well, richer than us anyway, not that that is anything unusual. She wants us to leave, and go to the city. I want to go with her. I can't go now because of Mother's illness, but even after that...' He paused. 'Even after that I don't know if I want to go. My friends are all I will have left. Soon everything will be different. Mother will be gone and I must choose between my friends and my girl. This town is all I have ever known.' He had begun speaking partly in jest but now he found that for the first time his vague anxieties had coalesced into something more concrete. 'I must admit I am a little afraid of the things that are going to happen. I was happy as I was. I expect things were simpler in your day, old one.'

'If I had lips I would spit at you,' hissed the old voice, unheeded. 'The world doesn't give a shit about your problems, Idiot. I died lying in my own filth with no-one to help me. Why should I care to listen to your problems? Don't be so weak. Count your blessings and leave me alone.'

As though he had heard her, the boy continued, 'I suppose the world doesn't care. It's like when you have a great weight on your shoulders and somebody is complaining about their small problem. You want to scream, "Screw you! That's nothing! You think you've got problems!" I think that is how the world sees us. We are tiny next to all the other things that scar its surface and asking it to care will just make it resent you.'

Somewhere in the dust and shadow memories began to stir and the old voice spoke again, 'I used to love and laugh and hate and fight. I can almost remember. It's like waking from a dream and trying to hold onto the feelings as the images fade away. I can just remember. There was a house, a small house and a boy, a little older than you. Mine. He was mine. There was such a lot of noise and movement. Now there is silence and the flicker of light as days go by. Your whining has stirred the memories of memories. I can almost recall what it felt like to touch another human being. To taste and smell. To be kissed. Even to feel the pain of loss. To feel something more than this envy.' The venom in the voice ebbed away. 'The young don't appreciate what it is to be young any more than the

4

living realise what it is to be alive and I hate you for it. Idiot. If only you could realise how weak I am and how bright and strong you are. I can't help you. You must do as you think best and try to do as little harm as possible. But you won't. You will blunder along, breaking things as you go, as everyone does. I am glad I can't be in the world any more. I can sense it on you. It is on your skin and in your breath. It has changed a lot, I can tell, but people never change. Your story is the same as every other idiot boy who has sat in this room.'

The boy looked around the room slowly and back at the box containing the skull of his adopted ancestor. He thought again of his boyhood trips here with his mother and grew sad. Soon, he thought, she would be gone and he must leave and all the remnants of his childhood would be gone. The only tangible sign that his family had ever lived in the town would be this anonymous skull in its box, surrounded by the memorabilia of generations. As this occurred to him, he longed for their guardian to be real. Even in the days of mobile phones and parking tickets something in the core of his being still clung to the superstitious ways of his forebears. 'If you are there, please help my mother if you can.'

'Your mother will get what is coming to her, as we all do, for better or worse.' The unheard voice softened. 'And bothering me won't help.'

The boy stood at the doorway looking out into the light. He knew that his life would be changing; it permeated every feeling he had, but as he glanced back at the room and its contents he knew that change it must. 'I will be leaving town soon. There will be no-one to visit you any more. I am sorry.' All he could do was face whatever happened with courage and humility as his mother would wish. Too soon it would all end and he would join his ancestors. 'It's nice and cool in here,' he said vacantly as he crossed the threshold back into the full glare of the sun, 'too hot outside.'

'Enjoy the warmth while you can, Idiot.' If he had been able to hear the voice he might have perceived affection in its tone. 'Now leave me alone so that I can fade like the rest.'

5

Ossie's Circus

by K S Dearsley

There was something magic about the Big Top. From the outside it was only canvas and rope, but on the inside there was another world where, in a few hours' time, people would forget the drab routine and monotony of the megapolis's sprawl of office and domicile blocks in the colour and wonder of the circus – and the animals. At the moment, however, it contained only Osbert Lucas, ringmaster and owner of Ossie's Circus, putting Esther, billed on the posters that showed her angry and dangerous as the only elephant outside the last remaining patches of wild. The reality bore little resemblance to the image, but few things about the circus did. Man and elephant seemed to be taking part in some elaborate courtship. After so many years their movements were a ritual that made life outside with its cares drop away. Only they existed.

"It's no good hiding in here!" The Amazing Karina, the world's most daring trapeze artist, stormed into the ring, the canvas flapping in her wake. Behind the façade of dye and make-up she was old, but her eyes still snapped fire.

Ossie threw the whip he never used to the ground. "I'm not hiding!" His eyes met hers and dropped guiltily.

"Am I really such a hag?" Her voice was small and hurt.

"Of course not!"

"Yes I am. It's having to do the thinking for both of us. We should've had a family, then we'd have someone to lean on."

"The circus is our family, we don't need anyone else." Ossie busied himself with Esther. The circus was shrinking. There were the Flying Rinaldis, the clown Popps – barely enough acts left to form a queue let alone make a grand entry parade, and as for the animals – Popps's terrier Nipper, the parakeets, Esther and Sultan. Goosebumps came up on Ossie's arms at the thought of the indifference in the tiger's eyes, as if it had judged and dismissed him. All of them were irreplaceable. Ossie slapped the elephant's side. That much about the posters at least was true.

Karina watched him with hands on hips. "And when we're too old? Or when the Protection League finally gets us shut down?"

Ossie made a rude noise. "Protectionists!"

"You can't brush them off so easily. There're more of them all the time. There's even one outside the arena now."

Ossie had seen her; a thin-faced woman who patrolled the entrance with a placard, like a wading bird stalking the shallows, shrieking dire prophecies in a voice to rival the parakeets.

"And what do you do about it?" Karina threw up her hands.

"What do you want me to do?"

Esther started nuzzling Karina's neck. She pushed the questing trunk away. "You and this elephant – maybe you should have married her instead!"

Esther changed tactics and began pushing Karina gently in the back.

"All right! I'm going. I can't fight the pair of you." She turned and they noticed a figure loitering in the shadows of the canvas walls.

He cleared his throat. "Are you the owner?"

Ossie groaned: not another civic official.

"I thought you'd got all the permits," Karina said through a smile that had dazzled audiences around the continent.

"I'm here about your animals." The gangling frame in the ill-fitting suit did not look like someone in authority. Compared with Ossie's dapper figure he resembled an untidy spider.

"Protectionist!" Karina hissed.

Ossie would feed whoever was on ticket-box duty to Sultan. An image of the tiger pacing his cage and spurning the manufactured protein that Ossie was forced to give him instead of meat made his shoulders slump.

The intruder's arms tangled with the ropes and banners in his haste to wave away Karina's accusation. "No, no! I'm a scientist. I want to study the way people react to animals."

Karina and Ossie shared a look.

"My findings could be helpful – show officials that contact with the animal kingdom could be beneficial. Hygiene isn't everything."

"My animals are clean!"

"Findlay Todd." The intruder held out his hand, not even noticing Ossie's outrage. His gaze was fixed on Esther and his smile was one of pure delight. "I won't get in the way."

Ossie had seen that expression before, usually on the faces of children in the audience. The scientist was smitten. Ossie looked at Karina. She rolled her eyes.

"You're the ringmaster, do what you think, as usual, but... " She turned to Findlay Todd. "You'll have to make yourself useful about the place!" The glare Karina turned on Ossie as she left warned him that the same went for him too.

"Roll up! Roll up! See the last performing tiger in the world. Gasp at the agility of the Flying Rinaldis. Get your tickets here. Roll up! Roll up!" Ossie stood on a box waving his top hat to punctuate the well-rehearsed lines.

It was going well. With half an hour before the start of the performance the Big Top was already two thirds full and a long orderly queue stretched from the ticket box. Ossie jumped down and started pushing his way towards the Big Top. A placard waving over someone's head caught his eye: 'Warning: Animals Can Damage Your Health'. Beneath it Ossie recognised the birdlike woman, who had continued to stalk the entrance to the arena as relentlessly as Sultan did his cage. Too late he realised what she was up to. She jumped onto the recently vacated box just as Ossie reached it.

"Friends! Think again! Keeping animals in captivity is wrong. Where is it that disease comes from? How is it spread? I tell you, this is a place of death."

Ossie hesitated. People welcomed any entertainment they could get and many paused to listen.

"Consider friends, before you enter, what caused the black death? Animals. They didn't die, but people did. Yes, thousands! All over the world. Who hasn't heard of the horrors of rabies..."

A few listeners began to murmur. Time for Ossie to intervene.

"Then can you explain, madam, why I'm still here?" He turned to the crowd. "Osbert's Circus has been touring the continent for three generations and, with hand on heart, I can say that we've never lost a performer through the animals – except a former strong man, and he should've known better than to try and lift an elephant." There was a trickle of nervous laughter. "Look at me – a picture of health! We're all pictures of health." Ossie moved towards the Big Top as he spoke, drawing the crowd after him.

The Protectionist continued to rant, but without an audience.

Behind the curtain Ossie found an argument in progress between the Flying Rinaldis and Popps, whose dog had cocked its leg up the acrobats' seesaw. At his entrance the hubbub ceased. The ringmaster glared a warning look.

"Where's the scientist?"

They shrugged. The answer was obvious. Ossie found Findlay Todd standing in front of Sultan's cage watching the tiger restlessly padding to and fro, his stripes like rippling shadows of the bars. The scientist's face was painted in a tragic expression that failed to hide the wonder. The mop-head wig and outgrown clothes of a clown coupled with his lost manner made Ossie want to laugh outright. Todd was a natural.

"What do you think of our star performer?" Ossie asked him.

The scientist's blush glowed under the greasepaint. "Different from the screenings I've seen. Close like this it's, it's... "

"Real?" Ossie's voice was husky with awe and affection.

"Why does he do that? To and fro, to and fro."

Ossie could not meet Todd's innocent expression. "No time to watch him now. You're on soon."

Todd's head drooped. He stared at his hands as if he had been trying to count his fingers and could not make ten.

Ossie slapped his shoulder, shepherding him towards the ring. "Popps and Nipper will look after you."

Todd looked at the terrier, which was scampering about the feet of the performers, adding to the confusion and generally enjoying itself. He smiled weakly. Ossie left him and peeped through the curtains. He swallowed the last-minute panic which still rushed to his throat after so many years, and stepped into the magic circle.

The show got off to a good start. The Flying Rinaldis bounced and somersaulted their way into the audience's hearts, sailing higher with each boost of applause. Each generated and fed the energy of the other. By the time Ossie re-entered the ring he was floating on waves of excitement from the audience. The animals felt it too. Nipper chased around the two clowns, easily outwitting them, and Esther was at her most whimsical. Even the parakeets seemed supercharged. Ossie had difficulty controlling them. Between tricks they made chuckling noises to each other and repeatedly left their perches. When he asked one to choose from a variety of scarves the colour which matched its feathers, it settled instead on the shoulder of a little girl whose plaits were done up in ribbons of the same hue. Ossie smoothed over the mistake, inviting the girl into the ring as his assistant. The audience loved it all.

Only Sultan remained above the excitement. He prowled around the ring, eyeing the audience with disdain through the hastily erected bars. They fell silent. Ossie cracked his whip and shouted commands. The tiger obeyed, but indifferently. The ringmaster had to flick him with the whip before he would snarl. Sweat began to trickle down Ossie's neck. More than ever he was sure that to the tiger they did not exist. The amber eyes saw only lost jungles and dead mates. With more trepidation than he had felt in a long time, Ossie placed his head in the tiger's mouth. He was glad when the act was over.

Only one more remained. The strong man fought a tug-of-war with Esther. The elephant let him win, but not before they had got the audience on the edge of their seats shouting and cheering. When it was over Ossie felt old; as old as the look in Sultan's eyes. He lingered by the restless beast's cage. The sounds of the other performers' tired congratulations reached him there, but the ringmaster was years away. By the time Karina persuaded him that he ought to sleep his mood matched the tiger's.

Ossie was staring gloomily at the big cat once more when Todd found him the following morning. The scientist's excitement made him appear to have an extra set of limbs, so wild were his gestures, but Ossie no longer saw anything comic.

"It was fantastic! Just great! The applause! How can I ever thank you?"

"Thank me?" The bitterness in Ossie's voice made Todd hesitate.

"There's no other feeling that comes close. Who needs food and drink when you can have applause?"

Ossie scowled through the bars, away from the scientist's puzzled face. "What about the animals? I thought it was them you were interested in."

Todd looked injured. "Of course. I just wanted to thank you, that's all."

10

"Don't! This is a dying world, can't you see that? No children, no more animals. Sultan and me, we'll be the last." Ossie glared at the scientist, his fists clenched at his sides. Shock shattered Todd's expression. Ossie relaxed. "Just find me a theory that'll keep him alive." He nodded towards the cage. "And you can keep your thanks."

The two watched the beast in uneasy understanding. It lay sprawled on the floor, its eyes unseeing.

"Hey! How's the new star?" Karina called cheerily as she approached. Todd blushed at the compliment. "I laughed so much, I still ache. Are you sure you're a scientist?"

Todd exchanged a look with Ossie. Karina saw and misunderstood. "You leave the man alone to study, Ossie, he doesn't need your opinions. Anyway, I need you to come shopping. We're running low on everything."

"Not today." Ossie spoke quietly and Karina looked about to protest when Todd intervened.

"I'll come. There are a few things I wanted to fetch from my domicile anyway."

Karina shrugged and the pair left Ossie alone to his dark thoughts.

Donning his ringmaster's outfit for the performance acted on Ossie like water on a wilting plant. He anticipated another bout of verbal sparring with the Protectionist with glee. No sooner did he start his routine than he spotted three placards approaching above people's heads. His opponent had brought a flock of reinforcements. Ossie's eyes gleamed with mischief. No doubt she would find the comparison to a bird the greatest insult. This time Ossie took care not to relinquish his vantage point.

"Ah, here you are, madam! So nice to see you again, and you've brought your friends with you tonight. Ladies and gentlemen! Let me introduce you to my most loyal fan. She hasn't missed a performance since we arrived."

A space opened out around the embarrassed protesters. The birdlike woman's face grew redder than the parakeet's feathers. There were cheers and boos from the delighted crowd.

"Murderer! Child-killer!"

Ossie gestured her insanity to his audience.

"That's right, laugh, let him make fools of you! But murderer I said, and murderer I meant."

The noise began to die down.

"You!" She stabbed a finger at a startled man, whose child was tugging at his trousers for attention. "Don't you love your child?"

The man looked indignant.

"And yet you'd let him fall into the clutches of this evil man. Don't risk him coming into contact with his infected beasts like my misguided friend here." The Protectionist put her hand on the shoulder of one of her companions, a pasty-faced woman whose hands constantly tied and untied themselves. At the touch the woman began to sob. "Last night one of that evil man's beasts settled on this poor woman's daughter. Now she lies at death's door."

Ossie's brain raced. She must mean the girl with the ribbons. Karina and Todd had returned from their shopping trip with some such rumour. A wild tale put about by the Protectionists to scare people.

"Death's door!" he snorted. "A summer cold, a mere sniffle! I've certificates of clean health for all my animals, signed by a civic inspector."

A murmuring started in the crowd and some people began to push their way towards the exit. The distraught mother's sobs and cries of "My poor baby!" sounded above the worried hum. There was an uncomfortable feeling in the pit of Ossie's stomach. He changed tactics, slapping his adversary on the back.

"This lady herself is the best advertisement for our safety. She's been here day and night since we came and see how well she is? What good colour she's got!"

There was no laughter, only the mother's sobbing.

"Hurry along, then. That's the way. You don't want to miss our first act, the fabulous Flying Rinaldis!" Ossie led the way to the Big Top, talking all the while, but this time not everyone followed. A group remained listening to the Protectionist's poison.

Every night the queue shortened. Not unusual in itself; interest always fell off after a week or so, but the girl really was seriously ill and no one was sure why, except the Protectionists. The group around them grew. Ossie did not need the second visit from the civic inspector to know that it was time for the circus to leave town. When

12

he announced that the evening would see their last performance there, Todd's face fell.

"Perhaps I could come with you. My studies are far from complete."

Ossie's look was full of sympathy, but he shook his head. "You'd never get the permits in time. Anyway, it's people you should be studying. Animals are quite straightforward really." Ossie was grooming Esther as they spoke. Now she nodded her massive head.

Todd swallowed. "I'd better go now, then. After the show it would be... I'll go and tell the others."

The ringmaster made no attempt to stop him. A few minutes later, the scientist shambled from the arena followed by shouted good wishes from the performers.

Ossie shook his head and slapped Esther's flank. "This won't do, old girl. There's packing to get on with." Ossie took a deep breath and joined the activity around the tents.

There was another matter on his mind. Whilst gingerly placing his head between Sultan's jaws the previous night, Ossie had spotted an angry swelling above one of the yellowing fangs. It must be causing the beast torment. This time he needed no encouragement from Karina to 'do something'.

Late that afternoon the ringmaster hurried over to the restless cat's cage, his shoulders hunched against a fine drizzle that made him think longingly of warm winter quarters. The carnivore scarcely glanced at him as Ossie replenished its supply of drinking water. He held his breath as the cat lapped daintily at it. At least the suspicious tiger had not rejected it, as Ossie had feared, but had he laced it with the right dosage? Sultan left the container and resumed his patrol. The tiger's limbs became heavy and clumsy. Finally, the cat flopped onto its side, its eyes half-shut. With an economy of movement that was the opposite of his usual flair, Ossie leapt into the cage.

The business was easier than he had feared. The tooth appeared sound. Lancing the gum and a generous application of antiseptic should be all that were needed. Afterwards, Ossie squatted on his haunches, running a hand through the luxuriant fur, alert for any flicker of consciousness in the cat's eyes. His thoughts were interrupted by a sudden hubbub. Turning, he saw Findlay Todd disentangle himself from a clatter of buckets. The scientist flailed about as if a demented puppeteer had control of his limbs.

"No time! There's no time!"

The performers converged on him, their questions adding to the din. Ossie muttered a curse and went to investigate. As he pushed his way to the centre of the group, Karina's voice rose above the others. The ringmaster had quailed under that tone many times. Suddenly there was silence.

"Stop babbling!" Her fierce eyes held the scientist's. He stammered a couple of times, then took a deep breath.

"She's dead. The girl who held the parakeet. She died this morning. You've all got to get out of here."

"We're leaving after tonight's performance," Ossie cut in.

"There's a mob on its way here, and they won't stop at wrecking your tents." Todd threw a desperate look around the circle of performers.

Ossie opened his mouth to reject the idea, but caught Karina's expression. For the first time he noticed how lined her face was. He shrugged. "We'd barely have covered expenses anyway. All right, everyone, the Big Top comes down."

There was immediate chaos made worse by the fading light. Ossie wished he could crack his whip and bring the performers to order. He felt his legs suddenly grow weak. The whip – Sultan! He gestured Findlay Todd to stay back, uncertain of what he would find. He turned to the scientist with a face as white as a clown's. The cage was empty. The door swung back at his touch.

Todd's eyes widened needing no explanation.

"How much time do you think we have before the mob gets here?" Ossie asked.

"When was the performance due to start?"

"So! About an hour, then. Enough if we're lucky."

The massive bulk of Esther standing beside Ossie was reassuring. Together they watched the trucks carrying his past rumble out of the arena. Without the presence of the elephant, the empty bowl would have swallowed him. Less of a comfort was the scientist, who had ignored Ossie's protests and stayed to help. They waited until the sounds of the trucks had died away. More than anything, Ossie wished for the familiar prickle of danger than told him Sultan was

14

near. The ringmaster clamped his jaws firmly together and the two men mounted the elephant. They had to find the tiger first.

A gentle command sent Esther forward to search the streets. If the ringmaster guessed rightly Sultan would keep to the darker places. All they could rely on was Esther's instinct and sense of smell. The elephant's progress was quiet for so large a beast and Ossie began to hear a distant murmur of voices. Todd tapped his shoulder.

"Protectionists. They'd come this way," he whispered.

Ossie redirected Esther along a parallel route. Then the sound changed. There were shrill cries. Without urging, the elephant headed towards them. Coming suddenly on a junction with the main highway, Ossie pulled the elephant back. The acid glare of streetlamps made the scene unreal. It could have been a yellowing still from an old film.

The mob had fallen silent, held in the contemptuous gaze of the tiger. Ossie could smell their fear and so could Sultan. The amber eyes were alert, eager. At the edges of the crowd a few of the bravest broke away. With exaggerated stealth, laughable compared with the cat's easy grace, they got on either side of it, wielding heavy pipes and wooden clubs but taking care to stay out of reach.

Todd stirred about to dismount, but Ossie stopped him. The tiger caught their scent and looked towards its master. It rose onto its hind legs, pawing the air and snarling as if in the ring, then turned its back on its enemies. A club thudded onto its head. The tiger stumbled and was lost under a deluge of blows. Shouts of triumph from the watching crowd drowned the sounds of violence. The butchers drew back, heat fading from their expressions. The proud star attraction of Ossie's Circus was no more than a pathetic mess of blood and ruined fur at their feet. One of the women struggled away, hand over mouth. Someone further back retched. All traces of exultation drained. Those at the front glanced about them uneasily. The press thinned.

Ossie took a ragged breath. He turned to Todd. "You've got to get away."

The scientist brushed away tears. "They've done their killing."

"And now they've got to justify it. You have to set the record straight for us. I'm relying on you."

Todd clasped Ossie's hand and dismounted. He leaned against Esther for a moment, drawing strength from her bulk, then walked off into the darkened streets.

"That's that then, girl." Ossie's voice was choked and unsteady. "Hail and farewell, Sultan!" For a moment Ossie could see the orange and black fur blazing in the gloom of a jungle – free.

Esther raised her trunk in salute, then they too turned away.

Memoryfest

by Martin Badger

My sister, Madeleine, has insisted on accompanying me. I'm very glad of that, though it does underline my invalid status. She says, 'Nonsense, you came with me for that root canal.' It seems I went with Maddie three times to the dentist as recently as a year ago. Of course, I don't remember that.

I don't remember anything.

Well, that's not quite true. I can remember a few things now. A very few. Nothing about the accident or the period right afterwards – well, I was in coma – but since I came out of the hospital a few weeks ago everything is more or less in place. The doctors tell me that's a God sign and I suppose they're right. I meant 'a *good* sign.' Are typos significant? I'm told I'm not at all religious but passing the church, St Michael's, not far from the hospital where I'm now only an outpatient, I've several times pulled up and stared at it, as if it were significant. This puzzles Maddie – she says she can't remember me ever going inside.

As for what happened before the accident… I can scarcely remember a thing. It's as if my mind were an iceberg and the tip is after the accident but all else is submerged. I told this to Mum and she thought about it and smiled. "Well, don't worry Tom, at least the water is clear. Beautifully clear." But I can't be sure of that. Is there something murky back there I'm keeping back? Is that why the process is so bloody slow? Perhaps on some level there are things I just don't want to recall. My best friend, Gareth, smiles at this. "You haven't got that many levels, Tom," he says. I'm not offended. He only means I'm not complicated, not that I'm stupid. Gareth doesn't seem to have a malicious bone in his body.

This whole business is Maddie's idea and she's the one who's organised it. When she saw that going through the family albums with me, showing me DVDs of Liverpool matches and getting old mates to call round wasn't working, she changed tack. Now she's set up this memoryfest at *The Duck*. This is my all-time favourite pub and it's in Allerton, which is apparently my favourite part of Liverpool. Both of these details I have no problem believing; Maddie

17

has taken me to *The Duck* before and walked around Allerton with me and I felt good in both places.

She's been very busy, my younger sister: texting away, sending emails, blitzing *Friends Reunited*. The idea is that just about everyone I've ever known, more or less, is to show up in *The Duck* tonight armed with any memories, souvenirs etc they think might help jog my memory cells. She checked it out with Dr Armstrong and he said fine, but don't expect too much. Considering how slow progress has been so far, I'm not expecting anything at all. But who knows?

We travel into Allerton by bus. Maddie is having driving lessons but hasn't passed her test yet. I went everywhere by bicycle, it seems. That was how I had the accident. A lady walking her Labrador found me crushed up to a lamppost. They think someone hit me and knocked me off the bike. My right shoulder took most of the impact but I got a real bang on the head too. Enough to put me in a coma. No, I wasn't wearing a helmet. I usually did, it seems, but not that night.

It's a short walk and Maddie takes me by the arm, perhaps fearing I might funk it. I clock a couple of jealous looks from thin, nervy-looking males. Maddie is good-looking all right and they probably think she's my girlfriend. It's not a long walk, but enough for my heart to start to pound. My God, who am I going to find in there? What blasts from the past are going to detonate inside my skull?

I'd forgotten how large *The Duck* is and expected 'our group' to fill the place. But no, they're on the far side at a few tables they've moved together. There are plenty of others in there. Something has been orchestrated because as Maddie leads me over everyone starts to say, "Hi Tom!" and, "Tom, great to see you!" with a rather exaggerated enthusiasm. I manage a rather vacant sort of smile as I look around for a friendly face.

But I see only faces, not friends.

A guy called Eddie has a horrible acne problem. It must have taken balls for him to show his pizza-like features. Poor guy. I was at school with him and we played Sunday League football too. I know I'm a good player but Eddie tells me three years ago I had a trial for Liverpool and that is something I certainly didn't know. Seems I was good but not quite good enough. Maddie bites her lip and I know she's kicking herself for not telling me this.

Jenny is so cool she seems out of place in our group. Rather gymkhana. Rather Katie Melua. She's the only one, myself included, without a Liverpool accent. I find her a real turn on. She's from nearby Childwall, the posh part, and I wonder how I got to know her. I don't want to seem to ignore the others, so I postpone asking her.

Dave is a powerfully built individual with a pint of Guinness in his ham fist. His face, voice and donkey jacket evince nothing at all in my mind, but it seems we once did a summer job together. I keep sneaking glances at Jenny as Dave tells me what a great time we had at Burger King and how he kept scoring but I couldn't get my leg over for love or money. Maybe he means it was a great summer for him.

I know instinctively there's something between Jenny and me, but I sense it hasn't gone very far. She looks at me and there's something in that look I really struggle to interpret. Something ambiguous. I try to picture the others gone and me sitting with my arm around her, nibbling at her curls. Can't quite do it.

Maddie has laid on some real surprises and chief amongst them has to be Mr Newton. Yes, Mr Newton. That's how he's introduced. He's at least twenty years older than everybody else and looks it. When I see that little twitch he has, I feel at once he's a teacher.

"I was very sorry to hear about your memory loss, Tom," he says. "I remember you very well from when I taught at Netherley. You were one of the most talented players we ever had in the school team. Now I believe you're doing well at catering college."

"Oh… right. Are you still at Netherley?" I ask, glancing again at Jenny, who is delicately putting a cashew into her mouth. I try to imagine her absently feeding me a nut and this time it works. I'm not really listening to Mr Newton but in his line of work he's probably used to that.

A couple of the girls there are really loud. They are also very visual, with bare midriffs, tattoos and piercings. Burger King Dave is clearly desperate to pierce either of them, but they make me feel slightly nauseous. I'm not entirely sure who they are so I'll have to ask Maddie when I get the chance. It's already been explained to me that people who are so in your face are not my type and I see the truth of it now. I can hardly believe Dave is interested in Sharon and

Mel when girls like Jenny and my sister are there. I mean, Maddie is so classy she puts nearly every other girl in the shade. But I guess Dave isn't looking for class.

The biggest surprise we have that evening is the one not laid on by my sister. It happens about nine-thirty, when everyone is on their third pint and chatting away. There's a match on Sky but it's only a Carling Cup tie between Fulham and Southampton and nobody's interested. I'm not really getting far in the memory stakes – none of the photos or stories stir anything – but I'm enjoying the evening. Then in comes Philip Clark.

He comes over to the group, a tall, stocky figure dressed in black, and says, "Excuse me, but is this the Tom Winter party?"

Everyone stops talking and looks at the newcomer and I notice he's got a cyclist's helmet in his hand. It's dark blue and I know at once it's mine.

"Yes," we all say.

"I heard about the gathering. My name's Philip Clark and I'm the parish priest of St Michael's." He has a round, red drinker's face, telltale spidery lines of red in his ample cheeks. Even Sharon and Mel fall silent for a few seconds.

"Sorry but... er, which one of you is Tom?"

"I am." I stand up for some reason and also put my hand out. I mean to shake hands but it looks like I want him to give me the helmet.

He does. "I think this is yours, Tom."

I look at the helmet, wondering how on earth it came to be in his possession. We've all talked about the helmet quite a bit, actually. About why I wasn't wearing it and what had become of it.

"I'm afraid I don't understand," I say.

"It was left in the church on the night of your accident. I've been meaning to return it. Very remiss of me, I know. I wasn't actually there at the time, but it seems you came in that evening and sat somewhere near the back. You must have left your helmet when you went."

"Oh..." I hardly know what to say. "How is that you know I was there? I mean, if you weren't there."

"Mrs Hawkes was doing some cleaning and she saw someone answering your description sitting a few rows from the back. She didn't find the helmet straight away, but when she did she left it in a box where we keep the stuff people leave behind and forgot to mention it."

"Does this Mrs Hawkes know Tom?" asked Maddie.

I thought a flicker of annoyance cross Father Clarke's face. Probably he didn't like being questioned. Who does?

"No, I don't think so. But you may remember there was an article about the accident in the local paper and a photo of Tom. She saw the photo and recognised you as the young man who'd come in."

I winced a bit at young man. But it was interesting news and helped to explain the strange affinity I'd felt with St Michael's. Had I been trying to find God or just searching for a bit of peace and quiet? Either way, something must surely have been troubling me.

"So, I must have left the church and then… had my accident."

"It would appear so. Well, I'll get off now but any time you want to come along to St Michael's, Tom, don't hesitate. I am usually there."

But was God usually there, I wondered. Was he more likely to be there than in this pub? I had plenty of questions but not many answers.

Again I found my eyes turning to Jenny, who was fortunately looking away at the time. Did Jenny have any answers? When she got up to go to the ladies', I decided I was going to find out. I stood up to get more drinks, declining anybody's help, and positioned myself at the end of the bar just a couple of paces from the toilet door. When she came out I would say something.

I'd just ordered the round – it was going to cost every penny in my wallet – when Jenny emerged. She looked surprised to see me standing there, but obviously guessed at once what I was up to.

"Hello, Tom."

"Hi Jen." I dried up. Had I always been this bad with girls? Girls I fancied, anyway.

"I had to come. It would have looked odd if I'd said no when everybody else was rallying round."

"Don't apologise. It's very nice to see you."

"Yeah, you've sneaked a few peeks, haven't you?" She smiled as she saw me starting to go red.

"I'm sorry… I… er… I hope you're not embarrassed."

"Don't be silly. I liked you a lot. You can't remember a thing, can you? That must have been some jolt you got. Does your head still hurt at all?"

"No. My shoulder does sometimes. When it's going to rain."

She laughed again. "You're turning into an old man. You still look good though."

The idea that I might look good to anyone was completely new to me. Whatever else Tom Winter had been, it wasn't vain. Maddie had told me I was attractive to girls, but I'd thought it was just my little sister being kind. Maybe not.

"You look very good, too."

Again she laughed. It came easy to her, though there wasn't much amusement in the sound.

"Being in a coma hasn't done much for your social skills. I think you did a better job the first time you came on to me."

"Where was that?"

"Right here. You told me I reminded you of a singer. I can't remember the name now. I'm getting like you."

"Probably Katie Melua. Wow, this is incredible. I didn't know any of this. Nor about St Michael's or the helmet. I feel I'm really getting stuff to work with. Maddie's idea has been a great success."

A shadow passed over her face. No, worse than a shadow. Something I'd said had pushed her into a dark place.

"What's the matter?"

She said nothing but her pretty face suddenly looked very cold: hard and set and even bitter.

"For God's sake, Jen! If you know something you should tell me. It might make all the difference."

She seemed to hesitate. What she was battling with I had very little idea. But at that moment Maddie came over.

"What are you doing with the drinks? People are thirsty over there. Come on." And she picked up a couple of glasses and set off, expecting us to follow, I suppose.

But after a moment, Jen, obviously deciding she'd done enough by turning up and putting in a couple of hours, said, "Bye Tom," and slipped out.

I stood at the bar for a moment, hanging on for support. I had a strange, disagreeable sensation of movement inside my head. Father Clark. The helmet. Jenny. It was all coming together.

22

Something just went then, like a seam ripping behind my ear. The past fell into place, hitting me like a succession of snappy Calzaghe jabs. Jenny's obscene and disgusting tirade about Maddie had overwhelmed me and I'd stumbled away from her. Gone home and picked up my bike. Blundered into St Michael's with some vague idea of finding someone to talk to. Or perhaps just sitting in the dark and quiet and thinking about madness and how it could be cloaked with beauty. But Father Clarke wasn't there and I'd lurched out, leaving my helmet, and set off for the park, where I could sit in the dark and think out what was to be done. Then Calzaghe let go with a trademark hook and my head came right off its shoulders at the final memory. The screech of a car in the gloom, Jenny's face contorted with rage as her Datsun bumped me and she was mouthing obscenities through the window as I flew through the air. A grotesque crunch and then darkness. Swimming ever deeper into the coma.

So far inside I thought I would never have to come back.

"Are you okay?"

I turned and tried to focus. Gareth looked genuinely concerned.

"You've been a long time."

"Yes, I'm fine," I managed to say. "Sometimes I go a bit… walkabout. Things slipping into place, I suppose. It's probably a good thing."

Gareth didn't look convinced. I probably looked terrible. What must Jenny be feeling? Guilt ridden? Terrified that it would all come back to me and she'd have to face charges? Still crazy enough – and jealous enough – to imagine that Maddie and I were… Dear God!

I went back to the group with Gareth and sat out the last round more or less in silence. My mind was racing too much to talk. People must have thought I was having a funny turn. Which I was.

Maddie and I wandered out into the dark about eleven. It was a fresh evening and the breeze was flecked with a few drops of rain. It felt wonderful. We'd been offered a lift but preferred to walk to the stop and catch the bus. I felt better than any time since I'd come out of the coma, certain at last that sickness was what I was leaving and health was where I was headed.

"I think it went well, don't you?" Maddie said. My little sister, always so upbeat. I decided, at least for the moment, to say nothing about what Jenny had done. She must have suffered the torment of

23

the damned since the accident and I didn't want anyone putting pressure on me to make it worse for her. Anyone could make a mistake, right?

Maddie had taken my arm as the rain came on a little heavier. Always so protective of me. Suddenly I felt protective of her, too. I slipped my arm round her and buried my hand in the back pocket of her jeans as we walked.

The Cleaner

by Robert Leonard

The Boss was covered in blood – none of it his own. He was standing in the middle of the room clutching a Samurai sword in one hand and a dirty great cleaver in the other. Both had seen recent and extensive action, borne witness by the three mutilated corpses lying at his feet.

I eased the safety off my revolver and asked quietly: "Boss – you okay?"

He was trembling from head to foot, but he nodded. That was good – at least he seemed in control of his faculties.

He tried to speak, but no sound came out. He coughed and swallowed and then asked: "Can you clean this?"

"Yes," I said, though I was by no means certain that I could, "But you have to do exactly as I say."

"What do you want me to do?"

Usually he was in charge, barking orders like a Sergeant Major. By that simple question, he was telling me that he was in my hands now and, for a while at least, he would do as he was told.

There then followed fourteen of the longest hours I've ever spent, but at the end of it, you couldn't tell that we'd ever been there.

"I'm getting too old for this," I said. What I didn't tell him was that I was thinking of retiring.

The Boss just said: "Make yourself scarce for a bit: take a holiday: wait for the dust to settle on this. I'll call if I need you."

I liked the notion of a holiday, away from the grime and unpleasantness of a job I had done for too many years, but was the only thing I was ever any good at. I hung around for a few days, though: just in case. Then I packed a small suitcase with a few 'essentials' and headed for Scotland.

The journey was a long one. First, the Intercity from London to Glasgow; then a local stopping train, along the banks of the river Clyde, past the giant cranes that stood like sentinels watching over the bleached bones of Scottish ship-building, to the little town of Kemrock at the end of the line.

I had never lived here myself, but I had family here at one time and had visited often when I was much younger.

I paused to watch the Dunoon ferry do a dramatic 'hand-brake turn' that allowed it to slide gracefully alongside the quay although the passengers waiting to board her had seen the manoeuvre too often to be impressed.

I dragged my small heavy suitcase in search of a taxi, but there were none to be found, so I made my way on foot through the town and along the coast road.

There were benches at intervals along the way and I stopped to rest a couple of times; first to look at the seawater bathing pool where my mother had learned to swim as a child. For some reason, the sight of it brought to my mind the smell of freshly baked scones. A little further on, I stopped again to watch the yachts sailing in the bay.

Finally, I reached my destination – a small guest-house overlooking the sea. I hadn't seen Dougie in ages, but we had exchanged cards at Christmas, over the years, and when he bought the guest-house the next card came with an open invitation for me to visit whenever I liked.

I had phoned a couple of days ago to make a regular booking: while I'm happy to impose upon my relatives, I try not to take advantage of the few friends I have left. Dougie had sounded strangely distant and distracted when I called him, but we agreed the date of my arrival, with my date of departure being left open.

As I approached up the garden path, I could hear a woman's voice berating someone in strident tones. I couldn't make out the words she was shouting, but she was clearly vexed about something.

I took a peek in at the window and saw Dougie sitting in an arm-chair. Actually, sitting is the wrong word, because he seemed to be trying to scrunch his six-foot two frame into as small a space as possible and appeared to be cowering under the tirade of abuse that was being hurled at him. Occasionally he would even flinch as a particularly barbed comment struck home.

I had to ring the doorbell three times and knock loudly before I was able to get their attention.

The front door was opened by a pretty, dark-haired young woman in her mid twenties who had recently been crying.

"We're not taking any lodgers," was all she said and then shut the door.

I rang the doorbell again. She must have heard, but chose to ignore the ringing.

After an entire minute of me leaning on the bell, the door was flung open; she filled her lungs to give me an earful, but before she could deliver it, I said: "I have a reservation."

This so took her by surprise that she forgot to breathe out. When she opened her mouth to speak again, it just sort of 'whooshed' out of her all at once.

"What do you mean, you have a reservation?" she demanded.

"I telephoned a couple of days ago," I told her.

She stared at me for several moments, then turned on her heel and marched away.

I left my case in the hallway and followed her into the sitting room where Dougie was wilting under the withering look that he was getting.

"Hello, Dougie," I said. "How are you keeping?"

Dougie just smiled apologetically, while the young woman's head went back and forth between the two of us as though she was watching a tennis match on fast forward.

"You two know each other?" she asked in astonishment.

"Oh, Dougie and I go way back," I told her. "Way, way back. Are you not going to introduce us, Dougie?"

"Oh; aye. Patrick: this is my daughter, Kaitlin – Kaitlin: this is Patrick. Patrick's an old friend from... way back," he ended, lamely.

"You can stay the night," Kaitlin said: "That's all. And I'll need to ask you to sign the register."

"I'll show you to your room," said Dougie.

"We'll be having our tea at six," Kaitlin told me: "You're welcome to join us."

Back in the hall, I signed the name 'Patrick Brown' in the register. I pointed at the last name and Dougie nodded his understanding. Then I added a fictitious London address before following him up the stairs.

Dougie handed me my room key, said: "I'll see you at six," and then scuttled off with remarkable alacrity for such a big man, leaving me to ponder on what might have caused such upset in the Douglas household.

I came downstairs on the stroke of six and was greeted by the delicious smell of home cooking. The three of us sat at the dining-room table and Kaitlin dished up an appetising spaghetti Bolognese.

"What line of work are you in, Mr Brown?" she asked.

"I'm retired," I said, evasively, but she wasn't to be put off.

"So what did you do before you retired?"

"I was a cleaner," I told her.

"What – people's houses?" she asked, sounding surprised.

"Sometimes," I admitted, "but I specialised in the disposal of toxic waste."

Dougie gave a snort of laughter, but under his daughter's piercing glance he quickly adopted a demeanour suitable for the bedside of a sick friend.

"I couldn't help hearing a note of discord as I came up the path earlier," I said to Kaitlin.

"You could hear us, could you?" Kaitlin said.

I noticed that she appeared slightly embarrassed. "They could hear you in Glasgow," I told her. "Would it, by any chance, have anything to do with Dougie's little weakness?"

"What do you mean?" she asked sharply.

"Dougie has always had a weakness for gambling. When we were younger, we couldn't let him out on his own, or he'd have come back without his shirt," I said.

"I thought he was over it," Kaitlin said, her voice choked with emotion. "It's been years... "

"What happened, Dougie?" I asked.

"The business hasn't been doing so well and, what with the recession and all, I just thought I'd have a wee flutter, you know; just to see if I could raise a wee bit extra cash. But then, one thing led to another and well..." His voice tailed off.

"How much did you lose?" I asked.

"He lost the house!" Kaitlin shrieked. And then, in a much smaller voice, she said: "Oh, Daddy: how could you? It's our home."

"But no casino would take a house as a bet," I said: "They'd lose their licence."

"Ah, but he wasn't in a licensed casino, was he?" Kaitlin said bitterly. "Daddy's been banned from every licensed casino in Scotland. This was some gambling-den in the back-streets of Glasgow."

28

"So – how long till you have to vacate the premises?" I asked.

Kaitlin just shook her head, so Dougie replied: "The end of the week, they said."

The rest of the meal passed in near silence. Dougie and Kaitlin seemed to have lost their appetites, which was understandable under the circumstances.

I helped with the washing up, despite Kaitlin's protests about paying guests not needing to do that sort of thing. Then, when everything was squared away, I said: "Come on, Dougie: take me to see this den of iniquity."

Kaitlin looked shocked. "Whatever would you want to do that for?" she demanded.

"They're businessmen," I told her. "What would they want with a guest-house? Maybe we can do a little business."

"Don't worry," I told her when I saw the look on her face: "I'll do all the talking – I won't let Dougie get in any deeper: he's just coming to show me the way that's all."

I could tell she didn't like it, but when Kaitlin raised no further objections, Dougie drove me to Glasgow.

The illicit casino turned out to be a detached house in a residential area. It was set in enough of its own grounds not to be overlooked by any other properties.

It was still early, by casino standards: there appeared to be only two customers and they were sitting at the bar. We asked to see the 'proprietor' and were led upstairs and shown into an outer office. We were kept waiting for around twenty minutes before being ushered into the presence of a man who wouldn't have looked out of place running a bank. As we entered, he was taking an index card out of a lockable filing cabinet.

He read what was on the card and said: "Mr Douglas; welcome back. Won't you introduce me to your friend?"

"This is Mr Brown," Dougie mumbled.

"And is Mr Brown a sporting gentleman?" he asked.

"I've been known to have a flutter," I replied. "But what we're really here about is Dougie's debt to you. We were wondering if you'd consider taking a cash alternative."

"What did you have in mind?"

"We could ask a couple of estate agents to value the property and then try and raise the cash," I replied. I was making this up as I went along. I didn't really expect him to accept my proposal; I just wanted to see how he'd react. I also wanted to take a look at his office.

His face took on a funereal expression and he shook his head sadly. "I'm afraid that would set a very dangerous precedent – very dangerous indeed. Unfortunate as Mr Douglas's case is, I'm afraid I can't make any exceptions. It was a foolish bet for him to have made: reckless even, but I'm afraid that he will have to live with the consequences and, hopefully, learn from the experience."

He placed two small stacks of chips on the table and said: "Have a flutter on the house, before you go. You never know: you might get lucky."

I shrugged, picked up the chips and said: "Come on, Dougie – we tried."

At the bottom of the stairs, I ushered Dougie into the gents'. I washed my hands and then hit the hot-air dryer to cover my words in case there was anybody listening. "Dougie: we're going to have a few hands of cards and then we're going to leave. When I decide it's time to go, I'll look at my watch and say that we'll just play one more hand because it's time we were away. Now listen very carefully because this is important: during that last hand, when I fold, you fold. Do you understand me? I don't care if you're sitting there with a royal flush: when I fold, you fold – got it?"

Dougie nodded and we headed off to spend our chips.

The card room had been decked out like an elegant Edwardian smoking room and Dougie and I ended up playing poker with the two guys from the bar together with the house dealer.

Dougie's luck did indeed seem to be changing and over the next hour his small stack of chips grew steadily larger. My own stack remained much the same size.

I consulted my watch and made a point of showing the time to Dougie, while saying: "We'll have to make this our last hand – we need to be going."

"So soon?" asked the man on my right.

"I'm afraid so," I told him.

When the cards had been dealt, I could see Dougie squirm in his seat – a sure sign that he had a good hand. I looked at my cards: two small pairs – not a great hand, but enough to keep me interested – that is if I wasn't playing another game entirely.

30

I made an ostentatious show of looking at my watch and said: "Fold."

Dougie squirmed in his seat even more, but eventually said: "Fold."

We cashed in our chips and left. I had seen and learned everything I came for.

The journey back to Dougie's guest-house was undertaken in silence, which suited me because there were certain things which I only wanted to reveal to Dougie once he was settled back in his own home – preferably with a large single malt in his hand.

We arrived back just before midnight and Kaitlin tried hard to hide that she had been frantic with worry.

"Well?" she asked.

"He said 'no'," Dougie told her.

"So what kept you so long?"

"We stopped to have a few hands," Dougie said without thinking. As soon as the words were out of his mouth, he appeared to shrink down into himself as though to encourage the floor to swallow him up.

"You did what?" screamed Kaitlin. "After all that's happened? Have you learned nothing?"

"They gave us complimentary chips – it wasn't my own money," Dougie said defensively. Then, turning on me, he said: "Why did you make us leave so soon? That last hand was the best I'd had all evening?"

"Yes," I agreed: "Three kings is a pretty good hand."

"Pretty good – it was... how did you know I had three kings? You never saw my cards."

I pulled out a playing-card that I had palmed back in the casino and placed it face down on the table in front of me. Dougie and Kaitlin both moved closer to have a better look.

"See that tiny dot there? If you weren't looking for it, you'd never see it, but that means this is a jack," I said, turning the card over. "Two dots for a queen; three for a king and four for an ace. You had three cards with three dots – so, three kings. The two jokers who joined us from the bar were in on it. They both folded good hands to make sure you won early on. That last hand, they had nothing to speak of, but they'd have kept on calling and raising to suck you in to making a large bet. If you discarded two cards, they might have fed you a small pair, just to squeeze as much out of you as they could."

"What was the dealer holding?" Dougie asked. If sound had colour, Dougie's voice sounded grey.

"A full house," I told him. "Aces over queens."

Dougie sank back into an arm chair. Kaitlin was white with rage, her fists clenched, her voice twisted with emotion. "They cheated us. They cheated us out of our home."

At breakfast the following morning, I said to Kaitlin and Dougie: "I think you should hope for the best and plan for the worst. In case you need to move out quickly, I should pack everything small and moveable that has commercial or sentimental value, so that you can load up the car at a moment's notice."

"What will you be doing?" Kaitlin asked.

"I'm going to go back to Glasgow and do a bit of research – try and find out more about what we're up against. I'll spend the night there and come back tomorrow morning. Don't leave the house and keep all the doors and windows locked. Don't use the telephone. I'll call you this evening to make sure that everything's all right. If everything's okay at my end, I'll ask to speak to Kaitlin. If I ask to speak to Dougie first, get out fast and get as far away from here as you can."

In the event, I got Dougie to drive me to the station as I didn't fancy lugging my small suitcase any further than was absolutely necessary. When I arrived in Glasgow, I checked into a hotel near the station, paying cash in advance for one night's accommodation, and then went in search of an internet cafe.

When Dougie and I were in the casino, I had taken the opportunity to note down the make of alarm system they used, together with where the sensors were sighted and the make of locks on the doors. Due to the nature of my work, I already had a set of skeleton keys for the locks: that just left the alarm to deal with.

I started with the manufacturer's own web site, by way of introduction, but quickly moved on to some of the more specialised user groups. Within an hour I had pieced together the sequence of steps that an engineer would use to turn off a rogue alarm when no one was available to deactivate it in the normal manner.

Armed with this information, I could now set in motion the rest of my plan. I made my way to a less affluent part of town and bought an old white van for cash. It was taxed and MOT'd till the end of the month. I got the number of a small insurance broker from the yellow pages and arranged insurance for the vehicle. I gave the address of a boarded up house a few streets away. The insurance broker said he would put a cover-note in the post and I said I would do the same with a cheque. This meant that now I wouldn't be highlighted on any automated systems as driving an uninsured vehicle.

Next, I went to a decorators' merchant and bought some five litre tins of paint, a selection of brushes and a large canvas dust-sheet. These I stored in the van which I now drove to a car-park that would allow me to leave the vehicle unattended over night.

I passed the rest of the day in museums, art galleries and the cinema, before returning to my hotel for the night. I phoned the guest-house and asked for Kaitlin, to let them know that everything was all right. She told me that they had finished doing their packing.

Early the following morning, I left the hotel and made my way to the car park where I had left the van. It hadn't been broken into and it still had all its wheels, so I set off for the casino.

There was very little traffic at that time in the morning, so I made good time. I drove into the grounds and parked so as to obscure the front door of the house. I got out the dust-sheet, paint and brushes and left them in full view to give any passer-by a reason not to be inquisitive. Then, screened by the body of the van, I went through my skeleton keys until I found one that turned the lock.

I slipped quickly inside, alert to the slightest sound, and went to the alarm control panel behind the reception desk. I pressed the combination of buttons that I had worked out from my researches on the internet, then went and stood by the door, ready to make a quick getaway in the event of my being wrong.

I stayed rooted to the spot for a full minute, all senses on high alert, before deciding it was safe to proceed.

I climbed the stairs to the boss's office that Dougie and I had visited so recently and used a stethoscope to deal with the combination lock on the filling cabinet. Inside, I found a mass of large index cards, each one detailing a punter who was in debt to the casino. In each case, name and address was recorded, together with amounts owed, payment dates and a list of personal details: sometimes very personal.

The cards were filed by date and many showed debts that had been paid off. However, the two categories that I was interested in were 'Current Outstanding' and 'Leverage'.

I riffled through the 'Current Outstanding' section to be sure that Dougie's card was there, then I put the whole of both batches into a plastic carrier-bag. I filled the gaps left with a batch of older cards from another drawer and closed the filing cabinet, being careful to reset the combination dial exactly as it had been when I found it.

Taking a last look round the office, to make sure I hadn't missed anything, I returned to the ground floor, reset the alarm and left by the front door, which I locked again behind me. Then I put my decorating gear back in the van and drove unhurriedly away.

Back at the guest-house, I showed Dougie and Kaitlin the card which recorded Dougie's debt to the casino. Kaitlin was all for tearing it up and burning it, along with all the other cards.

"Not yet," I said. "These could be useful." I turned my attention to the pile marked 'Leverage'. "Kaitlin, let's get onto the internet and try to identify some of these people."

"But they could be anybody," Kaitlin objected.

"No, I don't think so. I think some of these people are going to turn out to be pillars of the community: people that it would be worthwhile 'leveraging'."

While Kaitlin surfed the internet, I sat and took notes of her findings.

"What can I do?" Dougie asked.

"Keep us supplied with tea and biscuits," I told him. "This could take some time."

Two hours later, we had identified about a dozen people from the 'Leverage' list. There were two senior police officers; several people across a number of local government departments – planning being particularly well represented; a number of high-ranking and influential members within the business community; two lawyers and a doctor.

I picked up the phone and dialled the number on one of the cards. "Chief Inspector Standing?" I asked when the number was answered.

"Yes, speaking," came the reply.

"My name is Patrick Brown. I'm in the process of cleaning up a bit of a mess that a friend of mine has got himself into with respect to a certain unlicensed gaming establishment in Glasgow. During the course of my enquiries, I've come across some information pertaining to yourself, together with a number of other prominent citizens. I was wondering if you might be interested in having these records expunged."

There was a pause on the other end of the line; then the Chief Inspector said: "How much would this cost me?"

"Financially, nothing," I told him. "However, some help, should it be needed, would be very useful."

"I'm afraid there's nothing I can do from where I'm sitting."

"That's all right," I told him. "Sometimes doing nothing can, in itself, be very helpful. There is something that you might be able to tell me though. Do you know who owns the establishment in question?"

"That would be Vernon Lews. Are you familiar with the name?"

"Only by reputation," I replied.

"Then you'll understand why my hands are tied," the Chief Inspector answered.

"Not entirely, no," I told him.

"He has very strong business and political connections. The casino isn't the only way he gets to people: it's just the tip of the iceberg. If he ran for mayor, he'd probably be elected unopposed."

I thought for a minute and then asked: "Could you tip off the casino manager that he's been ripped off?"

"I'm not sure how that would be in anybody's best interests – yours or mine," the Chief Inspector replied.

"How do you think he'll react?" I asked.

"He'll send a couple of his 'boys' round to retrieve what's gone missing."

"And when they fail to retrieve it – what then?" I asked.

"He'll have to report the loss to Lews. If he follows his usual M.O. he'll send a small army after you at about three in the morning."

"Thank you, Chief Inspector, you've been most helpful. Just one more thing: where would I find Vernon Lews – if I was looking for him?"

I noted down the address the Chief Inspector gave me and hung up the phone.

As I sat thinking, I was acutely aware of Dougie and Kaitlin looking at me. Eventually I realised that I wasn't really thinking at all; I was just putting off the moment when I would have to give them the bad news. "This goes wider and deeper than I first thought. You have to leave this place and you may not be able to come back."

"But why?" Kaitlin asked.

"All actions have consequences," I said. "In trying to clean up the consequences of Dougie's actions in losing the house, I seem to have stirred up a hornets' nest. This goes way beyond the casino."

"What'll happen?" she asked.

"Men will come. A few at first and then a lot of men, intent on doing harm – which is why you mustn't be here when they arrive."

"I'm not going," Kaitlin said. "I won't be driven out of my home by a bunch of thugs: I just won't."

She stood there with her fists clenched and a look of defiance that transcended reason. I resigned myself to the fact that, for the time being at least, they would be staying.

I went up to my room and took two silenced revolvers out of my suitcase. Then I went back downstairs and stuffed one down the side of the sofa. I sat down and laid the other on my lap, covered by a newspaper. I was careful not to let the others see me doing this.

While I sat quietly on the sofa, Dougie and Kaitlin paced the house in a state of restless agitation.

In the event, we only had to wait about an hour, though to Dougie and Kaitlin it must have felt like days.

We heard the crunch of car tyres on the gravel drive followed by the noise of two doors being slammed. Kaitlin visibly jumped when the doorbell rang.

"Dougie," I said, "You answer it."

A few moments later, Dougie walked backwards into the lounge followed by two men of less than savoury appearance. One was every bit as big as Dougie himself; the other individual was a little weasel of a man with slicked-back hair and small darting eyes.

The big man was addressing Dougie. "A little bird has told us that you've made off with a bunch of stuff that doesn't belong to you and we want it back."

I coughed to announce my presence. The big man looked at me; looked away, and then did a classic double take. If he could have jumped out of his skin, he would have done.

"Flaming Nora – they didn't say you'd be here!" he exclaimed.

"They don't know I'm here," I replied.

The big man seemed confused. I recognised him and he clearly recognised me; I just couldn't quite place him.

"What; you're not here to pick up the what's it then?" he asked.

"No. I'm here on holiday. I'm visiting my good friend Dougie and his daughter, and while I am here they are under my protection."

His wiry companion was looking between his colleague and me. Finally, he asked: "You know this geezer, Harry?"

Harry! That was the big guy's name. I knew him from the old days – well, knew of him really – we were never actually introduced. I'd heard he'd moved to Newcastle – must have missed the turning and kept on going.

Harry didn't answer, so the weasel said: "Come on! Let's just get the gubbins and go – the boss is waiting."

"Hang on," Harry told him: "I have to make a call." He took out his mobile and speed-dialled a number. "Boss? It's Harry. We're at the address you gave us, but there's a bit of a problem. You remember Slasher Jack's West London mob? Well, his cleaner's sitting on the sofa not six feet from me: the prince of darkness his very own self. Says he knows them. Says they're under his protection. What do you want us to do?"

Harry listened dispassionately to the casino manager ranting on the other end of the phone. All Harry said in response was: "You're having a laugh." Then he hung up and said to the weasel: "I'm off home. If you've any sense, you'll do the same."

"What did the boss say?" the weasel asked.

"He said he doesn't care who's sitting six feet away, we're to find the stuff and get it to back to him pronto."

The weasel grabbed Kaitlin and had a knife to her throat before you could blink. But before he could say anything, I was off the sofa and across the room, pressing the barrel of my gun against his temple.

"I'm not even going to count to three," I said. "Put your knife away and leave."

He withdrew his knife and I eased Kaitlin out of his grasp and steered her towards Dougie.

"What happens now?" I asked Harry.

"The boss'll have to call Mr Lews."

"What's he like, this Lews character?" I asked.

Harry thought for a moment and then said: "He's a bit like Slasher, but without Slasher's sunny disposition."

Slasher had been accused of many things (mostly acquitted), but no one had ever accused him of having a sunny disposition. "How many will he send?"

"All of them, I expect," Harry said. "And they won't be nice friendly types like me and Paul here; they'll be the real deal – real nasty like: you know what I mean?"

I nodded. I knew what he meant.

Once Harry and his pal had left, it took some time to get Kaitlin settled after the shock of what had happened to her. When she had finally stopped shaking and crying, I sent her and Dougie to the kitchen to cook us a meal. This was partly to distract Kaitlin, but mainly because we all needed some hot food inside us.

We didn't bother washing up afterwards. "Take the car-ferry across to Dunoon," I told them. "Find somewhere to stay and don't go out alone, especially at night. Remember, crowds are good. Don't use your phone – I'll call you in the morning."

I watched them drive away and then started on my preparations. There was a box on the side of the front porch which held the electric meter so that it could be read without having to go into the house. I opened this and switched off the mains electricity. I went back inside and broke the glass in several light-bulbs, without removing them from their fittings, and turned their switches to the 'on' position. Next I turned the gas on low in the kitchen, but didn't light it.

I checked to make sure that the 'No Vacancy' sign was showing and then left the house, wedging the front door closed with a small wad of paper, and set off into the early evening traffic. I had half a mind to leave the van parked outside as decoration, but in the end I decided against it. Ordinarily, I would have stayed to watch things unfold, but I needed to be in Glasgow, at the address Chief Inspector Standing had given me, by the time that Lews' men had arrived in Kemrock.

I had to admit, things were getting a lot more complicated than I was comfortable with, but I was looking to simplify things considerably by the end of the night.

Lews' lair wasn't some well guarded manor house in a remote area where he'd be able to see me coming a mile away. It was the top floor of a large red-brick tenement block in a run-down part of the city. My battered old van didn't look out of place in these surroundings, so I parked a couple of streets away and settled down to wait.

At half past two in the morning I set off on the final part of my night's work. The air smelled of old chip fat, ethnic cooking, beer, piss and vomit and at this time of night, the streets were mine.

I entered the tenement and made my way up the stairs. The place had a lift, but I didn't use it; in the unlikely event that it was actually working, the noise of it would have wakened everyone in the building. When I reached to top floor, I pulled a silenced revolver from my pocket and stood listening intently for several minutes.

There was only one door on the top floor. It had a decent lock, but it still only took me a few moments to open. I slipped silently inside and paused to listen once again, straining to hear the slightest sound out of place.

I was in a long passageway. It smelled like an old people's home and was lit by forty watt bulbs. Half way down the passage, a door was slightly ajar and I could hear somebody talking on the telephone. I moved closer to listen. I assumed that it was Lews talking to his army, which would be in Kemrock by now. As he had the phone on loud-speaker I was able to hear both sides of the conversation.

"There's no lights on – the place is all dark."

"It's the middle of the night, you moron: of course it's all dark. Now get inside and get my property. Squeeze the girl if you have to – squeeze her hard – squeeze her anyway, whether they give it up or not. Then kill them. Kill them all and kill them hard – I want an example setting for this. Nobody who rips me off should expect to die easy – now get in there."

"Here, the front door's open."

"The lights don't work."

"Course they don't work, the power's off at the mains. Here, get out the way, I'll do it."

There was a noise like a huge dog giving a single, monstrous bark. Then silence.

I could hear Lews saying: "Trevor? Trevor – what was that noise? Trevor, answer me – what's happening?"

I stepped into the room and said: "Trevor can't hear you."

We stood looking at each other. The years hadn't been kind to Mr Lews. I've learned to size up men like him pretty quickly. Broadly speaking, they fall into two categories: those you can do business with and those you can't. The first type you can negotiate with and reach an agreement that will satisfy both sides. The second type won't rest until you, and all those dear to you, are dead, no matter what the cost to themselves.

Lews was the second type. He lunged for the gun on his desk and even managed to get a shot off, which buried itself in the woodwork, while I put three bullets into his chest. I knew he was dead, but I still put another two into his head – just to be sure.

Keeping well clear of the desk and the area around it, I did a quick sweep of the apartment. There was money all over the place in notes of varying denominations. I stuffed two carrier bags full of five, ten and twenty pound notes and then left.

I didn't see anyone as I made my way back downstairs. Even if anyone had heard the gunshot, I dare say that time and experience had taught the other residents that loud bangs and screams were best ignored. I returned to the van and sat in the back, waiting. If I set off straight away at that hour, I was likely to be pulled over by the police just to relieve the boredom.

It was six in the morning before I deemed it safe to drive away. By now, there was a thin but steady stream of cars and pedestrians and I joined the traffic, just another anonymous workman making an early start.

I travelled north for a couple of hours before phoning Dougie and Kaitlin from a lay-by. We agreed on a time and place for a rendezvous and met up later in the day. I took Dougie to one side and filled him in on some of the details. Kaitlin wasn't best pleased at being left out like this, but there were some things that it was better she didn't know.

I left the van in a lay-by with the keys in the ignition and squeezed into the back of Dougie's car, which was still stuffed full with their belongings from the guest-house, which I strongly suspected was now in need of considerable repair, if not rebuilding.

While Dougie drove us to a town with a railway station, I told them the plan. "Keep as close to the truth as you can. Say that two men came to your house yesterday saying that you had something of theirs and they warned you that others would call later that night to get it back. Say that you didn't believe them and didn't know what they were talking about, but you packed up your valuables and moved out for the night – just in case. Go back via the same ferry to keep your movements consistent. Don't mention casinos or gambling debts. If they ask about any guests staying with you, show them the register. You can tell them that I stayed one night and left yesterday. If your home has been damaged, and I'm afraid it probably has been, call the police and your insurance company, in that order. If I'm right, the police will have been round there already, but you're not to know that."

We drove in silence for a bit and then Kaitlin asked: "Are we safe?"

"Yes," I said. "You're perfectly safe. But remember, Dougie, all actions have consequences; so no more gambling – I might not be able to clean things up for you next time. Those index cards with the gambling debts on them: when the dust settles, go round to every person individually and give them their cards. Tell them who you are and that their debts have been cancelled. Don't ask for anything in return – Kaitlin; you make sure that he doesn't. You'll end up with several dozen new best friends. They'll invite you to join the Masons, I shouldn't wonder. Start with Inspector Standing."

When we arrived at the station we made our farewells brief. I promised to be in touch every day to see how things were going and then Dougie and Kaitlin set off to see what remained of their home. It might be in ruins, but at least it was still theirs and it could be rebuilt. Meanwhile, I made my way onto the platform to wait for the train that would take me back to London. Apparently I wasn't ready for retirement just yet.

The Unfortunate Case of One Garry Lumbergut

by Mary-Jane Wiltsher

Garry Lumbergut was a cumbersome and grotesque man. He had the clammy, protruding eyes of a toad, and the wet folds of his neck slumped over the collar of his nylon shirt, like a dank flesh-coloured jelly fresh from its mould. He weighed 17 stone, ate Nutella and fried egg sandwiches for breakfast, and loved nothing more than to bully his tiny mouse of a wife, Patty.

Now, Patty Lumbergut had never been struck by her gargantuan brute of a husband, but she feared him nonetheless. He was coarse, self-centred and foul-tempered: a vile, overgrown child who could launch into a hellish tantrum at any given moment. When they had married – a rushed, perfunctory affair – his arrogance was less overt, but with age his male pride had ballooned along with his belly, moodiness sprouting deep lines across his forehead, indicative of a growing disgust for the world around him and all it encompassed. So far as Garry Lumbergut could ascertain, the people and places he had encountered in his existence to date held very little discernible worth, and it was in this frame of mind that he took to a life of gloomy solitude and gluttonous consumption, muttering slurs against humanity through the crusts of his pork pies.

But there was one thing in particular which aggravated Garry more than anything else, and this was the very notion that something, anything, might have the capacity to impinge on him. Not so much that it could succeed in warming the cockles of his shrivelled black balloon of a heart (anyone who had encountered G. Lumbergut would acknowledge that this was a veritable impossibility), but more that something might serve to frighten him, to dislodge him, to shake his vast fleshy form to its core.

"Ain't nuffin' that'd scare me," he boasted, on regular occasions. "Nuffin'."

Patty Lumbergut would rarely respond. She had learnt a long time ago that passivity was her friend in situations such as this, and that Garry did not respond well to disagreement.

It was 1970, and this mismatched, unhappy pair lived in a long row of brown-brick terraced houses in West London, and on the far corner of their road stood a ramshackle second hand shop called

'Junk & Disorderly'. The proprietor of this tatty odds'n'ends store was Mr Higgins – a tall, mild-mannered man with a kind, lopsided smile and hair the colour of sawdust. For some years now, Patty Lumbergut and Mr Higgins had been in love, but it had always remained the unfulfilled, unspoken kind of affection which one usually encounters only in the delicate pages of yellowing novels.

What Patty loved most about Mr Higgins was how instantly he saw the good in something: the worth in its antiquity, or the inherent beauty in its ungainly design. The curious collection of bric-a-brac in his higgledy piggledy shop ranged from tiny, decorative items (squat brass animals, silver trinket boxes, garish coronation mugs) to bigger household pieces (ancient kitchen dressers, battle-scarred from the hustle and bustle of a family dining area, or prickly horse-hair armchairs with cushions permanently dented by the substantial buttocks of elderly ladies). Few people would have understood the appeal in much of Mr Higgins' stock; even the owners of other second hand stores in the area raised their eyebrows at some of the items he deemed deserving of care, attention and re-sale. The back room of Junk & Disorderly was filled with specialist polishes and balms: pots of thick brown grease that made drawers slide smoothly on their runners, and homemade concoctions in plastic spray cans that could make silver cutlery twinkle the way it first had when it was given as a wedding present in the 1940s. Mr Higgins had always striven to be a conscientious man, and he scrupulously applied such principles to the abandoned items which arrived through his door twice a week. Yes, Mr Higgins could well recognise something precious that had gone unloved for a horrifyingly long period of time. And of course, this was what he saw in Patty Lumbergut.

There was a resigned exhaustion in her face he found unmistakable, though she masked it thinly with her enchanting, but always fleeting, smile. He observed the manner in which she twisted the waist belt of her long green mac around her thin fingers as she spoke, and the astounding grey-blue of her shyly averted eyes. It was not that her sorrow was what made her beautiful; there was something distasteful about such a simplistic correlation. But the utter magnitude of Patty's loneliness made Mr Higgins angry with mankind, and the depth of such resentment was something he had not felt for many years. She captivated him more than any woman he had ever encountered, and he wanted nothing more than to mend her hopelessly broken heart, and to adore her as thoroughly as she deserved.

But it was not to be. These two were a quiet pair, and their adoration of one another was not one of scandalous melodrama. There would be no illicit affair, no furtive embraces, no secret elopement to some exotic, far-off country. Instead, the two remained alone, despite living only a few hundred yards from one another, while the shadow of Mr Lumbergut weighed down on them, an oppressive black cloud that could never be ignored.

The years slipped slowly by. Garry Lumbergut grew even fatter, developing a penchant for deep-fried spam, which he obtained from his local chippy. In contrast, Patty seemed to almost shrink in stature, as though her continual cowering had forced her to fold completely in on herself. Down at Mr Higgins' shop, time ticked exasperatingly away on twenty different clocks – carriage, grandfather, pocket. The more disheartened he became, the more ludicrous stock he compulsively acquired, hell-bent on working his magic on all things uncherished. But it was a fool's mission. Takings had slumped, and Mr Higgins was fast becoming penniless. The higher his stock piled, the more he saw through his idiotic attempts to create a distraction from his ultimate predicament, and the more frustrated he became with his lack of gumption. Stuck behind the irregular wooden counter at the back of his tiny shop, Mr Higgins wondered for the first time if there might be something fundamentally wrong with him. His life seemed an irredeemable mess. He was a coward. A joke. Something had to be done. On March 16th 1974, the sign in Mr Higgins' shop door still dangled the word 'closed' to passers-by after 9am. Nobody noticed, though it was the first time it had happened in over ten years.

At the far end of the road, Garry Lumbergut sat in his chair and rustled his chip packet. The greasy paper cone was empty, but its contents had not satisfied him. In discontent he extended a chubby arm over to the sheet of newspaper that his portion had come wrapped in, hoping that a few chips might have strayed into the headlines. He had no luck, but something else caught his eye: **'MOST TERRIFYING MOVIE EVER MADE'**, bellowed a particular section of print. **'THE EXORCIST – IN LOCAL CINEMAS FROM MARCH 16TH.'** Garry Lumbergut surveyed this item of news as one might regard a dog turd. He rarely bought

44

newspapers, believing them to be a source of wasteful expenditure, and his eyes wandered down the page very slowly, unused to the trials of small print. **'Get ready for one of the most genuinely horrifying experiences of your life**.' The moist grooves in Garry Lumbergut's forehead deepened, and he squinted hard at the review. *What a flamin' load of bollocks*, he thought to himself, and began to crumple the sheet into a ball with his breezeblock fist. But something stopped him. He couldn't understand why, but the review infuriated him. Challenged him. What soft bastard had the audacity to proclaim that this piece of rubbish was something *he*, Garry Lumbergut, would shit a brick at? He shifted restlessly in his armchair, unfolded the paper, and read it again. His outrage deepened, and he glanced up at the clock. On March 16th 1974, Garry Lumbergut waddled down his front garden path. Nobody noticed, though it was the first time it had happened in over ten days.

When the front door of her house banged shut at 9.30pm, Patty Lumbergut rose cautiously from the sofa and moved out into the hall. She had been surprised to find her husband absent when she returned home from grocery shopping – this happened rarely, and it would generally be a matter of minutes before he returned, armed with a sugary treat from the newsagents, or cursing an acquaintance at the betting shop for misadvising him on a particular horse. But on this occasion he had been gone several hours, and whilst she was perhaps not fraught with worry, she was certainly curious. As he struggled to manoeuvre himself through the narrow doorframe, she threw him a questioning look.

"None of your naggin', woman." He puffed, and barged passed her to the kitchen, wheezing from the excruciating endurance that the short walk home from the local cinema had demanded of him. Leaning over the sink as far as his gut would allow, he slurped water straight from the tap like a thirsty bulldog then straightened, face purple. Giving him a side-long glance from where she now stood by the stove, Patty noticed something inexplicably strange in her husband's face. His eyes shifted in a way she had never seen before, and his usually stagnant physique was positively twitching.

"I'm bloody knackered. Might turn in early," was all he said, before wiping the damp residue from his upper lip and retreating upstairs.

At 11.30pm, Patty Lumbergut slipped into her side of the bed. She knew her husband was not asleep. Normally she waited for the gravelly tones of his pugnacious snore to carry through the house before she tiptoed up the staircase, but tonight that had not happened, and she was simply too tired to wait any longer. Knowing she would gain nothing from enquiring as to his well-being, she stayed silent. At quarter past midnight, she drifted into an uneasy slumber.

Garry Lumbergut lay wide awake in the dark, his chest quaking. Outside, a fox emitted its distinctive shriek of a bark, and he flinched. He had felt fine entering the cinema. Admittedly, his heart thudded, but this was due largely to the strain of standing in a considerable queue, which extended right through the doors and down the street. He was not used to carrying his own weight for prolonged periods, and it had put him out immensely. Thinking his industrial sized vat of popcorn would provide partial compensation, he made his way into the shadowy auditorium. But something was not quite right. His heart continued hammering like that of a stricken rabbit, and he peered nervously around as he lodged his considerable behind between the arm-rests on either side of his chair. There were stifled giggles from all angles: a group of teenagers pelted his thick neck with wine gums. Garry Lumbergut was not used to contact with the outside world; he was a gruesome hermit, and the sound of this ill-contained laughter felt like a thousand pinpricks in his waxy, grizzled ears. As the film began, he sensed his whole body churning. He yearned to leave this confined social space – there was something thoroughly repellent about the very essence of the cinema experience. It wasn't just the wide-eyed young girl in the picture, with that satanic voice emanating from her frail body and projectile vomit spraying from her mouth in all directions. No, it was everything. Sitting with strangers. Hearing their pathetic screams. Their damp, whispered words. Couples snuggling against each other in corners. Everyone reacting unanimously to the giant, flickering screen. His pulse quickened and he clutched at his armrest. Something deep in his chest tightened. Half an hour before the end of the picture, Garry Lumbergut fled the auditorium, spilling his uneaten popcorn up the aisle as he went.

By 2am that night, the neighbourhood streets were deserted. It was not until then that Mr Higgins crept down from his maisonette above

Junk & Disorderly and into the workroom which stood behind his wooden counter. His expression was haggard, his palms moist. He was not a reckless man, and though his plan seemed carefully thought out, this gave him little assurance, doing nothing to relieve the terrible feeling of slow-sinking guilt which consumed him.

Given that his shop was positioned on a corner and backed onto disused garages, he only needed to concern himself with one neighbouring house. This, he gathered, was left by an elderly gentleman to his innumerable grandchildren, but had stood uninhabited ever since his death. Nevertheless, Mr Higgins calculated that by making an anonymous call to the emergency services in good time, the adjoining house could be spared any significant damage, but that Junk & Disorderly would suffer to the extent he desired for a hefty insurance claim. There was a small electric heater in the workroom which he always used in early mornings during the colder months, and next to this he placed the bag of bone-dry rags he collected for polishing. The notion of a dusty heater mistakenly left plugged in seemed to him a viable one, and he hoped that the singed remains would be noted. Added to this, an old chest stood against the nearby wall, the drawers of which were full of tissue paper he had not yet emptied. This seemed to offer the whole set-up further validity. He winced inwardly at his own disgusting logic and ran a limp hand through his pale hair. Gazing around the room, he took the box of matches from his pocket, closed his eyes, and cursed his newly acquired wretchedness.

He left through the rickety back door. Pulling a cloth cap low over his brow and checking each way for unexpected passers-by, Mr Higgins retreated across the main road and up one of the side streets opposite, where he knew there was an overgrown area by an abandoned sweet shop, sheltering a telephone box. From here, he could survey his shop with the small pair of binoculars he had obtained from his stock the previous day. He would telephone 999 when necessary, proclaim in a vaguely inebriated voice to have spotted the blaze whilst walking home from a party, and put the phone down before giving a name. Ducking into the shrubbery, he looked down at his wrist watch. This was where he would wait it out. Everything seemed very still, and Mr Higgins became aware of his own shallow breathing.

Somewhere, a cat mewed disconsolately.

A few hundred yards away, at the very end of the opposite residential street, Garry Lumbergut had just let rip his first few resounding snores.

All around, people slept soundly up in their rooms, their stomachs rising and falling beneath the duvets.

In Mr Higgins' deserted maisonette, his old cooker stood quietly. A brass nut at the end of the gas connection cable – which had loosened over the years since its original botch-job fixture – was silently permitting a small, but steady, emission of town gas.

The explosion was colossal. The front windows were projected from their frames and shattered across the tarmac. Mr Higgins' blackened stock was strewn over the pavement – up-ended furniture billowed smoke from where the shop entrance had once been. The parallel house had half its porch and upper balcony blown off, and the windows of the Chinese takeaway opposite splintered and crashed inward. All that was left of Junk & Disorderly was a smouldering cave. Sirens wailed under the smoky night sky. Up by the telephone box, Mr Higgins lay in the spot where he had fainted beneath the overhanging shrubbery, the receiver dangling above his head.

The sheer force of the blast reverberated right up every neighbouring street. Far enough away to have the noise of the explosion considerably dampened, Garry and Patty Lumbergut awoke to a disconcerting jolt and an ominous *thud*. As Mr Lumbergut opened his eyes and raised a hand to his pounding chest, it seemed that the whole house was shaking from its very foundations. The curtains had rattled partially open, letting in a strip of moonlight which cast elongated shadows along the wall. Items were falling from all around – paperbacks tumbled from the bookshelf, a glass crashed off the bedside table. Pulling the duvet over his head like a distressed infant, Garry Lumbergut became convinced that the bed frame itself was vibrating. *What the hell was this?* Oozing sweat and squeezing his eyes tight shut, he suddenly recalled a horrible scene in the movie in which the possessed girl's bed had levitated from the floor. His violent pulse thundered away in his eardrums, and his entire body seemed to involuntarily spasm and seize up in terror and agony.

"Garry?" Patty Lumbergut pulled back the duvet and rolled her husband's doughy body toward her. "Garry?!"

But it was no good. Garry Lumbergut was stone dead.

Several years later, a greying Mr Higgins was escorted by a portly policeman out of Wormwood Scrubs and allowed to walk free from its towering iron gates. Miraculously, no one had been harmed in the blast, but racked with self-loathing and mortification, Mr Higgins had admitted everything when questioned at Ealing police station, making his plans for insurance fraud entirely plain. His sentence was shortened as a result, and having served his time with placid acceptance, he had now been granted early release. Squinting forlornly into the bright sunlight, he realised there was a lone figure standing on the corner of the street. It was her. A slow smile eased the sadness from his tired face, his pace quickened, and then he ran to her.

On a pleasantly mild day in 1981, Mrs Patty Higgins was perusing a newspaper in the living room of her airy suburban home, when something caught her attention. **'CONTROVERSIAL VIDEO RELEASE OF 'THE EXORCIST''**, read a headline: **'MEDIA HYPE OVER ULTIMATE HORROR'**. Patty Higgins wrinkled her nose. She did not like horror films, and had absolutely no knowledge of this particular picture. Lowering one corner of the paper to ask her husband if he knew anything of the movie, she realised to her amusement that he was sound asleep in his armchair. Their extensive collection of clocks – grandfather, carriage, and more – softly chimed six. It would soon be time to start preparing supper. Smiling to herself, she ruffled her newspaper, turned the page briskly, and began reading something much less unsavoury.

Miniature Beacons in the Purple Dusk

by Claudia Boers

You sort of stuck out your arm with your thumb half up, but then you changed your mind and tucked away an imaginary strand of stray hair instead. The traffic glided past you like an articulated tin snake. You knew you should have waited and taken the bus with the others, but you were also enjoying the heady sensation of freedom. You'd been greedy for this part of your life to begin and now here you were, the sun on your shoulders and the cool blue Atlantic glittering like a promise in front of you.

Your friends were still fussing over bikinis and hairlines and which tank tops to wear with which shorts when you'd given up waiting and decided to go. When you'd announced that you would see them at the beach they'd stopped their flapping and stared at you like four quizzical hens.

"On your own?"

"Yes, I'll be fine. I just want to get there before the sun sets."

They didn't like your sarcasm or the fact that you were breaking group code (after all, they were your best friends and this was your end-of-school holiday) but you didn't care. You told them to find you on Fourth Beach, slung your bag over your shoulder and strode out of the cottage.

But when you got to the bus stop and checked the timetable you realized you'd have to wait fifty minutes. You worried that your friends would find you there, a sailboat without wind, when they eventually turned up. You hopped from one foot to the other as you rechecked the times, willing them to be different, but they were the same. It wasn't a long way to the beach, only a fifteen-minute drive along the coastal road, but it was too far to walk. The gulls mewed and the unfamiliar air smelt salty, faintly wild. The breeze played with your hair and for a moment you felt like a girl in an advert for an exotic shampoo or perfume. In that impulsive instant you decided to hitchhike instead.

You walked away from the bus stop and only stopped once you were beyond the crossroads, just in case your friends turned up in time to catch you breaking one of the cardinal rules. Though you were confident you'd get a ride long before they ever appeared.

50

After pretending to shake a stone from your sandal and then rummaging aimlessly in your bag, you held out your arm again. But this time, spurred on by the thought of your friends turning up, you stuck your thumb straight up into the sunny air. You tried to block out the sound of your mother's outraged voice and you wondered whether hitchhikers should walk, or stand still, or face the traffic and smile, or look away. You decided to stand still, but not to smile because you wanted to look cool. You tugged the hem of your shorts down, but fluffed up your hair.

Everybody stared at you as they drove past, and one man even hooted, but nobody stopped straight away. You started to feel a bit silly and began to think you might walk back and meet your friends after all, when a Volkswagen van started slowing down. For a panicked moment you considered walking off and pretending you hadn't really been hitching after all, but you didn't.

The van was perfect, tangerine and cream with shiny chrome trim. It even had an original wooden roof rack with two surfboards strapped to it. It was like something out of a movie and you felt a flush of pride that this was the car that had stopped for you. The engine sputtered in a friendly way as it pulled up, and you felt a corresponding thrumming in your veins. There were two guys in the front, slightly older than you, all tans and teeth and sun-bleached hair. You couldn't believe your luck.

The driver leaned out of his window. "Where you going?"

"Fourth Beach." You tried to sound laid-back. You weren't sure whether to say please or not.

"Hop in, we're going that way!"

It was that easy.

The side door slid open and it was only then that you became aware of three more guys in the back. You hesitated, your heart suddenly hammering like hail on a tin roof. You thought, I could just run, but pride kept you rooted to the spot. You stared at them, wishing you hadn't worn such a skimpy vest, or such tiny shorts. You took in their sunglasses and golden-haired arms. You smelt their curious male musk, a combination of deodorant and hair gel and sweat. In just a few seconds you decided that they were okay. You thought you could tell. You climbed into an empty space and the guy nearest the door slammed it shut.

At first the van felt too small and close and hot. You kept your knees pressed together and dabbed your damp upper lip on the back of your hand. You could feel the backs of your legs sticking to the leather seat. But as the van picked up speed and a breeze washed over you, you began to relax. You could still see the deep band of ocean and lighter blue sky through the window. The guys, who at first glance had seemed like a faceless pack, became more distinct. They were friendly, interested in you.

"What's your name?"

"Where are you from?"

"How long are you on holiday for?"

You began to feel all floaty and happy, like when you and your friends secretly drank vodka or cider. You noticed how fancy the guys' sunglasses and watches were, how nice they all seemed. Your friends would never believe you when you told them.

"How come you're hitching?"

"On your own?"

"You shouldn't, it's not safe."

"If I caught my sisters hitching they'd be in for the high-jump."

"Ha! As if Georgie and Emma would ever hitch."

And you pictured Georgie and Emma - two wilting wallflowers - and it made you feel carefree and bold. But there was a mild envy towards them too.

"But it's true, it's dangerous, you're lucky it was us that stopped."

The guys all nodded in agreement. You shrugged in response, nonchalant, though you'd never felt so popular or cherished in all your life.

The guy in the Diesel shades next to you clapped his hand over your thigh, as if to emphasise a point, and said, "Hitching's just asking for trouble," but then he left his hand where it was, searing hot on your naked skin. You were uncomfortable, but you thought maybe he was just being friendly. You didn't want to be rude, so you didn't say anything.

They were engineering and medical students, and already you craved more of their intoxicating charm. Maybe they would ask you for your number when they dropped you off, or better still, decide to come to Fourth Beach too. What would the girls say if they turned up and found you sitting in between all these third year guys?

52

Diesel Shades started rubbing his thumb in tiny circles on your thigh and you were sure that at least one of the others must have seen. You could feel your face burning and for some reason you wondered whether he would be trying it on if it were Georgie or Emma sitting next to him.

"Which university are you going to next year?"

"What are you going to study?"

Maybe nobody had noticed what he was doing. You wavered as you thought of the technical diploma you would start in February. Then you surprised yourself and said maybe law, but that you weren't sure and were taking a year off to decide, as if luxuries like that existed in your family. You had never said anything like this before.

Diesel Shades moved his hand a little higher and you squeezed your legs together more tightly to try and stop its advance, but he was persistent, as if it was a game and you were just playing shy. You caught one of the guys behind you, the one in the *Stussy* tee shirt, glancing at your lap. You felt ashamed. You pushed Diesel Shade's hand away, but you smiled at him too, so he wouldn't think you were rude. He gave a smirk that seemed to say, ha, one of those uptight types, and then drummed his fingers on the back of the seat in front like he didn't care.

You felt relieved and bad and you fiddled with your hair, twisting it into a knot and then letting it go. You could feel their furtive stares and you were grateful for your green eyes and long brown legs.

"Hey, I'm sure I know you."

You looked at the guy, sitting next to the driver, who'd spoken. He reminded you of an eager Jack Russell.

"Really? I don't think so."

Subconsciously, you were already certain you would not know any of these boys.

"I'm sure I do," he persisted, scrutinising you.

But you shook your head, though you wished you could put yourself in their world and say, yes of course, we met at so-and-so.

"Do you know the Lloyds?" he tried.

You told him you didn't.

"Hhhmm," he mused. "It'll come to me."

You smiled prettily and then shouted to the driver, "Cool van."

"Thanks."

"It was a gift from his folks," said Diesel Shades.

Wow, you thought.

You hadn't noticed Diesel Shade's voice before. It was smooth and round, like the fine bitter chocolate you've come to savour since then – so subtle you can only appreciate it after it's melted on your tongue.

"I know!" shouted the guy who thought he knew you. "Richard Parker's twenty-first."

Richard Parker. Your initial reaction was panic. Panic that your mum would find out you'd been hitching because Richard Parker's mum and yours were sort of friends. Your mum was a nurse, who helped Mrs Parker with her ancient mother-in-law. You sometimes went along too and waited outside the old lady's cottage in the Parkers' garden. Occasionally, if Richard or his sister, Olivia, were home during the holidays, you'd knock a tennis ball around the court together. And you were always invited to their birthday parties, which is why you'd been at Richard's twenty-first the year before.

You still didn't recognise the guy, but you realised he must have been one of the dinner-jacketed St. Lawrence boys at Richard's party. You'd all danced together in a marquee on the lawn.

"Ah, now I remember you," you fibbed, forming your words with care.

"Did you also go to St. Margaret's?" he asked.

St Margaret's had been Olivia's school.

"No." You dreaded the next question.

When it came you were tempted to lie again, but this time you couldn't think quickly enough so you told the truth, flinching inwardly. In your mind, the name of your mediocre state school made you nothing more than the type of girl who would hitchhike alone in a strange city. Exactly the type of girl a St. Lawrence boy would not want to know. The type of girl a guy could try to touch up.

After that, even though things seemed to carry on just as before, you were convinced the boys would not ask for your number or join you at the beach. And you were right. When you reached Fourth Beach the driver pulled over, the door slid open, and you were disgorged onto the pavement with nothing more than a cheery chorus of goodbyes and a merry peep-peep as they roared away. You couldn't have felt more tainted or flat as you stood and watched the orange and cream van disappearing.

You trailed down the stairs to the beach, and with each wretched step the hot, black feeling of disappointment lodged itself deeper inside you.

When your friends arrived you told them nothing, as if the whole thing had never happened. They'd forgiven you for leaving without them and they marvelled at your luck in getting a non-scheduled bus.

"I brought your towel," said Jane.

"And we made you a cheese sandwich and some juice," said Sue.

You were grateful, but you were also irritated by the humbleness of their offering. You longed to go to the bar at the back of the beach and buy a hamburger and shake.

As you all lay positioned to maximum tanning advantage, you felt glad of your friends' distracting banter and uncritical company, though you couldn't help thinking how trivial they sounded too. You didn't join in. Instead you stared dully at the relentlessly churning breakers far out to sea.

"Want to play beach bats?" Liz asked you when the others went for a swim.

You studied her flat face, her coarse springy hair.

"No." You couldn't keep the scorn out of your voice.

Her eyes grew wide. "What's wrong?"

"Nothing," you muttered and stared out to sea again.

When the others returned and flopped down on the sand, glistening wet and giggling, you couldn't take it any more. You stood up wordlessly and walked away. When you reached the water you dived straight in, relishing the sharp cold shock. You began pulling yourself through the waves, kicking furiously, swimming as hard as you could. You wanted to lose yourself somewhere in that endless ocean.

You swam beyond the furthest swimmers and then beyond the last buoys, but you didn't stop there. You didn't care about sharks or undertows. You struggled on through the breakers and into the shadowy swells on the other side, and even then you didn't slow down.

Eventually, when your throat stung and your chest heaved so much it ached, you stopped. You treaded the murky water with jellyfish limbs while trying to catch your raggedy breath. Then you floated on your back and shut your eyes while the ocean gently rocked you. After the bright sunlight you could sense crimson circles slowly spinning against the backs of your eyelids, but when you tried to study them they vanished, like a trick of the mind, a false reality.

When you finally lifted your head and looked towards the shore, you were startled at how far out you were. The world looked like a stage set, or a child's game: just a narrow strip of moulded beach dotted with tiny specks of people and little houses perched on a play-play hill. The absolute silence around you made it even more unreal. You imagined you could just reach out and pick up the plastic trees or dinky cars or matchstick telephone poles and rearrange them, exactly as you wanted to. The little people too.

By the time you started swimming back, the sun was just a wobbling half-peach behind you. You used breaststroke this time because there was no hurry, the world would wait. Your breathing was even, your heart clear. You moved through the water like a languid seal. In the distance, against the fading backdrop, a scattering of lights had begun to twinkle like miniature beacons in the purple dusk.

The Next Face

by Roy Swanepoel

Ernst had told Mona to wrap their silverware in clothing so that it didn't rattle when they climbed the stairs to their flat that night. Yet little had gone right for the Meiers since they'd crept away in the dark two weeks before, fleeing the expected invasion. When Ernst was transferring the suitcase full of heavier clothing to his right hand and the treasure case to his left, one catch snapped open. An embossed crystal dish screeched out between the clasps, clanged against a granite step, struck another, dashed and sent shards of glass tinkling down the dark stairs past the children. "*Auwa*," Hansi yelled when a piece of glass bit into his bare shin. Mona's forefinger was still at her lips quietening him when their neighbours' door swung open and the obese Herr Müller, with a fire poker in his right hand and his hair up like prairie grass, appeared in silhouette in the door-frame. He clicked a switch, the lamp blazed and the Meiers stood in white exposure on the stairs below. Mona raised a shielding hand to the light and Ernst, immobilised by the suitcases, blinked from beneath his hat.

The lamp above hissed briefly, then it was utterly silent.

Ernst's lips tightened over his protruding upper teeth, and his black moustache prickled outwards in a painful simulation of a smile. "*Aabig*, Herr Müller," he said in a phlegm-obstructed voice. "It was just the suitcase." He gazed up at him expectantly, in seeming readiness to interpret anything he said as humorous.

Herr Müller shuffled forward into the light, his one brown patent-leather slipper squeaking as he moved. He stopped and stood splay-footed above them. His brown face, rosy jowls, holey white vest and sun-browned forearms created a nauseating impression that he was peeling, peeling all the way down to the watery white of the skin.

"We'll clean it up," Mona said.

Her small sensitive nose crinkled as a faint whiff of stale sweat reached her.

Herr Müller ignored her. His gaze was fixed on Ernst, his narrowed eyes concealing and revealing his attitude towards him.

A silver moth buzzed against the light and dropped like a stone onto Ernst's hat.

"So, so," Herr Müller said in a slow drawl. He nodded slowly. "What's this I see? Gertrud," he called loudly over his shoulder, "look who's come back."

Mona winced at the sudden noise.

Little Bettina, tired and impressionable, sensed rather than understood the tension and clutched at her mother's skirt, her lower lip trembling in preparation for tears.

"It's bleeding," Hansi said, frowning accusingly at his father and pointing at his shin.

Gertrud, her pink curlers anchored by a paisley head-scarf tied beneath her chin, looked around the door, like a strange fish from behind a rock.

"*Ja wa*," she said. "The Meiers."

"They didn't switch the light on," Herr Müller said. His words hung in the air. In them was an echo of earlier encounters there on the stairs.

Ernst was a well-paid accountant for the renowned Betschart A.G.: Max Müller was a caretaker and an assistant something-or-other at the gasworks. The Meiers couldn't help their slightly lofty behaviour towards them; it seemed to go with their five-roomed flat and the important board meetings Ernst attended.

"Well," Ernst said and cleared his throat. "The children are tired."

"I'm not tired," Hansi said rebelliously.

Bettina, who invariably echoed Hansi, said, "I'm not tired either."

"Yes, you are," Mona said.

In the grip of discovery, Ernst had forgotten the half-open suitcase. Now aware of it, he rested the heavy suitcase on a stair. The weight dislocation unsteadied him, and the sudden lift of the treasure suitcase caused his silver trophy for the two-hundred-meter sprint to tumble out of the suitcase, strike the stair with a clang, then stop dead against the stair wall as though magnetised. Too late Ernst grabbed at the lid. A roll of silver cutlery, topped and bottomed by pairs of Ernst's underpants and bound with elastic bands, thudded down beside his foot.

Gertrud peered around Max to see what it was.

"Their silverware," she said.

"Quiet down there," a man yelled from the upper flat.

58

"Oh, really," Mona said, making small vibrating movements with her hands. She snatched up the roll, squeezed past Ernst, halted at their door and, with the silver under her arm, began rummaging in her handbag for her key, her shoulders heaving.

"Fetch it, Hansi," Ernst said, gesturing with his chin towards the trophy.

"My leg is bleeding."

"Fetch it," Ernst said with an edge in his voice. He turned to the Müllers. "If you've quite finished staring, I'll thank you to mind your own business."

Gertrud shrank back with large eyes. "*Na sowas*," she said.

Max was unmoved. He remained as he was, his chin out and his eyes narrowed and speculative.

"Come, children," Mona said, pushing their door open. "Come."

"Don't forget to clean up the glass, Frau Meier," Gertrud said from behind Max. "I'm certainly not going to do it."

Ernst glared at her, clamped the suitcase under his arm, hefted the other and turned to their door.

"Your army friend was here to look for you on the day of the mobilisation," Max said.

Ernst stopped.

"So was your boss, Herr Betschart."

Ernst swung back towards him, alarm on his face.

"Herr Betschart?"

Max scratched his neck.

"He said he was having the books checked by a ... what do you call it?" Max said.

"An auditor," Gertrud said.

"Yes, an auditor."

Ernst flinched as though fire had blazed up before him. "Having the books ...?"

"Yes," Gertrud said. She frowned in concentration to recall the words. "He also said he'd have the police after you if the books weren't in order, didn't he, Max?"

"Yes, that's what he said."

The clothing suitcase banged down beside Ernst.

The faint look of malice that had crept into Max's eyes during the telling faded as he saw the torment on Ernst's face. He dropped his gaze guiltily, and a roll of fat appeared beneath his jaw as he looked down at his brown slippers.

"Your soldier friend kept saying, 'It can't be true that he's run away'," Gertrud said.

"Come," Max said, and eased her back into the flat.

"What?" she said.

The door closed behind them.

Ernst shut his eyes and stood motionless on the landing. When he opened them again, the stair light had gone out.

"It's bleeding more now," Hansi said petulantly as he passed with the trophy. There'd been a new tone in the boy's voice since they'd left, an insolence and disrespect that hadn't been there before.

Ernst followed him into the flat and kicked the door closed with the sole of his shoe.

Mona stood in the hallway, her fists clenched before her.

"I'm not going out there again to clean that up," Mona said. "I'm not. That impossible woman. She can say what she likes. I will most certainly –"

"Shut up," Ernst said. The words clacked in his mouth. "Just shut up!" Spittle appeared on his lips. He dropped the suitcases dramatically to the floor. "You did this," he cried, throwing his hands up in the air. "You and your … and your …."

Mona's cheeks puffed out. She was a plump woman of thirty-five, prettier across her wide-set green eyes and high cheekbones than around the stiffened ridges of her mouth. "Me?" Her voice screeched up the scale in disbelief. "My fault?" She grabbed the roll of silver from the hall table and shook it before him. "It doesn't rattle," she said shrilly. "It doesn't."

Ernst gaped at her incomprehension and at the preposterous underwear being waved before him. He grabbed her wrist. She tried to struggle free. "Oh, so it doesn't rattle, eh?" he yelled, his face ablaze. Abruptly he let her go and backed away as though her face had suddenly blackened before him. Mona stopped waving. Fright filled her eyes. Ernst swung away, stalked into the lounge and slammed the door behind him.

Bettina's wail – sharp as a thorn – penetrated every ear.

Ernst flung his hat towards the olive-coloured sofa. It bounced, struck the wood panelling, fell to the floor and circled to rest before the fireplace. He rubbed his eyes and stood for a moment with his palms on his cheeks. The room appeared strangely disproportional. The window seemed farther away and the walls nearer than he'd remembered them in the poky room they'd all shared at his cousin Herbert's home in Winterthur. How he'd hated that room. There'd been a smell in there, a smell more unpleasant to him than the odour of soldiers together in a barracks or bunker. Had it been the children? Had it been him? He crossed to the windows and pulled them open to freshen the stale air. A cool breeze rose from beneath the curtain and crept up into his open jacket. Bettina's crying faded by degrees.

To his right stood an oak-and-glass cabinet. Four panels were decorated with paintings of soft tranquillity – farmers, gleaming ponds, hayricks and benevolently rounded mountains. He poured himself a kirsch, tossed it back and stood looking at his reflection in the glass. His teeth gritted and a tear welled in his left eye in sympathy of the sting. Behind him hung a photograph of his parents. The left side of the picture was melting, sliding down like wax, as though they were disappointed in him.

He took the bottle and glass, placed it on a low table beside his armchair and sat down, unconsciously straightening the creases of his trousers as he did so. He leaned his head against the backrest and for some moments dwelled in the lingering warmth of the kirsch and the coolness of the tear in his eye. The air was better. His gaze turned to the photograph of his parents on the wall. Berta, his mother, had warned him against marrying Mona. "She's weak and selfish," she said. "She'll bring you nothing but trouble."

Only now that he was back in his own armchair could he see the whole harrowing affair from beginning to end. In Winterthur it had been so fragmented. Everything appeared so torn by Mona's frantic efforts to keep him there, by Herbert's scorn that he didn't report back to his battalion and by his own doom-black thoughts about certain German invasion of Switzerland. He could still hear himself and Mona, not three weeks before, expressing their disdain for those who were evacuating. Then he foolishly told her the rumour Karl, his friend, had heard about a well-camouflaged battery of howitzers at Oberbargen with their guns trained on Schaffhausen. In the steadily rising tension of the German build-up on their border, Mona fixated on the notion of her children being blown to bits before her. She kept repeating this, growing more theatrical, asking if he wanted to see it.

It was incomprehensible to him, the power this phrase, this 'blown to bits', had over them in the next days. Although he detested hastily-made plans, one night he spontaneously decided to remove them to Winterthur, some thirty kilometres inland. He had every intention of returning the next day, as soon as he saw her and the children in safety, but he didn't.

Bettina had fallen silent. As he poured another tot of kirsch, he heard the front door open. He closed his eyes and shook his head. Mona would clean the stairs because she thought this was why he'd shouted at her. It undid him that her focus invariably fixed on the side issues. It was never there, never on the thing it was about. To this day he still didn't know whether she did this on purpose or not. He sipped at the kirsch and held the small glass between his hands.

Each time he'd prepared to leave, she'd set upon him with every fantasy she could muster. Out of the muddle of her thoughts came the absurd notion that he was having an affair with Fräulein Frei at Betschart's and wanted to return to her. What did he care about his children being blown to bits? And even if he found her ugly, and hated her hairstyles, she – unlike him – gave herself up entirely to the love of her children. Lucky she was, lucky not to have his selfishness. And he shouldn't think she didn't know, because she did. She knew he wished she'd died quickly of her heart ailment, so that he would not have been forced to spend most of their savings on her medical care.

On the morning of the tenth of May, Herbert rushed into the room to tell him that Germany had invaded Holland and the whole army was mobilising the next day He immediately started packing his few things, charged with apprehension that he would arrive back too late and not be with his comrades at the crucial hour. Mona was all over him, crying and pleading. When he didn't respond she ran into the kitchen and began swearing at Herbert's wife and calling her a bitch. Ernst was shaken into the realisation that she was trying to force Anna to throw them out. Mona knew full well he would never leave them out on the street with nowhere to go. Anna obliged immediately and twenty minutes later they were all out on the Römerstrasse with their suitcases.

Ernst was overawed by Mona's intense determination. He wasn't weak by nature, but he'd always chosen the path of least resistance. And this was where it had led him.

He found a room in a guest-house. They stayed there, running short of money, waiting for the invasion. It didn't come on the fourteenth of May, as everyone expected it to. And it didn't come on the fifteenth either. Slowly it began to dawn on him and on everyone else that the threat of invasion had been a deception, a distraction to mask the Germans' intention of attacking Holland. The Germans had not invaded Switzerland, but they'd destroyed his life. He hadn't called Betschart because he thought it was pointless. He hadn't responded to the mobilisation and he hadn't taken a stand against Mona. That night when they were eating a makeshift dinner in their room, he could hardly get his sandwich down in his remorse at not joining the mobilisation. In a warningly harsh voice, he said they were going home the next day. Mona said not a word.

He tossed back the remainder of the kirsch and felt his mood change. Damn it, hadn't he been one of the first to report for duty when the border guard was called up on the twenty-eighth of August the year before? Hadn't he spent five weeks after the first mobilisation slaving to the point of exhaustion each day, digging trenches, chopping wood, marching, shooting, training and with sleep-heavy eyes guarding their bunker at night? And who was again one of the first at the gathering point when the border guard was summoned on the sixth of March that year? Add another four weeks. Then he goes away for a little while at the wrong time and what do the bastards do? They wipe his slate clean. They have the bloody audacity to obliterate his life without even listening to reasons.

Snatches from directives given out by Schaffhausen's local parliament came to him: 'Voluntary evacuation on your own responsibility and at your expense; only possible and permitted when no hostilities imminent; destination must be registered with local community by twentieth March nineteen forty at the latest.' He grimaced at the thought of the snide comments he would hear and the derisive laughter behind his back.

A knock sounded at the door. It opened and little Bettina came in, wearing red ribbons on her pigtails. She'd worn white ribbons before; he was attentive to such things. He also knew that Mona had opened the door. Bettina, small as she was, always made such a racket of it.

"Papa," the little voice said. "Mama cleaned the stairs."

He held his hand out to her and she ran towards him, her face bright with excitement, her sorrows in the corridor long forgotten.

"Careful," he said and placed his glass on the table before taking her on his knee. He noticed wet spots on her collar where the tears had run down, and his throat constricted at the thought of her being blown to bits.

Mona looked around the door. He glanced towards her. Her brown curls were neatly combed and she wore fresh lipstick. He stroked Bettina's hair. Mona came in. There was a clatter of feet in the corridor and Hansi appeared beside her.

"Shh," Mona said. "It's late."

The clock read five to ten.

They all seemed to be waiting for him to say something. When he didn't, Mona cleared her throat.

"I'll … I'll say it was me who made you stay."

He swung towards her in astonishment, unable to recall a single occasion when she'd admitted responsibility or blame. The dread in her eyes shocked him. Abruptly, like a hot rush of embarrassment, his sense of control returned. It was there again, in his shoulders and in his neck.

"No, you won't," he said.

Mona squeezed her hands together.

"You can tell them you got sick in Winterthur and that's why you couldn't come back. You were sick. I mean all those outbursts. It wasn't you."

Ernst felt Hansi's gaze on him.

"Put Betty to bed and close the door when you go out," he said to Mona. "Hansi and I have to talk."

Mona lifted the lolling Betty from his lap. He saw in Mona's fine eyes a softening of tension, a return to the illusion that all was well. She went out.

"Sit down there, Hansi." He indicated the chair opposite him.

Hansi obeyed in his reluctant, stalling way.

"When it's possible for the schools to open again, the boys may tease you about me, say I'm a coward. I'm sorry about that."

Hansi, kicking his legs up and down before him, didn't look at him, but at the tips of his shoes and the plaster on his shin.

"Do you think I stayed away because I was afraid?"

"Yes," Hansi said.

Ernst studied him for a while. "Maybe you're right. Whatever the reason, I have to report to our battalion tomorrow. I'll see my comrades' faces and hear what they have to say about me."

Hansi dabbed at his plaster, his ruddy face and fierce eyes attractive in his pretended disinterest.

"Aren't you going to say you were sick?"

"It's a possibility, isn't it? Some people may even believe it. I thought about it, of course. But I'm a bookkeeper, Hansi. Debits and credits and balances. It's just the way I see the world. And in that world you can't correct one mistake with another one."

Hansi jumped up, crossed to the mantle-piece and took a glass ball back to his chair. He shook it and watched the snow fall on a little blue house in the centre of the ball.

"What are you going to say then?"

"There's nothing I can say. I've lost their trust. Yes, that's what's happened. I never really knew what that meant, you know – the trust of the people around you. I had to go away to see what it was."

For some minutes they sat in silence, watching the snow falling in the ball, looking into another world.

"I'll just have to start all over again and try to win some trust back."

"If you die fighting for Schaffhausen, then they can't say anything," Hansi said.

Ernst nodded.

"Yes, that's a comfort, isn't it?"

Hansi glanced suspiciously at him, then hid a small smile behind the glass ball.

The clock on the wall began to chime ten. It was a warm sound, reminiscent of a cloth-padded drumstick tapped on a cymbal.

"Well, it's late," Ernst said. "Go to bed now, son."

"What are you going to do?"

"Me? I think I'll polish my tunic buttons and buckle."

"Now?"

"Yes."

"Oh, all right," Hansi said with a great show of weariness. "I'll do the buckle."

"Aren't you tired?"

"I'm not tired," Hansi said sharply.

Early the next morning Ernst went out in his grey uniform with his kitbag, bayonet and rifle. He descended the stairs and, on a whim, walked out to the rear of the building and stood looking at their tiny allotment garden. The salad had died and the asparagus was gone. Down on the road below, a horse strained up the rise, pulling a cart loaded with bags marked with white crosses. Mona was asleep when he went to bed. For long hours he stared up at the ceiling. Then at breakfast he hummed appreciation at the taste of Mona's coffee, the way he'd always done.

He heard the door open behind him. Max Müller stood in the doorway with a plastic tray in his hand. Max shuffled closer, his gaze flickering over Ernst's uniform. "This is your asparagus," he said, holding out the tray.

"Is it? Thank you." He examined them. "I'll leave them here in the shade." He placed the tray beside their salad patch. "My wife will be down soon. It will be a pleasant home-coming surprise."

Max stood with his hands deep in his trouser pockets, looking at the stolen asparagus. Then he turned and shuffled away.

Ernst walked out onto the Neustadt. The wood-and-barbed-wire barriers – the 'Spanish riders', as they called them – were still there at the end of the street, but placed against a wall. Twice along the street he saw familiar faces. All Franz Bauer said was that his whole family was down with the flu, and old Katrin Kuhn merely asked him to remind Mona to call her when she next went to the drying installation with her fruit and vegetables.

Ernst walked on, waiting for the next face. He wondered how long he would be doing that, waiting for the next face.

Flashpoint

by Judy Walker

I don't like the warden. He's a skinny bloke, straight back, short dark hair and a mean frown – ex-army, I know the type. He lets me know he was in the army as he's signing me in, to warn me like – 'don't think you can mess with me'. As if that would have me shitting my kegs.

"I don't care what your background is, mate," he says. "I treat everyone the same here, as long as you stick to the rules. I'll play fair with you, if you play fair with me."

There's a silence. I don't look at him.

"Okay?" He's obviously wanting me to acknowledge that I will 'play fair'.

"Can I see my room?"

"Follow me." He jerks his head down the hall.

I don't have to share – I'm pleased about that. The room's not much different from what I'm used to – bed, desk, chair, lock on the door – except this time, I get the key.

"Dinner's at six, sharp. You make your own breakfast – there's cereal and bread set out ready. I expect you to help keep the place tidy too. You have to be out by ten in the morning and you can't come back in till four."

"Suits me, I'll be off early, anyway."

"Got a job, have you?"

"Yeah."

"I lock up at twelve, so if you go out in the evening, make sure you're back by then or you won't get in. Oh and no visitors, right?"

"I've got no one wants to visit me."

"Well, you sound like the ideal guest, pal."

I look at him, but he doesn't seem like he's taking the piss. I like rules, me. I've got to know where my boundaries are. That's why prison suited me because everything was ordered. There was always someone to tell you what to do next. I think I'll be all right here.

I go down to the dining room dead on six. There's a queue already, so I join it, pick up a tray, wait my turn. The woman serving takes my plate, spoons the dinner on and passes it to me. I look at it and then at her.

"Is that it?"

"You what?"

"Is that all I'm getting?"

She shrugs. "If there's any left you can come back."

I'm getting a flash in my head, so I walk away. I choose a seat in the corner, so I'm looking out at the room. I don't like to have my back to people. I like to see what's going on.

The food's not that bad, actually. I take the opportunity to size up the other blokes while I'm eating. There's a couple of young lads with washed-out tee shirts, and beads round their necks – ex-crackheads probably, the rest are older, in their fifties or sixties I'd say, most of them. Two or three will have done time, but the rest look like professional dossers. I see them sneaking a look at me, deciding whether to bother trying to touch me for a fag or a fiver.

When I've finished I go back to my room and lie on the bed – it feels as soft as a sack of tits compared to what I've been used to. Christ knows how my back'll cope with it.

It's my first day out today. They say they look after you better nowadays when you leave prison – probation officer and social worker, all that crap, but really once you step out the door, they couldn't give a toss about you, glad to be rid. They put a train ticket and a map in my hand and that was it.

I didn't like the train – you never know who's going to come and sit down next to you. I was on my own at first – in one of those seats around a table but then this woman got on – old biddy she was – with another one a bit younger – her sister probably. They sat opposite me and when the conductor came round she was all over the shop trying to find her bloody ticket. I kept getting the flashes – so I got up and went to the corridor bit between the carriages to have a fag. The pair of them walked past me, heading for the buffet, so I went back to my seat. I got out the map and studied it, worked out my route from the station. My probation officer said I could get a bus, but I'm better walking.

It was getting dark by the time the train got to Bolton, but I found the hostel without having to ask for directions. It's down a side street, past a couple of cheap hotels. There were cardboard boxes and bin bags stacked all along the pavement and I had to step over the remains of a takeaway curry to get to the door. I wasn't expecting the Ritz but I thought it'd be better than this.

68

I'm down at six in the morning. I have a bowl of cornflakes and a couple of slices of toast. It's set out, like the warden said, but I still have to get the milk out of the fridge and put the bread in the toaster. I'm up and down like a bride's nightie, so that doesn't put me in a good mood. I look at my map for where I'm going. It's about six miles, the probation officer told me, so I'll need a good hour and a half to walk it. I pass a couple of blokes coming down for breakfast, as I'm on my way out. They nod at me, but I don't make eye contact. That's the first thing you learn in prison.

I'm back by half five, knackered. I thought I was quite fit but I tell you, a day's labouring and a six mile walk at the end of it has finished me off. I get washed and lie on my bed till six, then I'm down to queue up for my grub.

"Hello love, had a hard day?" she says, as I give her my plate.

"Not bad." I move away quickly. What's she after, wanting to know my business? Some bugger's in my seat, so I have to sit at a different table, which I don't like. I'm half way through my dinner, when this bloke comes up to me and leans over the table.

"I had to clear up after you this morning, you dirty bastard," he says.

"What are you on about?"

"You left a right fucking mess all over the kitchen, didn't you?"

The warden's coming over. "All right lads, what's going on? Let's try and sort it out nice and peaceful eh?" He tells me I'm meant to clear away my own breakfast stuff in the morning.

"But I'm going to work," I say.

"It's the rules, mate," he folds his arms.

"You never told me. You didn't tell me that." I'm standing up now.

"All right, all right, no need to get fussed. I did say breakfast was self service, didn't I?"

"Yes, but I didn't know I was supposed to clear up as well as get my own grub – bloody hell, I'm paying to stay here." I'm getting a really strong flash.

"Well, you know now. Breakfast is DIY – make it yourself and clear up yourself. You get your dinner served, so you just need to take your stuff back to the serving hatch."

"Clear away? After I've been out working all day?" I stand up, scraping back the chair. Everyone's looking now, so I know I've got to give them something to look at. I pick my plate up and fling it on the floor, then my tea mug and the tray.

"I'm fucking paying to stay here," I shout. "I don't expect to have to clear up – that's someone else's job, that is." Another flash.

"Right, that's it." The warden comes towards me, but I spin away and we stand apart looking at each other. I look him straight in the eye. Then the serving woman comes over, just quietly, and starts picking everything up and putting it in a plastic bag, wiping the floor with a cloth.

"You don't have to do that, Eileen," says the warden.

"I don't mind," she says. "He's just had a bad day. He's new, give him a break, can't you?" She's dead calm, just gets on with it although her face is all sweaty.

There's a long silence. I'm waiting for the warden to tell me to piss off somewhere else. He's standing there chewing his bottom lip, frowning so hard his eyes have almost disappeared into his forehead.

"All right lads, back to your seats, the show's over." He turns his back on me while the other blokes shuffle back to their places. When they've all settled down again, he comes back.

"Okay, Ray. I'm going to let it go, just this once. But anything else, any other incident – I don't care what it is – you're out. Okay?"

I walk away. I go outside, walk round the block till I come to the back yard. I go in the gate and stand against the wall, light a fag. The door opens and Eileen comes out with a bag of rubbish. It's dark so she doesn't see me at first. When she does, she jumps.

"Oh, it's you. You gave me a right fright."

"What did you do that for, in there?" I ask her.

"I don't like trouble, that's all."

I offer her a fag and she takes it, comes closer while I light it from mine, then stands next to me and leans her head on the wall. I haven't been close to a woman for years. She's nothing to look at – mid forties, dyed blond hair, running to fat, and when she lifts her arm, I can smell sour sweat.

"Just out of prison, are you?" she says.

"Shows, does it?"

She shrugs. "You'll have to watch out, you know, if you want to stay here. Mr Thomas is a mean bugger – I've had a few run ins with

70

him. If I didn't need the money so much I'd be off like a shot. He won't think twice about chucking you out. He can let the rooms ten times over, so it's no skin off his nose."

"If he thinks I'm kowtowing to him, he's got another think coming."

She turns to look at me.

"What?" I say.

"You remind me of my dad, you do."

"Why's that?"

"He was always getting into arguments, fights. He'd come in from the pub, full of beer and start arguing with my mother, throwing things. He never listened to reason." She takes the fag out of her mouth and tosses it on the ground. "I hated that so I'd do anything to try and keep the peace. That's what it reminded me of tonight, when you started."

She gets her own packet of fags out and offers me one. We light up and stand for a bit. Then she says: "Mind, she deserved it half the time – never let up on him."

"Eh?"

"Me mother. She were always nagging on about something. I used to say to her: 'Mother, just leave it – you're provoking him,' but she couldn't see it, so the pair of us usually ended up with a good slapping off my dad. I've still got a deaf ear where he slammed me against a wall once." She rubs her left ear. "So what were you in prison for?" she asks me.

"I killed a bloke."

"Been in a while then, have you?"

"Fifteen years. It would have been less with good behaviour."

"So you didn't behave, then?"

No, I didn't behave well in prison, not for a long time anyway. I made trouble whenever I could because I didn't want to give those screws an easy life, or anyone else, come to that. I was known for my temper. I did more time in solitary than anyone in that prison.

"You're lucky to get a job, mind," she says. "Where are you working?"

"Just labouring on a building site up near Banstead. It's about six miles from here, do you know it?"

"The forty-six takes you straight there, you know. The bus stop's just across the road."

"I'd rather walk," I say. "Too many people on a bus. I'm not good around people, they get on my nerves. That's why I think I'll be all right with this job. I just keep myself to myself, get on with my work."

I keep my head down in the hostel for the next few days. I get into a routine, so I'm all right. I know where my boundaries are. I do keep getting the flashes though.

I have a couple of fags with Eileen out the back again one night and she asks me if I think prison did me any good.

"The only person who ever really tried to understand me was my last governor, Mr Webster," I tell her. "'Ray,' he said, 'you're not going to solve any problems with violence,' and he was right. You don't get anywhere going down that road, not in prison, because the authorities can deal with that, see?"

"Putting you in solitary confinement, you mean?"

"Yeah – and other stuff, you don't want to know. But Mr Webster, he was the one that introduced me to negotiation, seeing things from other people's point of view, that type of thing. I'd never done that before. He was the one that arranged for me to meet the daughter of the fella I killed."

"What was she like?"

"Nice lass – early twenties she must have been, I reckon. She was nine years old when it happened. Her mother's still on tablets she said, for her nerves."

"Was she still angry with you?"

"All she wanted to know was why I'd done it. And I couldn't tell her, couldn't give her a reason – because there wasn't one. That was the first time I saw the result of what I'd done from someone else's point of view. It sounds corny, I know, but that really was a turning point for me."

"So you've learnt your lesson then?"

I shrug and toss my fag end on the ground.

I come in early from work one day and I hear the warden shouting at Eileen. He's in the kitchen with her, mouthing off about the state of the place. I just want to sit down and take it easy but he's started on me now.

"You're supposed to help around here. The floor could do with a sweep and you can get those ashtrays emptied."

72

"Fuckin' hell, I've just done a day's work. Can't you leave me alone? I just want to fucking relax for half an hour."

"It's not Buckingham Palace, you know. Everyone has to pull their weight here, and you're not. Eileen!" he shouts. "Fetch the broom."

He's wagging his finger in my face. I think of the rock I've got in a sock up in my room. My hands shake. The meat cleaver goes into his head. I count the number of times – five, six, seven. Blood spews over his hair and down his face. He's on the floor, just lying there.

I sit down at the table and Eileen joins me. I offer her a cigarette and we both smoke in silence till a beeper goes off.

"That's the potatoes," she says and gets up, goes into the kitchen. I can see her through the hatch. She drains the pan, puts the potatoes in the chafing dish and slides it into the oven. Then she comes and sits back down.

I look at the warden. I know he's dead.

"I'll ring for the police," I say. She nods and says she has to get on preparing the dinner.

When the filth arrive, they take us both down to the station. We're there for hours. I don't see her again till we're in court.

She gets ten years.

Recognition

by Sarah Evans

The pub was mass market. Simon hated these places with their sticky wooden floors, wood-worm beams and bright tapestry seats. His eyes skimmed over the groups of employees huddling in their uniforms of dark suits, then swept past the couple in the corner.

Stopped.

Flicked back.

Flicked down to the beer-splattered boards, and back.

The woman looked a bit like Josie. But it couldn't be. Too much of a coincidence. Same golden sheen of hair. Different style. Like a stuck record, his eyes kept going back. A familiar angle to her chin. An unfamiliar bend of body. He was always imagining he saw her. Right flow of feminine clothes. Colours brighter than was usual.

Oh God!

Recognition spliced through him. It was; it was Josie.

Usually Simon avoided the drink with colleagues on Friday nights. But he'd decided he ought to make more effort. Already, only twenty minutes in, he'd run out of shop talk. The others had moved on to things more personal: the progress of football teams and tennis players; films and reality TV that they offered strong opinions on. Simon's mind was blank. He'd been planning to make a discreet exit. Now his heart was somersaulting.

He'd instinctively sat further back, breaking the line of vision. He didn't want her to see him, not yet. He wondered how long she had been there, sitting within reach and him not knowing. Now he leant forward, needing a clearer view, needing to double, triple check, wanting to see who she was with and how she looked and to absorb the full impact.

She was with a man. She was dressed in a sleeveless top and a skirt that billowed out to dust the floor. Her face was in profile. He could see the guy full on: thick-build, scalped hair. Thuggish looking, he would have said. Or was that just because the man's voice had risen, and Josie was trying to twist away, and the man seemed to have taken hold of her arm, and to be preventing her from getting up. Simon caught his colleague's eye as he turned back, realised Tim had been looking too. Tim raised his eyebrows, as if the couple were providing a diversion.

Simon's fists clenched.

He stood and had zig-zagged half way across the crowded floor before realising that he hadn't thought through what he was doing, and that this might not be a good idea. The guy she was with appeared more menacing as he got nearer. Simon's hands remained tightly angled.

'I should go.' He heard her voice, low and urgent. 'Really.'

'C'mon, where's the harm? Stay a bit.' The man's voice was half-threat, half-wheedle. His hand still gripped her wrist.

Simon reached them. He touched her shoulder lightly.

'Josie,' he said as he crouched down beside her, away from the guy.

She turned to look at him, a moment's confusion switching to a beam of pleasure.

'Simon! What are you doing here?'

He shrugged, and waved behind him. 'Out for a drink with people from work. You?'

She grimaced back.

'Who the fuck?' the guy was saying.

Simon kept his eyes trained on her, ignoring her companion. At least the guy had let go of her arm, which she brought forward and started to rub. His own hand had come to rest on her elbow, hovering awkwardly beneath it, but he was reluctant to relinquish even so slight a hold.

'It's good to see you,' he said. Oh God, it was good! She looked thinner, he thought, edgier, still beautiful. He thought about when he first knew her, his astonishment that she might be interested in him. 'I've been meaning to get in touch.' This was only half a lie. The thought had circulated relentlessly, an ill-formed intention, never realised into action.

The guy was standing now, forming an edge-of-vision blur. He was stockier than Simon, but shorter – except Simon was at a disadvantage crouching down – his forearms bulged, and were covered in blue tattoos under thick black hair. Best not to look at him directly. Simon raised his arm, touched her shoulder again. 'How have you been?'

'It's good to see you too,' she said. 'I'm good. Fine. I was just thinking of leaving.' Her eyes twitched sideways towards the guy.

'I'm leaving too. I'll walk you to the tube.'

'Have it your own fucking way,' the guy was muttering. He kicked the table leg, setting the glasses clattering, and carried on with a series of expletives. Simon's knees creaked as he rose to standing.

Josie stood as well, and his arm floated behind her as she walked with him. He left her at the door to grab his coat, jerking a thumb at the exit to Tim who was now deep in conversation with the others. It was clear enough that he was leaving.

Outside, he hesitated.

'Thanks,' she said. 'I'd been out with people from work. I just got talking. I stayed when the others moved on. Not a good idea as it turned out.' She smiled ruefully. 'Anyway. Thanks.'

'So the tube.' He looked left and right trying to figure out the best direction. 'Or. Have you eaten? We could get something?'

'Oh. I mean no. I don't know.'

He stared down. Her hardly-there shoes, tapering to a sharp point, triggered a smile. He'd never understood why she wore such uncomfortable looking footwear. *Please, please say 'yes'*. He thought of all the times he'd made that plea, as if just by thinking it, it would influence her decision.

'Please,' he said. 'It would be nice to catch up.'

'Okay.'

'Where to?' Every nerve tightened as he remembered the last time they'd eaten out together.

'You'd better decide.'

'Okay. Pizza Express?' Hardly inspired, but he'd passed a branch on his way here. She used to like going there; he could remember what she usually ordered.

'Fine.'

He held back from hugging her, felt stupidly happy when she let him take her arm.

'You're looking well,' she said.

'You too. How have you been? I mean really?'

'Better. Much better.' Her mouth turned down. 'Well not better. Obviously. You know that. But managing better.'

'That's good.'

She laughed. 'Maybe not entirely managing. That guy. Not one of my better decisions.'

'No.' He wondered what would have happened if he hadn't been there. Nothing probably. Surely she'd have left anyway.

They were seated in a quiet corner. The glass table between them supported a thin vase containing a single flower whose stem was coiled round with wire.

'So how's it going? The new job?' she asked.

'Good. Really good.' It had felt impossible to stay working at the Treasury, risking bumping into her at the lifts or in the canteen. But he'd been overdue a change anyway. It had all happened very quickly. 'Long hours. But paid well. And stimulating.' He started talking about his current project, a complicated merger. He doubted any of what he said was interesting. 'And it's different,' he carried on. 'Working for a small company. None of the red tape. Consultancy is hard work, but involving. Feels worthwhile.' For the last six months he had immersed himself in work. He overheard his new workmates chatting at the coffee point the other day, their conversation bumping to an embarrassed halt, but not before he'd caught snippets of the exchange: '...devoid of personal life...' '...never mind personality...' He was the one always volunteering to travel, willingly working weekends, staying on late into the evening.

The waitress was hovering. Neither of them had looked at the menu. Anxiety clenched. The last time they'd eaten together, they had had a huge row. He'd been so certain at the time that Josie was the one acting unreasonably. He looked up at her.

'Did you want a bit longer?'

She was frowning with concentration.

'No. I don't think so. Have you decided?'

'Yes.' He couldn't have cared less what he ate.

The waitress was tapping her pen meaningfully.

'The *Four Seasons*,' he said.

'I'll have the same,' she said decisively and shut the menu.

He hadn't quite known what to expect, but it wasn't that. The waitress had moved on before he suddenly thought, 'It has anchovies. You don't like anchovies.'

'Oh,' she said. 'No.'

'D'you want to ask for it without the anchovies, or d'you want to order something else?'

She gazed back, eyes drawn together, mouth slightly open. He remembered the look, and what sometimes followed.

'Shall I sort it?'

She nodded *yes*.

Before, his attempts to help had always made things worse. *Managing better*, she'd said earlier. What did it mean?

He caught the waitress as she headed for another table, watched her look of disdain as he said they'd both changed their minds.

'Kitchen might have already started,' she said, her lips tight.

'They'll have to start again then.' If they insisted that he pay twice, he'd do so. He wasn't going to offer.

He asked for the *Four Seasons* without the anchovies, and ordered the *Fiorentina*. They could share. Or she could choose.

Choose! Oh God!

She was staring at that awful flower when he returned, her fingers tracing the metal coil.

'It's one of my strategies,' she said. 'Ordering what the other person does. My therapist suggested it. It's hard letting go, even of small decisions like that. Better than the alternative though.'

'Yes. I guess.'

That last time she had taken forty minutes debating three different restaurants, whose menus had struck him as practically identical. She had quizzed an increasingly exasperated waiter for almost half an hour, wanting precise details of ingredients and flavours and calories. She had ordered. Changed her mind. Changed her mind again. He walked out. Later she refused to accept that her behaviour was odd. If she was paying for something why wouldn't she want to know what she was getting? 'It's you, you're so uptight,' she'd accused him.

'Your therapist?' he asked now.

'Uh-huh. Cognitive behavioural therapy. Amanda suggested it. Remember my sessions with Amanda?' Her fingers raked through her hair and he caught sight of the white ridge of scar behind her hairline. 'Therapy doesn't address the underlying issue, of course. It's about trying to find ways of behaving. Finding strategies to cope.' She smiled slowly. 'To cope with my *disability*.' She drew the word out. 'Disabled. That's what they've decided I am at work.'

He breathed in the garlic-scented air. It wasn't a negative word. His diversity training at the Treasury had defined it so widely it might encompass anyone.

'Does it bother you?' It shouldn't bother him. It did.

'It sort of helps. They get brownie points for the disability stats. I get special consideration. My boss talks to me slowly and clearly.' She articulated the last phrase very deliberately in demonstration. 'But that's better than before.' He remembered how things had appeared to be rising to a crisis the last he knew. Not helped by the fact that all those tests showed that she was fine. 'It gives her a way to cope with her frustration.'

Simon flinched. *He* should have coped. He was the one who cared.

'D'you still see Amanda?' he asked.

'Occasionally. She got her article published. Accepted by *Nature*. I appeared as patient *AMN*. I could send you a copy.'

The lightness of her tone pierced him. As if she couldn't take it seriously.

'Did the study help?'

'It helped Amanda's career prospects. *Nature* is a big deal apparently. It sort of helped at work. Not that people really understood it. But at least it set out scientifically that there's something wrong with me; it isn't just me being deliberately awkward.' Her fingers were toying with the napkin, folding it into elaborate patterns. 'Perhaps it helped me too. Helped me accept what everyone was telling me. That I need to try and, I don't know, control how I act.'

'What did Amanda conclude?'

'You know the sort of stuff. Lots of theory about the pre-frontal cortex and its role in integrating rational thought with emotion and how the injury interfered with my ability to make decisions. But she managed to find some new things to say. Those tests she used to do with cards, apparently they helped prove some theory. But that bit all got rather technical.'

The waitress arrived back with the pizzas, asking which was for who. He pointed randomly.

'I thought we'd have half of each,' he said decisively. Josie bit her lip and didn't argue. Her passivity was easier. He wondered what was going on inside.

'So what about outside work? How have you been?' she asked.

'Fine.' He pushed the word out through half-chewed pizza, and swallowed. 'Actually not fine. Not really.'

'Are you seeing anyone?'

'No. I mean I have. A few dates. Dating agency.'

Her laugh was bright and vivid; he found himself drawn into it.

'I know,' he continued. 'It's just work doesn't leave much time, and I was never very good at meeting people.'

Her smile seemed to warm him from his centre. He thought of the last woman, Francesca. How perfectly she had seemed to match the detailed criteria he had set out, how similar their taste in films and art, how polite their agreement on political issues, how dreary the evening.

'I've spent every date wishing I was with you.'

'What, wishing you were with that mad woman who can't decide anything?'

'Wishing I was with you.'

He remembered the conversation with Francesca. He'd tried to be honest, or at least not to lie, when her tale of a failed marriage seemed to demand he reciprocate with a sorry story of his own. He tried to keep to the facts. A car accident. Hit and run. A head injury. Brain damage. The hardest bit was trying to explain the impact. How in so many ways Josie had seemed to make a good recovery. Intelligence tests showed she hadn't lost her high IQ. She could talk articulately about a whole range of issues. The changes were subtle.

Compulsive.

Obsessive.

He hated himself for using such ugly words to describe her.

'It sounds like you didn't have a choice. I mean splitting up. You weren't obliged to spend your whole life looking after her.' That was Francesca's conclusion, the conclusion he'd encouraged her to reach. He'd felt a pulse of pure dislike that she was letting him off so easily.

Josie was looking away, her face wistful.

'What about you?' he asked. 'Are you with someone?' He thought of the guy in the pub.

80

'One or two along the way. There was someone who lasted a month or so. Even moved in.' She grimaced. 'Something of a disaster, everyone thought. My parents think I'm not capable of being on my own. Want me to move back home.'

'I should never have left you.'

'You didn't. I left you, remember.'

'I let you.'

'I was driving you mad. We were driving each other mad. I don't see what else we could have done.'

'I should have persuaded you to stay. I should have helped.'

'It's not that easy. You know that. Anyway...' She gestured vaguely, as if wanting to waft away the train of conversation. 'Tell me more about what you've been up to.'

He told her about the places he had travelled to, the people he had worked for, the tourist trails he'd fitted in. With Francesca his voice had trilled with the fabulous art exhibitions, the exotic food, the buzz of achieving the impossible in a project. Now he stumbled on more honestly. The vapid blankness of hotel rooms. The eye-straining, back-aching weariness of sixteen-hour days. The bleakness of sitting in a restaurant alone.

'I miss you,' he said.

'You miss me the way I was.'

'I miss you.'

The waitress was there again, removing their half-eaten pizzas, offering them dessert menus, which he said *yes* to, even though he rarely ordered sweet food. He watched as Josie stared down, frowning at the effort. It had been hard to understand, no matter how much he read up, or how often the neurosurgeon explained it. The pre-frontal cortex is central to integrating emotion with rational thought. Decision making is more driven by emotion than people think. People usually decide based on imperfect information, using intuition. They're influenced by the visual image, by the misleading words. *Homemade* cake. *Real Italian* ice-cream. *Light and fruity*. They form an image beyond the facts. Decide on the emotion of the moment. It's why advertising works. That tiny alteration to Josie's brain meant she couldn't decide things, not any more. Trying to decide rationally, taking all variables into account, she'd find it impossible to choose at all. Or when she did choose, the choices would be odd. Choices that turned out to be wrong. That other people would say were wrong.

She looked up at him.

'It's no good,' she said. 'I can't.'

'D'you want me to?'

'Maybe.' She smiled ruefully. 'But you don't even like any of this stuff.' She reached into her jacket pocket, brought out a coin and spun it on the table. 'Another strategy.' It landed heads. 'Heads for not ice-cream.' She spun it several more times, eliminating possibilities. 'Looks like it's lemon tart,' she said eventually.

'But you don't lemony things.'

She laughed.

'No. At least I lose weight like this. Actually, I don't think I'll bother.'

He felt a sharp stab of disappointment. *Don't go! Not yet.*

'What about coffee?'

'More decisions!'

'Let me choose.'

She sat looking at him, her hands tightening then relaxing. He watched her breathe out.

'Okay. okay then.'

He ordered two lattes, decaff, glanced over at her anxiously, but her face was smooth.

'Are you still living in the same place?' he asked.

'No. The guy who'd moved in…I didn't know how to get rid of him. I sort of flitted. Had to leave half my stuff.'

'Oh God, Josie.'

Her laugh was short.

'Of course it upset everyone, my parents in particular, much more than it upset me.' Her hands were back toying with the flower. How fragile she looked, as if she also needed propping up with wire. 'I'm not unhappy. Everyone feels sorry for me, thinks what's happened is so awful. But I'm okay with things.'

Damage to the pathways for emotion. Not being able to feel deeply any more. He hadn't said that bit to Francesca.

When he said he loved her, her response felt blank. 'Do you?' she asked him once. 'I don't know what I feel. Not any more.' He hadn't tried to understand what it really meant. How did it feel not to feel? If she hadn't said that would he have been more patient?

82

The waitress arrived with the coffee and the bill. The restaurant was almost empty. Josie bit her lip.

'Everything okay?' he asked.

'Uh-huh. I'd have preferred dessert.'

'You still could.'

'No. This is fine. Really.' She smiled broadly. 'I'm not doing too badly am I? My therapist would be pleased.'

'You're doing fine.' He sipped the coffee he hadn't really wanted either. He wondered how he could draw out the evening.

'So where is it you're living?'

'Battersea way.'

'Nice?'

'No.'

'No?'

'It's cheap. The space isn't bad. A bit hairy returning late at night. Gangs tend to hang round. Just kids really. But still. And it can be noisy. The guy above tends to party at the weekends. Not so bad in the week. I don't usually sleep weekends.'

He could feel a thought forming, tried to push it back, not wanting to voice it in case she said *no*. 'Can't you move?'

'Could. I mean will. Only it's a six month contract. Three months to go. I can't afford... I mean Mum and Dad would help. It's just they've done so much already.'

'I could help.'

'You?'

'It's only money.'

Her expression locked. 'Yes. But...'

The waitress was looking over at them meaningfully. 'I can at least pay tonight.'

'That would be okay, I think. I mean, yes. Thank-you.'

'Come home with me.' He blurted it out. He could hardly bear to look at her. 'I mean, I don't mean...' Except of course he did. He had a horrid vision of himself as no different from that bloke earlier, preying on the sense of her vulnerability. 'I mean I can sleep in the spare room. If that's what you want. We'll just talk. You can get a good night's sleep. I'll even bring you tea in the morning.' The way he used to.

He remembered how when they made love it had felt like nothing had changed. Even after days and evenings fraught with tension, in bed she would curl towards him. Touching would provide the apology they hadn't voiced. He would hold her afterwards.

He'd wake beside her in the morning and she'd smile to see him there. He'd make tea, bring it back to bed. They'd bat back and forth comments on the rain battering the window, or the birds that had been chattering since five am. A moment's sweetness would envelope him and he'd allow himself to believe that everything was going to work out fine. But as the clock clicked forward, his dread would slowly grow. Soon they would have to get up.

What would set her off this time?

Getting dressed. Sometimes she would select easily. Other times he'd get out of the shower to find every item of clothing she owned heaped on the bed and her detailing the pros and cons of every item. *Does it matter?* he tried to say. He'd offer suggestions: why not this blouse, how about that skirt? *That doesn't help*, she'd tell him coldly. *I'm not a child.*

Or it might be deciding what to have for breakfast.

Or what to take into work for lunch.

Or whether they should meet up after work for dinner or just come home.

Or how they should spend the day that stretched out before them.

Weekends were the worse. There were a lot of decisions to be made at weekends.

She was looking very directly at him. He had no idea what was going on inside, what factors she might be considering.

'Just tonight?' she asked.

He hesitated. He hadn't thought beyond the simple fact of not wanting the evening to end. 'I don't know. Do we need to decide that now?'

'No. I mean I don't think so.'

'Just decide about tonight. It can be whatever you want it to be. We can take it from there.' Could they try again? She was managing better now. He would try harder. Could the memory of the fact that she had loved him once be enough to get them through? The questions cycled round.

She looked down, slowly picked up her coin and spun it. It landed heads. She continued staring down.

'What does that mean?'

'It means I don't go home with you.'

He dug his finger nails hard into his palms, trying to think of an objection. Like the random bad luck of the hit and run, like the skull fracture that had penetrated just a fraction too far, like the coincidence of bumping into her tonight, his whole life seemed to rest on luck no more substantial than the flipping of a coin.

When she looked up at him, she was smiling gently.

'But it isn't a coin-spinning type of decision is it? And sometimes the logic all points one way. I don't want to face the walk back to my flat. It's comfortable at your place, and quiet. And I trust you.' She paused, her face serious. 'The problem is, some of my very worst decisions are when I'm sure.'

He felt his own decision form, the recognition that had been settling all evening: even now, she was what he wanted.

'Come home with me.'

'Okay then,' she said. 'Okay.'

Softly Now

by Cate Manning

The ward round was just finishing when a nurse from Violet ward bustled over to Dr Lonsdale.

"It's Bernie," she muttered to the doctor. "She's had to be taken to seclusion. Can you see her?"

"Of course, Maggie." Dr Lonsdale turned to us. "Do you want to come? It will be a good learning experience." She picked up the files of patient notes from the ward round and began to make her way to the nurses' station without waiting for us to reply.

We hurried after her. Of course we would come. Almost everything that happened here was a good learning experience, by medical students' standards. This morning's ward round had been broken up by a patient throwing a cup of hot tea at her nurse while he was describing an incident in which she had been found spitting out her medication. I had frozen in my chair while the team had set off their alarms and rushed to remove the cup of tea and try to calm the patient while back-up was on its way. They called it 'de-escalation': the process by which they dealt with patients on the ward who had become disturbed. The woman had been physically removed from the room by four strong nurses. She was not struggling by then. Her anger had died down and she looked forlorn and a little frightened. It was a typically impulsive act by a patient with borderline personality disorder. That's what Dr Lonsdale had said. I was still gripping the sides of my chair with white fingers long after the patient had left the room.

I was ashamed of my fear. It was a common public perception to think that one had to fear the 'insane'. That is what we had been told in lectures. The vast majority are no more dangerous than any person you might meet in the community. The risk that they might hurt you is far less than headline-grabbing newspapers might have you think.

In spite of this knowledge, I was most definitely afraid. I could not quell my sense that there was something terribly unpredictable about the patients. I felt somehow adrift in their world. I wasn't convinced that the rules by which society was governed were applicable here. I wasn't sure there were rules at all in this world and if there were, I had no idea how to negotiate them. And I was most afraid that the patients would sense my fear and it would either offend them or encourage them to see me as an easy target. Or both.

I had not made things easy for myself, either. I had chosen to come to a forensic psychiatric unit for four weeks of my psychiatric placement. The patients here were those who had either committed violent offences, or been too difficult to manage in a 'normal' psychiatric unit. I wanted to face my fear and teach myself that I could cope with the challenge. Instead, my anxieties were worse, if anything, and I could not relax for a moment. I was glad to be on the placement with Michael, even if I did suspect that he found my nervous disposition somewhat irritating. But at least I was not the only medical student – there was safety in numbers.

We hurried after Dr Lonsdale as she made her way to Violet ward. In the women's unit, all the wards were named after flowers, as though that made them seem gentler, sweeter. Whenever I saw the ward's name written down, I found myself wanting to read it as 'violent'; the delicate purple flower was the last thing I associated with the ward reserved for the most disturbed and difficult-to-manage patients.

We had to pass through four locked doors which could only be opened with the heavy keys that the staff kept chained to their belts. Everyone had to have a belt in the secure unit. You looped your alarm around it and then, if you were cleared to have keys, they followed after the alarm. If you came without a belt, you had to be issued with one at the front desk. It was the safest way to ensure the keys could not be taken from staff and used as a weapon, or to escape. *Abscond* was the word they used for patients who had left the unit without permission from their clinical team. Perhaps it sounded less worrying than *escape*; it certainly sounded more clinical.

The atmosphere on Violet was tense. We followed Dr Lonsdale to the seclusion wing – behind a further set of locked doors. There were four rooms here, each designed so that the furniture was either unmovable, or so heavy as to be impossible to lift, and there were no items that could be used by patients to hurt themselves or others. They were horribly imaginative at finding ways to self-harm in the women's unit. They could use bed sheets, ripped up, to tie ligatures around their neck or limbs. They could swallow anything small enough to fit in their mouths: batteries were popular because of their toxic acidity. They could break cds or dvds and use the sharp edges to cut. If they had old wounds, they could reopen them with their nails. Sometimes they inserted new objects into old wounds; one patients had pushed a biro pen into an abdominal wound during the ward's community meeting that morning. Their capacity for self-destruction was beyond my understanding.

We had gone to see a patient on Rose ward with Dr Lonsdale a few days ago. When she had finished asking about the woman's symptoms, and dealt with her concerns, Dr Lonsdale had said to the patient, "Jane, these medical students are here to learn about us and what we do here. I know one of the problems you often have is when you go to the emergency department with self-inflicted wounds, they don't understand why you've done it." Dr Lonsdale turned to Michael and me. "The patients are often treated quite badly in A&E: left waiting for hours, given stitches without any local anaesthetic, or told that they are wasting NHS resources by being there. It is very distressing for them." She turned back to the patient. "In a few years' time, Jane, these students might be doctors in the emergency department. So I was wondering if you might explain to them why you self-harm, to help them understand more if they ever have to treat someone with similar problems."

The patient nodded. "Yes, Dr Lonsdale, you're right. They don't understand. They get angry with us there." She looked at us now, her eyes darkening. "I hurt myself because it's the only way to stop me from hurting anyone else. It's either me or whoever's near me and I'm trying to stop hurting other people."

"And you don't feel you have any other option?" Dr Lonsdale asked Jane.

"No. If it gets to that point then I have to do something, I don't have a choice."

"And one of the things we're working on with Jane is trying to persuade her to come to see us when she feels like she's getting close to that point, but before she's reached it – isn't that right Jane? That way we can try to help you avoid getting to the point where you don't have any other choice."

The next patient that was asked replied, "I can't express the pain any other way. It's in me and I need to get it out of me. And," she admitted, looking guiltily towards Dr Lonsdale, "there are times when I do it because I feel like no one's hearing me. Like there's no other way to get their attention, but if I tie a ligature then they know I'm serious."

Another patient had said, "It's the only way to get the tension out of my body. It just builds and builds and gets bigger and bigger. You can't bear it. It's like – it's like you can't be inside your body and feeling this; it's too much. We call it my volcano." Here she half-smiled, half-grimaced at Dr Lonsdale. "The cutting... it lets the tension go, it's like a release."

After that woman had left the room, Dr Lonsdale turned to us. "Kayla lights fires. She's come to us from prison. This is her last chance – she's got six months to prove to us and the courts that she can engage in treatment, otherwise she'll be going back to prison." The consultant paused, "She cuts herself... down below. She has a history of sexual abuse." She didn't say anything further – she didn't need to. The symbolism of that particular form of self-damage was stark enough even for us to grasp.

Violet's seclusion wing was busy. There were two nurses in the corridor and three more nurses in the bare room where Bernie was being de-escalated. When Dr Lonsdale walked into the room there was a collective sigh of relief.

They all rely on her to have the answers, I realised. *She walks in and they expect her to solve it. She's so young.* Dr Lonsdale seemed only a few years older than me, though I knew that was not the case and it was only because of her bright eyes and youthful energy. She was good at her job. Like all consultants she was expected to have the answers and like all consultants, she took on that responsibility with apparent ease. But unlike the surgical and medical consultants who I could understand might actually know all the relevant medical facts to help them solve a given problem, Dr Lonsdale faced much more nebulous crises, where the way forward was not necessarily clear and there were no facts one could memorise to tell you what to do.

Bernie lay on the sheetless plastic mattress writhing in anguish, tearing away from the hands of the nurses who sought to prevent her from scratching herself with her nails. She was sobbing brokenly, making no attempt to wipe the tears and saliva from her face.

It was the rawest expression of distress I had ever seen. I felt a lump in my throat. It was difficult to be witness to another human brought so low. I pushed my fingernails into my palms. I must *not* cry.

Dr Lonsdale moved gently towards the agonised woman.

"Bernie," she called out soothingly. "Bernie, it's Dr Lonsdale."

Bernie continued to sob, but her writhing slowed down and she turned her face towards the doctor's voice.

"Bernie, what's wrong? Hmmm? What's wrong, Bernie?" Dr Lonsdale continued to talk gently and calmly though Bernie appeared to be unable to answer her questions.

Slowly, the sobs quietened, all the while as Dr Lonsdale spoke to her as one might speak to a young child.

"She's been in secure institutions for the past twenty years," Dr Lonsdale had told Michael and I the first time we met Bernie. "It started when she set fire to some leaflets in a waiting room. A cry for help... and she ended up in prison. From there, she was sent to the high secure hospital in the north. She has not been discharged from hospital since then. We don't even know if that's possible for her now."

On that day, Bernie had seemed in good form. She was a small woman with the typically overweight body habitus of so many psychiatric patients. One of the many unpopular side effects of the antipsychotic drugs was to increase appetite and alter normal metabolism. Weight gain was almost inevitable. Her wiry brown hair was streaked with grey, which, along with the weary lines on her face, made her seem much older than her forty-nine years. She had smiled at Michael and I and chatted freely to Dr Lonsdale. She told us that her hallucinations took the form of a strange sensation of water trickling down her body. She was so wholly altered before us now that it was hard to recognise her.

Bernie lifted her head slightly from the mattress. Her eyes were red and dull from crying. She began to motion with her hand, a sharp twitching movement which I did not understand at first. Then she began to plead.

"Kill me. Kill me. Kill me." I realised with a jolt that she had been miming cutting her throat for us. Showing us what she wanted to do. "Kill me. Cut my throat. Kill me. Kill me." Her words began to build in volume as a kind of hysteria took over and she began to shake and try to scratch herself once more.

"No, Bernie. We're not going to kill you." Dr Lonsdale's voice was sympathetic, but still calm. "I'm so sorry you're feeling this way. We're not going to let you hurt yourself, Bernie." The nurses held her hands away from her face.

The sobbing started again, but it was quieter than before. Soon she lay still on the mattress, perhaps exhausted, or finally accepting the futility of her desire to harm herself.

"Bernie, we'd like to give you a shot of your meds, is that alright?"

Bernie nodded heavily, now curled up in a ball.

One of the nurses stepped smoothly forward, holding a syringe and an ampule of the drug. The two other nurses helped Bernie lower her trousers – the injection had to go into muscle and the buttocks were a good location – while Dr Lonsdale drew up the medication. It seemed like the final indignity: her naked pain now mirrored by physical exposure before her silent audience. She hardly seemed to care. After twenty years in one institution or another, I guessed this was not a new experience for her. She lay back down on the bed and stared vacantly at the wall on the opposite side of the room.

Apart from the bed, there was no other furniture present. There was a separate toilet, but it had no door. One of the other doctors had shown me the system of mirrors that allowed the nurses outside the room to see the patient while they were in the toilet. There was nowhere to hide here.

"I'll come back and see you in a couple of hours, Bernie. Is that okay?" Bernie nodded blankly without looking at Dr Lonsdale.

We left the room, heading to the nurses' station so that Dr Lonsdale could write a summary of the incident.

"What started it all off?" asked Michael.

Dr Lonsdale sighed. "We've been trying to lower her medication so that she's on the minimum dose to keep her well. She hates being on it at all. It's a difficult balance and it seems we went a little too low to keep her symptoms under control."

"And what medication did you just give her there?" he asked. I tried not to show my frustration at the question. It was a typical medical student response. Show us someone suffering and we'll see a learning opportunity. And not a *learning about humanity* sort of opportunity. A *what drugs do we use to control this* kind of opportunity. It made me angry, but I wasn't yet able to speak. The horror of the scene we had witnessed had not yet left me.

"Haloperidol, intra-muscularly," Dr Lonsdale replied, only half paying attention to us while she scribbled furiously in the notes.

It was five thirty and we both needed to get home. We left Dr Lonsdale on the ward and were let out by one of the nurses. After I'd turned in my alarm, I swept out of the building hastily before Michael could try to talk to me. I was in no mood for dissecting what had happened, especially not with him.

"See you Monday, Emma," he called after me.

"Sure. See you." I hopped onto my bike and pedalled as fast as my legs could bear. My thighs were burning and my ears were stinging before I slowed down to a more sustainable pace. It was a bitterly cold February evening and a biting wind had me craving my warm front room and a cup of tea.

It would take more than a cup of tea to drive the memory of Bernie from my mind. I did not know if I even wanted to. Should I be holding on to that experience as a lesson in... in what? I was not yet able to make sense of it. I was not even sure if I should be trying to make sense of it, if that was even possible.

Next Monday we were back in the men's unit. It suddenly seemed like an oasis of calm. The patients, though detained in a secure facility because of a history of serious violence linked to their mental illness, were mostly extremely stable. There was little self-harm on their wards and the high-octane emotions I had seen in the women's unit were largely absent here.

I reflected on that for a long time after I finished my psychiatric attachment. The male patients' offences tended to have been against other people; when removed to a secure facility, they no longer had access to easy victims to target and thus, they stabilised. The women, on the other hand, often targeted themselves as their own victims. Removing them to a secure unit, therefore, did not isolate them *from* their victim, but rather *with*, and so they did not stabilise, but continued their attacks. Indeed, now they had even more reason to loathe the target of their attacks – they could now lay the blame of being detained on themselves. Society was confirming their already pitifully low opinion of themselves and appeared to be telling them: you must be removed from our world, you are not good enough to be here.

It was not as simple as that, of course. Society was presumably intending to tell them something along the lines of: you are worth protecting and we will protect you from yourself if that is what it takes. You are worth all the resources we will spend on you, we value your life even if you do not and we think we can help you.

But, *twenty years in an institution.* Did we really think we were still helping at that point? Well, by then it had gone too far, we couldn't turn back. Bernie could not survive in the real world on her own now. Not as things stood. I couldn't decide if we had broken her spirit or saved her life. Perhaps both.

It shook my internal compass. This was one of the first times I had been forced to confront the damage that the medical profession could do, whilst simultaneously helping someone. The paradox was painful to get my head around and once the idea lodged itself in my consciousness I began to see it everywhere. In the elderly gentleman who demanded of his medical consultant to be allowed home as we did our ward round: he was not well enough, he was told. He died that afternoon. In the young woman who took an overdose of antifreeze, whose story was not believed by half of the staff on the intensive care unit where her consequent kidney failure sent her. When she mentioned that the arterial stabs in her wrist were painful they contemptuously complained behind her back that she should have thought of that when she poisoned herself. In the middle-aged man who had to have both his feet amputated due to devastatingly poor blood supply to his lower limbs: when he was still struggling to cope with his new identity as someone who needed a wheelchair at his six month check-up, the surgeon scolded him impatiently. How could we, the medical profession, seem to be doing so much good, whilst at the same time inflicting so much damage?

It was almost a year later that I met Dr Lonsdale again at a teaching session in the medical school. She remembered me, which was unusual. Most consultants see so many medical students that they no longer bothered to learn their names, or if they did, they forgot them as soon as the attachment with them was over. It was understandable: there's only so much energy one can put into getting to know students who merely pass through, staying for a few weeks before moving on to the next speciality.

Dr Lonsdale recognised me, though. I suspected that few students voluntarily spent time at the secure psychiatric women's unit. It was not a necessary part of our core medical training and it had none of the glamour of the more popular obscure specialities like neurosurgery or intensive care medicine.

I knew her, of course. She remained as bright-eyed and energetic as before. It was good to see someone enjoying their job so much. I was beginning to lose faith in the idea that medicine was right for me. I was beginning to lose faith in medicine.

"Hello Emma!" she smiled.

"Dr Lonsdale. How are you?"

"Excellent, thank you. And you? Finals coming up?"

"Yes. Well, a few months yet, but we're all cramming. So much to learn!"

"Well, I'm sure you'll do fine."

"Thanks. How are things at the women's unit?"

"As ever. Busy. Messy. But we're muddling along."

"And – " I hesitated, but I needed to ask. "Bernie, umm, that patient Michael and I saw with you. In seclusion. Umm, is she – how is she?"

"Oh gosh. Yes, I remember, she was going through a difficult patch when you were with us."

I nodded.

"I'm afraid we had to send her to a specialist unit that provides enhanced care for very complicated cases like Bernie's."

There was a lump in my throat. "So she's gone back to a high security hospital?"

"It's not technically high security. It's just a place where there's considerable expertise in dealing with difficult patients."

"Oh."

"Well, it was lovely to see you Emma. I've got to prepare for my lecture – I'm up next. I hope you enjoy it."

I tried to smile, but I was sure it didn't reach my eyes. "Goodbye, Dr Lonsdale. Good to see you too." She was gone.

One of the patients I had met at the women's unit explained to me why she had stopped resisting her doctor's recommendations, even when they limited her freedom: "You can't fight the system. That's what I learnt here. The system always wins. You gotta work with it, you can't beat it."

You can't beat the system, I thought to myself, remembering Bernie's grey face.

Six months later, I left medicine.

White Snow Like Santa Marta

by Peter Webb

The hunger and stench receded as I dragged the snow and rock and melt-water to mind. It was a simple dream. That together we would go to the white mountains above Santa Marta, a great distance from the city. Beyond the swamp, up there in the clouds. We would plant olive trees and build a finca with a veranda. But instead I stood in a blindfold. There was a pit in my stomach. And a bullet was coming to break my face. My mind broke into spasm. Then a thousand fragments span away and I was searching for Lena.

In one such fragment of memory my mother was taking me to the seminary. She wore shoes of unfamiliar shiny leather and a cotton jacket. My shoulder was close to the hem of her skirt. We sat on a pew and my shirt was stiff. I wanted my brother, but he was not there. The echoes of the Holy Father were bubbling around the arches. And the smoke from the charcoal was intoxicating. A choir filled the vault with their fine, clear sound while the collar chafed my neck. Beyond the altar I saw a window ajar, and beyond that, if I tipped my head, there were snowfields.

Then another fragment came spinning across. I stood in my well-worn choir gown. The congregation was bent in prayer. My frustration at their cycle of guilt and repentance grew hot. Something snapped – and I was driven to the most logical of all conclusions: an irreversible rejection of God.

"Why all the guilt if they know they'll do it again?" I cried.

"It's bullshit!"

With that I discharged myself from the choir stalls, leaving my friends in church.

Then I saw Lena. It was night time and my neck was damp. Her nose was sharp and her ringlets alive on her shoulders. There was sweat cooling on my back.

"Thanks for the dedication," she said, and smiled.

Her eyes were laughing. Her friends had gone.

"A drink?" I said. There was sand in my shoe.

The beer was cold and we danced in a hot press of bodies. Then the shoreline was quiet. The Caribbean washed on the pale sand, and the white ghosts of the mountains thrilled us from across the bay. Together we agreed.

"One day, we'll go there."

Then one last snapshot. I faced Lena to say goodbye, her face and camisole were warm from the duvet. The thick of the night was around us still, and the neighbours' deranged cockerel had not yet woken. Lena was half asleep. I'd been sick through turning all night, obsessed by Lena's revelation. That she was pregnant. That was not our plan. What did she expect? (And how did it happen?) I wanted all my options open but now, overnight, we'd been transformed from a transitory couple into the strong likelihood of a permanent trio. The countless potential outcomes of the story of my life-time were cut in that instant. Now I faced the prospect of just one, and only one, real ending. And that left me desolate. Was Lena both the beginning and the end? To stay with her now would annihilate all, except the last, of my untold possibilities. At the door now, preparing my farewell, I leaned my forehead into hers. Her neck smelled, like always, of warm almonds.

"You see flaca, I'm not ready for this; you have to take it out."

To me this seemed like honesty, but there was terror in her face.

"Y el bebé?" she said, imploring with her eyes; and the baby?

"Hablamos después de eso." I said; let's talk about that later.

"Y Santa Marta?" She said; and what about Santa Marta?

"Ahora, me tengo que ir. Hablamos después." I said again; closing her out.

"Y de nosotros?" She said; and what about us?

"Ya está." Already that's it, I replied.

I squeezed her arm and smelled her neck, then broke for the dark street with my treachery, not allowing time to qualify those words, nor giving her the chance to start or finish anything more. On the street the taxi was running, its cab was musty and warm. How strange that on this fine, clear morning, our world was at its end. Then the demented cockerel in the neighbours' property cried out. And my last thought before the crack of the rifles was of my treachery. Darkness fell around.

Six months before the firing squad, my view of the world was not blessed by such simplicity. The timing of the call to that rig at Barranca had been routine. That is to say, they called shortly after midnight. After Lena's revelation that I would be a father it was a deliverance to leave at the first cock crow. The taxi driver cut through the streets of the capital with ease, and my relief at escaping grew with the distance the car put between Lena and myself. The action at the rig beckoned and I looked forward with anticipation, because out there life would be straightforward, and the wind would be fresh.

Through the morning, the taxi cab warmed up and the tyres hummed on the open road. As yet unaware of the firing squad waiting in the jungle, it struck me that I'd promised Lena nothing. We were both young and yes; we'd played with the dream of Santa Marta, that one day we would go there; but that had been a game. Did Lena think ours was so much more than that, or was she remembering our fun in a way that was partly invented? Whatever else, she was terrified. So much so that it scared me. But our youth! We had so much to see, to do, there was so much out there. There were so many other girls, that was for sure. I'd been wanting to cast around and leave myself to the night again, to go with the music and small drinks, and the narcotic of the dark girls' perfume; to fall in love with goodwill and optimism. Then recover my sense of reality in the morning and let the world take care of the rest. It would be something to do that again. The warmth in the cab made me drowsy.

When I awoke, the driver was descending from the altiplano, down to the great rivers of the interior. The daylight was strong and hot air brought humidity from the trees. The rig was out there, waiting, and I was trying to put the doubts from my mind. How was it that I loved her, but had to leave her? What would life be without … us, without her as an anchor; one sure bond to so many other things? I thought about the summers in Santa Marta, my great hopes for the band, of days learning my grandmother's accordion, and nights singing the tunes of Diomedes Diaz. It was special, that time we lived. And now I had to cut away and leave it behind. That would be difficult for her, more difficult for her than me, to cut away the child inside her, but better that way. Better to have the opportunities and Life than a kid we didn't want. If I was sure of just one thing, it was that we shouldn't have that child. So Lena would need a procedure but I put that from my mind, she was a big girl. She would find somebody. And there were plenty more souls out there for both of us. Beyond the window colourful fruit trees streamed into a blur.

Where does that love go, that love we don't need any more? The tears, they go to the ocean. And sighs of regret go to the wind. A poet said that. But the love when it stops, where does that go, perhaps to the mountains? I watched the turbulent Magdalena spilling down the valley. All those dirty tears crashing to the sea. And the love? It can't just vanish. If there was one thing I was sure of; it was that I did not want that child.

I loved Lena but I did not love her enough, did that make sense? Or did that make me a coward? What if my inadequate love turned, one day, into full love? What would happen then? It might be too late, but hell. She was a big girl, she could cope. And one day I'd fall in love, bang, and that would be me for the rest of my life. There'd be no hesitation, no doubt, no looking back. That's if I held out long enough. I slept again and this time it was fitful.

We arrived at nightfall and a terrifying swarm of insects pitched at the arc lights above the rig floor. The taxista turned his vehicle for home, he would sleep on the roadside. That would be uncomfortable, but these journeys he did for us petroleros, the oilmen, they were good money for him. After a warm farewell he drove away.

Meanwhile my crew in their orange coveralls were on the catwalk. I changed into rig boots and casco, ready for the derrick, and by then the winch man was already signalling to the tool pusher. Together they raised the top sheave with the draw works by degrees. It was delicate work to rig the cables above the drill floor and to prepare the sondes for the oil well, but this was my regular crew. We'd done it on rigs all over the country and the winch man could handle this without supervision. All thoughts of town were forgotten as this industrial scale drilling operation came to a halt, and waited for us to discover what mineral interest, if any, lay buried deep beneath our feet.

Now that I had control of the rig, another million dollar investment, the safety of the drilling crew was in my hands. For that, Lena, and the life within her, was stacked in a dark recess of my mind. We had to send the sensing equipment down to Total Depth, six kilometres below, and recover it again. My mind focussed on the tools, the depths, the temperatures and the software. There would be borehole cave-ins in the seismic zone. That would be difficult, but we had practice.

We ran the calibrations, and then the cable was spinning off the drum. The ordered wraps uncoiled, flicking in steps from one flange to the other. Kilometres of cable flew down hole, then the wraps flicked back across the drum. The shrinking coils flew out into the night and the logging truck vibrated. That same cable-distance, many kilometres below, the electronic sonde nosed down through the hot dark mud before touching bottom and starting its long, careful ascent. If we made a good first run then tomorrow we'd be back in town, back with the warmth of humanity that seemed so distant. And I'd be back near Lena.

Thirty waking hours later, in the broad light of the second day, my adrenalin was dying away. The job with its habitual complications was almost finished, and the lads in their dirty coveralls were on the catwalk, waiting to rig down. I whipped my head from side to side, trying to shake the sleep away, ignoring the sensation of steel nails driving through my skull. At the rig table the tool pusher squinted upwards and gunned the diesel engines to bring the travelling block back down, and the winch man worked the heavy action of the clasp to release our sheave wheel. I held out my left wrist to the rig supervisor.

"Son las dos," I said; it's two o'clock.

"Son las dos," the supervisor confirmed.

I'd been holding out against the knots in my stomach, but now the job was almost done the anxiety over Lena returned. I drifted. And smiled at the thought of her. It was bizarre, this warmth at her memory while hating her for the confusion we both faced. She had to go through with it, with taking it out. But now that I had time to myself, I imagined I was back at her door with another chance to say goodbye. Then I caught myself, the job was almost done. Almost was the word. Samples had to be labelled, the well reports printed, the time sheet signed and the invoice approved. I faced hours of focussed activity before I could let myself go. I braced myself against the driving steel nails and checked the crew had food from the canteen. Then I started my final edit of the well report. If the printer didn't jam, and the company man signed the service record first time, then I'd be done in two hours.

Later, after it all, I took a clear black coffee and found a quiet corner. Rather than lean back in the easy chair I pulled my wallet from my jacket. In the wallet was a photo, creased soft around the edges. I brushed its corner with my thumb. A younger Lena smiled back at me from a photo booth in Santa Marta. She was burned dark by the sun and there was sand in her hair. We'd been out on the beach after the noise of a concert, that last summer. I turned the photo and remembered abandoning my small musical success for the excitement and razzle-dazzle of drilling rigs, for the petrodollars. I turned the photo over and over. When does half love become full love? I asked myself. She seemed more alive in that photo than before.

Is it that I don't love her enough? Or that I do not love her at all? To have that question repeating and repeating, was too much. And not having an answer was worse, so I made the less-than-rational decision, to return to town, right then, through the night that was coming. I had to see Lena, and find the answer, despite the persistent sensation of nails through my head. If Santa Marta was my destiny then I had to know it. Was it the fatigue that made me think like this? Whatever it was; I had to go back and talk. So with relief at my decision to leave, I rolled up the mud and oil on my filthy coverall, changed my shirt and pulled on fresh jeans.

I asked the winch man; did he want a ride into town?

"Pero jefe, la guerrilla?" He was concerned; But boss, the guerrilla?

"Y bueno," I said; whatever.

"Estés loco jefe? Por la noche?" Are you mad boss? Through the night?

With a shrug I kicked the pickup into life and, spitting gravel with the wheels, I turned out of the drilling location. The cab grew warm and I fought sleep with the FM radio and a wide-open window. The damp air washed my face. Then I was thinking about Lena and the thing we had to find out about. What if my inadequate love grew into full love? Then we might want that child. As I put the kilometres behind me I prepared to bid my youth farewell. That baby would need a father.

The sun dipped out of sight, and the coming dusk fell like a shroud over the forest canopy. The palm fronds and prehistoric trees grew from greens and yellows into greys, then the jungle turned black like oil, with an occasional pair of eye lights shining back from the undergrowth. Finally it was pitch out there, except for the tunnel of my headlights. I recalled this long straight, across a flood plain, and I let the throttle of the pick-up go so the kilometres on the clock clicked and clicked. Gravel chipped on the chassis and the night was out there, beyond the warm bubble that carried me home, the darkness opening up to let me through, then closing up behind. The kilometres clicked on the clock.

After the long straight I braked for a corner. I was braking late when the undergrowth moved up ahead. A branch fell into the tunnel of my headlights. I snapped awake, dragging my locked tyres through the mud. A man in the road was raising his open palm; I released a profanity.

"Ahh-iiie, paisano, I'm fucked."

Grey figures, with masks and attack rifles, stepped onto the verge. One boy stood up to the pick-up, he pulled back his mask and revealed one wide cheek cut in an ugly way. The others were uneasy. Fingers tapped on triggers. Chubby Cheeks clattered the muzzle of his rifle on my window. I opened my biggest smile for him. And waved my open hands. I was dumb. And powerless. But the guerrilla backed off. I stared up the barrel of his semi-automatic.

Don't pull, I was thinking, don't pull. I moved my hand by degrees to the window handle. Then wound it down. The pre-dawn air carried the smell of the boy soldier; like a dead thing or rotting food or months of sweat. He was smoking a roll-up. Then the piercing smell of adrenalin caught my nostril. Heat was pricking my neck. The guerrilla indicated the engine and drew his hand across his throat. I cut the ignition. A clatter of bullfrogs filled the trees. Then he spoke. The accent could have been Panama.

"Hey amigo, where'you from? Where'you going?"

He wanted to be friendly. I wanted to be calm. All the time he flicked the nose of his rifle. His boys were tapping their triggers. To calm myself I looked at the familiar plastic of the dashboard.

"I'm just a taxista, back from the petroleo location, no more. What'you wanting, amigo? I am nothing," I said.

"Un poco de la pesca, la pesca milagrosa," He grinned; a little of the miraculous fishing. He meant kidnap. My guts settled in despair.

"Y, que?" I said; and what of it? He said nothing.

"I'm a taxi guy, it's a yankee truck, I'm nothing to them, just litter," I said.

All the time I was smiling like an idiot; yes, of course, yes brother, I'm nobody, I just want to be your friend, brother. My

102

cheeks hurt. There was a glacial hole in my stomach. They did not believe. They smashed the laptops.

"Just cargo," I shrugged as they ransacked the pickup, looking for food and cash.

They found rope, used it to bind my hands, my feet. One pulled his scarf and tied a blindfold. In the darkness I was alone again. The first image that came was Lena. They pulled me away from the safety of the pickup and I lived six days in that blindfold. I lost myself to everything except the cycle of the daylight. Three days on mules, two days stumbling like a dog on a rope, and one day in camp. They did things and I was frightened they would do worse. They gave me aguadiente so I could drink myself stupid. I didn't take it, instead spilling it on the rash of bites where my shirt was open. The zancudos still landed on my skin but the alcohol cooled the rash of bites. After a day with sight and rest they led me by the rope and threw me in a cage. Outside the young boys had their rifles cradled in their arms.

The days passed and the weeks. All the time I was thinking about Lena and my rash decision to run back to her; was this incarceration my punishment for that? Or was it for my abandonment of the life inside her? What if Lena thought that I was not coming back through some hard decision of my own? What would she do then? Then she'd definitely take it out. That was unthinkable now. If I had run for her then my love must amount to something. What if there was more love to come? I had to get back: To Lena, and to save our child.

The kidnap training helped. Because in that time when I might have gone mad, or gone blabbing to the chief, to tell him how much my rich family and the big oil company could pay, I did not. Instead I played out scenarios and built escape plans, wanting Lena. Then one day a guard dropped his knife stone and that night I hooked it back, into my cage. I buried it deep for a fortnight. Then over the weeks I cut the chain attached to my ankles. So, four months after my first capture, I was on the run for less than one hour before the boy soldiers caught me a second time.

They threw me in a plywood box and left me to sleep in my own shit. My life before the camp, out there in the world, could have been on the moon. Any life that had been inside Lena would be unrecognisable now, be it a foetus with a heart that beat in time, or the remains of a tiny corpse, dead and gone. The thought of Lena on a surgical table rose over me, her legs apart, cut by a dirty steel, blood in her crotch. The imagined horror of some shanty town abortion was all the worse at midnight; the baby and the girl both cut and dying in the darkness. Lena was there, alone under a murderer's knife. I'd driven her to that, by running to the rig, then running home again. Caught on a road I should never have travelled.

Four of them came and took me into the night. Marched me to the field they used. My heart banged my ribs and my bowels turned to water. The life I was about to leave, my life, it reached back. Nothing more than half loves and missed opportunities. If only I could pray. Nothing came. The boys in their ragged greens took their rifles. They snapped the bolts. They shouldered the stocks and practiced their aim. I caught the smell of gun oil; then my own acidic fear. The camp chief stepped up and raised his firing arm. The boy with scarred, wide cheeks tied my blindfold. This was the second time. My face stretched back. My eyes were hot. The breath in my chest came in sharp irregular shots, crushed by my failure to make a life that was my own.

I stood and remembered the day my mother first took me to confession. I remembered the intoxicating smell of incense. I remembered the white snow of Santa Marta, and my treachery. Those last images flew before me. Then the darkness came. Flame flashed into the stars above the jungle canopy. A dam broke. With unexpected love I prayed without dignity;

Not this time, not now, I'll do anything for just one more chance. Please God. For You, just one last chance, for me.

The bullets were flying wide anyway. Still, I blacked out. Almost killed by the relief at my prayer, by the closure; by disappointment in the lack of man I was. Then my face was in the mud, my shoulder twisted under me. There was heat and light and damp air. The chain was back on my ankles.

Then Lena returned. I asked her, how could we plan so much when we knew so little? It wasn't bad timing that put us wrong. It was me and my obsession with freedom. How selfish was that? Before I slept, I willed Helena to come as she had been on the beach in Santa Marta. With a face that would launch a thousand ships. And I prayed that she knew what I had only just realised. I prayed across the expanse of jungle and across those six months. There was nothing more that I could do. Then I realised I must get on the radio to my brother. So I blabbed to the camp chief, the one thing I would never do, then I blabbed to my brother. Pay them; pay them all of it, whatever they ask, I said. Whatever the consequences, I said, I want to come home.

With that I had done everything. All I could do was to wait for release. And if it did not come, I wanted to die.

Months later, the sun cut through my bars and the warm day washed over me. One of the guards was there with a wet rag. He was rubbing my face. I stretched and the anxiety grew back. A can was steaming on the bare earth outside the bamboo cage. It was the first time they'd given me coffee.

That afternoon the guards were shouting and excited, the long wave radio was whistling and the chief was shouting into it. The guard who'd brought coffee came stepping out of the dusk, towards my cage. As he passed my rice he shook the chain and saw that it was loose.

"Don't work it, estupido, if you keep your head you may still live."

He left me to eat and think, while the radio in the main hut cracked into life. The chief was shouting then quiet, and then he came and reached into my cage. He shook me and struck me across the face. My cheek burned. He looked and held the bruise, then went to the open house with lights and a pool table. While I sucked my blood I heard him shooting pockets late into the night. The coffee guard came back.

"They made a deal," he said.

They came at midnight. Four of them bound my eyes, and then they drove me out on horseback. Trees snatched at my face. If only I could prepare myself. If this were the end then I would curl into nothing and deny my existence. I would send one 'goodbye Lena' and see you on the other side. But if I were going for freedom then, well, I didn't dare hope for that. From the silence of the men my life was in the balance, and at the end of this journey the scales would tip. Despite that, and the jolts of the pathway, sleep came. I dreamed I was falling into the night. Then they were pulling at my blindfold, cutting the line from my wrists and kicking me downhill into the first glimmer of dawn.

"You follow down the hill, and if you turn, you catch one." He cocked his rifle.

I teetered as the stiffness worked from my legs, and focused on the grey light in the trees. The noise of jungle daybreak was all around us; frogs, insects, birds and monkeys, all calling to each other. A leopard barked. One step, another, I counted, and then ran. Headlong down the path as the dawn breathed light on the trees. Breaking clear, I fell, blinking, and through my confusion I saw a bus waiting on a verge. A driver was there with the heavy diesel turning. This was no execution.

I stepped across the clay roadside, to the door, and up to the worn-shiny handrail. The bus was empty. Except for the back row where a man sat under a mat of dark hair. His sullen eyes were underscored by shadows. I stared. And he stared at me. Then my cheeks cracked into a smile, I ran, the passenger stood.

"Por Dios, hermano, que bueno verte!" My God, brother, it's good to see you!

His face was pale with dust, the ghost of the brother I'd been hoping to see. He smelled more of fox than the brother-smell I remembered. But when we embraced, the man in my arms was warm and real. It was my brother and we sat down. We slapped each other on the shoulders, looking around, not knowing what to do. So we waited. I tightened my jaw and my brother's temple twitched. I spoke.

"It's good to see you. You gave them the cash?"

He gave a nod. Away at the front, the driver turned to check. He closed the door and eased his bulging belly back behind the steering wheel, then stamped the pedals and reached for the gear stick. The tin-plate running boards vibrated and the gearbox crashed as the bus pulled away.

"You know where we're going?" I put the question.

"Home to Tigre," my brother replied.

"And Lena, where is she?"

"In Tigre," he said.

"Thanks be to God," I said, and went on, "And mama y papa? It must have been tough for them."

"It was bad for all of us, but they're okay. We prayed and cried but we found the money and you're coming home. Thanks be to God," he said.

We came to a village of wooden boards and plastic bags. Birds ran off the road and coffee berries lay in the sun. My brother put his hand on my thigh, and I put my hand over his. The driver's belly rested on the steering wheel. We all vibrated with the road, and the trees opened into fields.

"Did you find out about Lena?" I put the question.

"Yes, yes, we did," he turned quiet.

"And how is she?" I asked.

"It was tough, and that problem you left her with."

"What'you mean, you mean, she told you?" I said.

"She told us all, brother. It was so big when they took you, she had to talk, but you were not there. So she spoke to us. None of us knew if we'd see you again."

A rush of blood filled my neck.

"She waited? And then, what did she tell you?" I said.

"Yes, she waited; that's a big thing, new life. That you left inside her."

"And, what's her news?" I was burning to know.

"It's her news, she wants to tell you. I promised her," he said.

It was everything for me, and he held it back. Did that mean the news was bad?

The jungle came back to the road. Early morning creepers and coffee berries flicked against the windows. The bus descended down, and down, and the wheels clattered in trenches cut by rain. The thunder of white water rose over the clatter as we crossed an iron bridge, and then the engine boomed as we climbed the far side.

I closed my eyes. She'd heard me then. She'd been there, like on the beach at Santa Marta. I'd been right to the bottom, where there was nothing. In a world that was empty except for mud and guns, and memories and ghosts.

"Lena," I said. And the trees closed around me.

Hours later the first town spires came into sight.

Veil

by Janet Swinney

I first came to when I felt your fingers smooth the channel between my buttocks. Long, deft strokes you made, purposefully but not with force, so that my slow, inert flesh conceded willingly. You held my attention with your steady work. I caught my breath, and lingered somewhere between darkness and light each time you reached into the heavy fatigues slung low about my hips and paused.

I waited while you stroked my belly. Your hands swept to and fro between the blades of my pelvis, emphasising a gentle undulation that was obvious but not overblown. Deftly, and without fear, you opened the dark eye at the centre of my abdomen and looked coolly in. I liked your unhurried and yet thoughtful gaze. You made time, plenty of time, to hover, dipping your fingers tenderly in the pools of curving shadow that lay where flesh met bone. I had no thought of what your next move might be, only feared that I might lose my senses once again.

Your fingers unfurled my ribs one by one. I inhaled, arching upwards and to one side, the bones more apparent through the flesh here than there. The hollows of my armpits opened to welcome you: they shouted for your attention. You coaxed my breasts to fullness. The nipples – small, precise, precocious – rose to meet you. I gave myself into your hands. My back prickled at your touch. My shoulder blades flexed like wings. I fluttered with desire.

My wiry arms were raised and folded. In a slow and languorous dance that kept us intertwined for hours, you clothed sinew with substance. Long, slender muscles stirred beneath my flesh. You gave me a necklace that I took as a token of your love. When, at last, I felt your breath on my face, I could wait no longer: I opened my eyes.

From behind the thin gauze you had so carefully constructed around my head and forearms, I searched for your face. I found your patient, clever eyes, grey like stoats. As you stepped around me, I glimpsed a foam of golden hair, and white skin flecked with copper. I craved your kiss. I could barely conceal my passion for your touch. My face twisted with pleasure behind my veil.

You slathered me from head to hip with water. You caressed me fulsomely until I knew I must gleam like a beacon of sensuality. I

108

willed you to go further: to seek within, to coalesce with the gentle but insistent tongue of flame you had kindled.

I discovered longing.

I can hear voices. I have been sealed and seared and moved. Now there are two people talking in front of me. One of them is you. I half open my eyes.

'The men had difficulty getting her down the stairs.'

'Well, well done them. I think this is just the place to put her. It's time we had a focal point in this room.'

You nod.

'The place has been modernised so many times and not very well. The walls have always stayed blank, and we've never really shown off our students' work. But so many people meet here, we ought to show them what can be achieved. We should try to inspire them.'

You nod again.

'You must be very pleased with her.'

'Well...' You hesitate. 'I feel I've managed to say something of what I wanted to say, though you can always think afterwards of different approaches you could have taken.'

A little arrow enters my heart. For you, I have unequivocal love.

'Well, I think you've done extraordinarily well. You've really managed to capture something there. That moment of sexual anticipation, you know... I'm pleased to have her with us. And I'm not surprised at all you've won a scholarship. You absolutely deserve it. She'll remind us of you long after you've gone.'

My heart stirs again with this brittle news. From the slit between my arms, I watch the two of you drift away towards the hazy end of the room, you with your unkempt beauty and trailing clothes and a small dapper woman in a sharp jacket – I notice the Queen Anne turn of her leg – who is no match for you. The door swings idly after you are gone.

I discover betrayal.

There are rows of chairs set out in the room. They have been here since early morning. Now they are gradually filling, people with black or brown skin at the front, people with white skin further back, a bit of a mixture in between. The noise level is rising.

There's a man in the second row wearing a brightly coloured woollen hat. 'Oh man,' he says breathlessly. 'Where de hell dat ting come from?' The younger, hatless man next to him smirks salaciously.

'A real dog, man!' shouts a man in the front row. Just let her come down my way on a Friday night. We could do something real cool with the brothers!'

There's laughter all round. But this triggers a response from a black woman in an extravagant gele and extensive earrings.

'I don't know what kind of a gender equality programme you have running at your centre, my brother, but I don't think I would rate it very highly.'

'Ach. You Christians! You need to loosen up a bit,' says the man in the second row. 'It's just a joke.' The men snigger at the innuendo.

'Well I ain't no Christian, and I think Faith's right,' says another woman. 'There ain't no such thing as a joke when it comes to this subject. Where you bin the last ten years when you supposed to bin training? Here we are workin' with young people, trying to persuade them to respeck each other, and explaining the importance of safe sexual behaviour and here you are runnin off at the mouth like a dog in front of a bone. It's disgustin' and you're disgustin'. I don't know how that piece of pornography got here, but I'm not standing for it: I'm covering the bitch up.' And so saying she gets up, stomps to the front of the room in her baggy pants and wobbling shirt and slaps two pieces of adhesive paper – red adhesive paper! – across my nipples.

A sputtering of applause runs round the room. I am mortified. I am thankful that my face is covered and that no-one can tell I am trying to blush. Who knows what might have happened next, but at this point, the woman with the Queen Anne legs puts in an appearance. Silence falls. She marches to the front of the room, turns her back on me, unseeing, and begins a peroration. I do my best to hang on to my dignity until the gathering is over and everyone has departed.

Later you come to me. You remove the invidious stickers. You speak to me softly as you place a small, beautifully calligraphed notice on the wall: 'This is a piece of art work. You may hold any view about it that you choose, but please do not deface it in any way.'

I have discovered humiliation.

Today the sun is out. Patterns of light and shade flither across the floor. I am filled with optimism. Perhaps you will visit me soon. But here are two people whose mood is not so light. Two women stand before me, the woman with the Queen Anne legs, and another one of similar build in a fawn cardigan.

'I just don't think it's appropriate.'

'Why? It's been produced by a student who has done very well for herself.'

'It's the subject.'

'Well I know there's an element of sexuality about it, but I think it's a wonderfully uncomplicated representation of the female torso. I love the smooth furrows of the ribs on that side. See? And that groove just above the trousers. It says something to me about this young woman just discovering and celebrating her sexual identity. See the way she's just drawing up her T-shirt, but hasn't quite got it off. A sort of "coming out" moment. Don't you get that?'

'As a matter of fact, it's the breasts.'

'Eh?'

'Putting it here doesn't show any sensitivity.'

'What do you mean?'

The second woman twists her hands in the pockets of her cardigan and looks wretched.

'Well, there are women who've experienced breast cancer, you know.'

'You're not saying you...'

'No, not me. But we've got one member of staff who's off sick at the moment having chemo because she's had a breast removed. How is she going to feel when she comes back and sees this? And for all we know, there may be others among our students in a similar situation.'

Queen Anne Legs looks taken aback.

'I must say, I've never thought of it from that point of view.'

'Well I think you should,' asserts the cardigan wearer, making the most of her advantage.

'But,' says Queen Anne Legs slowly, 'if we follow that line of argument, it means we couldn't show pictures of cute little kittens either, just in case someone's cute little kitten has been run over by a bus.'

'Now you're just taking things too far.' The cardigan wearer is bristling.

'No. I'm genuinely struggling to see the difference.'

'If you want to show it, put it somewhere where only the Art students can see it. Stuff like this isn't to everybody's taste.'

'Oh?'

'In fact,' says the cardigan wearer, tears boiling in her eyes, 'displaying stuff like this is just another of your ridiculous ideas we could all do without.' She turns on her heel and makes for the door.

'So you're saying it would be okay to display it in the coal hole,' Queen Anne Legs calls after her. Then she turns back to me. 'Or maybe you're saying you'd rather display me in the coal hole,' she says sadly.

I discover bewilderment.

Now we have a ring of low chairs. And an unsteady three-legged stand with a pad of paper on it. Alongside me there's a table covered with a cloth, and cups and saucers set out in rows. A young woman brings in two silver canisters and some biscuits and leaves them next to the cups. Rain is snaking down the windows and the lights are on even though it's mid morning. People start to arrive in dribs and drabs. They shake their outer clothes off and leave them at the far end of the room. Some attempt to shake the cold off themselves. Someone goes to the stand, wrestles with it for a bit, and then writes on the pad in large, uneven print, 'Planning Meeting Equality and Diversity Conference' and then, underneath 'Aims, Objectives.' No-one is keen to sit down. Some come to the table and make themselves drinks. Two men – white – fall into conversation close by me. One is not so slender. His belly hangs over his trouser belt. His hair is thinning. He wears heavy rimmed spectacles. The other – thin, ginger, a few red pimples poking through stooks of beard – looks undernourished.

'Freezing out there.' The larger one jangles a spoon in his cup.

'You're not wrong there.' The ginger one brushes biscuit crumbs from the front of his fair isle jumper.

'Bit off the beaten track.'

'Yeah. But not a bad venue. Plenty of space – and cheap. Adam thought of it.'

'What goes on here, then? Is it a council building?'

'Oh yeah,' the ginger one ventures authoritatively. 'Night classes. My wife used to do tapestry here. Some pretty decent tack she turned out as well.'

The two of them fall silent for a while then, 'Will your lot show their faces at this conference, d'you think?' asks the larger one. 'Social Work aren't you?'

'Oh, yeah. They know that in our line of work you can't afford to put a foot wrong these days.'

The larger one sighs. His spectacles take on a gloomy cast. 'I have to be on the case all the time with my lot: "What the eff has this got to do with me?" they say. "I'm on the effin trucks all day. All I see is bins and the effin incinerator. Who am I going to equalise?"' He pauses for a moment and then leans forward confidentially. 'I dunno what they'll make of that.' He jerks his head up in my direction. 'She can come round my house any time for night classes with titties like that.'

'Ah.' The ginger one is only slightly phased. 'Whatever floats your boat. I suppose it's Art.'

They are busy contemplating this point when the door at the far end of the room swings open with force, unleashing a small tornado. A tall, gaunt man with a briefcase tucked under his arm steps into the room.

'Morning, everyone. Sorry I'm late. Caught in the traffic.'

He strides down the room amid a flurry of copious mackintosh.

'I'll just grab a coffee, and then we can start.'

He makes for the table, then veers right as his eyes fall on me.

He stops right in front of me. He glares up. I can see his eager-beaver eyes, and the hollows of his cheeks. His skin glistens from the rain and his dark, sleek hair is wet.

'Good God!' he cries.

He's wearing a badge on a clip. It says, 'Adam Curtiss, Equalities Officer.'

'No-one told me this was here when I made the bookings.'

He's forgotten the coffee.

'Well, we can't be having this!'

He performs a tight pirouette.

'The Muslims will go apeshit!'

After he's been gone for a while, an emissary is sent after him. When she reappears, the group gathers its stuff together and leaves in ragged formation. Coffee cups are abandoned on the floor and windowsills. The intended objectives of the equality and diversity conference remain undeclared.

I discover what it means to feel affronted.

A group of women, six or seven of them, in assorted garb – nylon saris, floor length coats and flowered headscarves, salwar chemise – huddle over a central table. They have exercise books in front of them and murmur quietly as they consider the exercise they have been set. Periodically they drive their biros or pencils into the page, sighing with the mental effort. A woman with gun-metal hair and a grey complexion wanders around the periphery of the group, peering between people's shoulders, and diving in here and there with a comment or a question. 'Good, Anima, good!' 'Oh, wait now, Shruti, what sort of ending would you expect to have on a word like that? No-o-o. That's right.'

The women labour on until their teacher goes to fetch more papers from her shopping bag. Suddenly Anima, who is sitting closest to me in a long brown coat and dappled headscarf, loses her concentration. She throws down her pencil and looks round the room impatiently, seeking something to distract her. She finds it. She sucks her teeth, and segues into a language it takes me a moment or two to attune to.

'Hey, Keka, I bet you wished you looked like that after your four babies.'

Keka also throws down her pen and swivels round to see the object of Anima's attention.

She clicks her tongue. 'You have some cheek. How d'you know I don't look like that? As a matter of fact that's exactly how I look.'

The others laugh. An older woman sighs: 'Look at her,' she says wistfully. 'I can remember when it was just like that. Waiting for

114

your husband to turn up. Waiting for him to undress you. Wanting to please him. Tingling everywhere. I was so innocent when I married him. I looked to him for everything.' She starts to croon softly in a low, mellifluous voice: 'Gungat ke patt khol re tohe piya milange.'

The others look at her blankly.

'What?' says Keka.

'Hindi?' says Anima.

'Yah, "Open the flap of your sari and you will see your lover."'

'Careful, Madhu,' says Keka, 'you'll embarrass our young sister.'

A young woman at the end of the table, her pale oval face encased in a tightly folded headscarf, looks down her long straight nose and blushes comprehensively.

'What? It's only a religious poem by the blessed Mira. My neighbour in Lalabazar sang it all the time. Anyway young sister will find out for herself sooner or later. All sweetness and light today, all dryness and dust tomorrow. I can tell you since what's-her-face wife number two showed up six years ago that's been the end of sweetness and light for me.'

'Count yourself lucky!' says Anima. 'I'm worn out with it. I've told that motherfucker of mine he can go and stick his stick somewhere else.'

They all laugh loudly.

The teacher, in her low-heeled shoes and drabbly skirt, pads back to the table. Madhu draws the pallu of her sari forward and pulls it down till it obscures much of her face.

'Now,' says the teacher – she places a pile of papers in the centre of the table – 'how are we doing? How have you been getting on making up those sentences with the adverbs of frequency in them? Let's hear one from you, Shruti.'

'My cousins always come round at the week-end,' reads the young woman bound in the headscarf.

'Good. "My cousins always come round at the week-end." And what do your cousins always do when they come round?'

The young woman pauses for a moment.

'They always play music.'

'Good. "They always play music."'

The young woman looks down demurely and allows herself a small smile.

'Anima?'

'I usually go the market on Saturdays,' says Anima confidently.

'Good. "I usually go to the market on Saturdays".'

'Madhu?'

'My sons like to go to the cinema.'

The others look at Madhu hard.

We can all tell that she's got it wrong.

There's a pause.

'No-o-o, not quite. Have another think.'

Madhu bows her head a little further towards the table. It's impossible for me to see her face at all now, but I can see the pale tips of her brown fingers planted doggedly along the edge of her sari as she props up her head with her hand and hopes for enlightenment.

There's a long and uncomfortable pause. It's evident to us all that she's not going to get it.

'We're talking about adverbs of frequency,' says the teacher gently. Things like "sometimes", "usually", "often", "always". We know your sons like to go to the cinema, but do they go sometimes, usu..."

'Often!' shouts Madhu triumphantly. 'They often go to the cinema.'

There's a collective sigh of relief.

'Good. That's the idea. "They often go to the cinema." Keku?'

'My husband sometimes does the housework,' says Keku primly.

Anima snorts.

'Good,' says the teacher.

'The bastard never lifts a finger,' murmurs Anima in her other language, 'except for you know what.'

The others shuffle in their chairs, suppressing their laughter.

Keku glares at her.

'Is something wrong, Anima?'

'I think she's made a mistake. I think it should be "My husband never does the housework".'

'It's right,' hisses Keku. 'He sometimes does the housework. He can make mogo chips.'

'Well,' says the teacher, 'men not doing the housework is a very common problem. Probably universal. So if he sometimes makes mogo chips, you're a very lucky woman.'

116

Anima and Keku raise their eyebrows at one another in mock defiance, and the teacher hands out the next exercise.

I taste the dust of second-class citizenship.

For days now there have been comings and goings. Tables have been set up and draped in colourful cloths, and items of curious shapes – many of which I cannot discern clearly – have been set out on them. Notices have been stuck to the walls and pictures pinned to boards. Coloured streamers – purple and green – drift from the light fittings. This morning, while the windows are still grey, the door flaps open and two women with lots of bags and several small children deposit themselves in a pile at the end of the room. One of the women draws a gadget from a bag and, working it steadily, begins to form brightly coloured globes that bounce and float erratically. The children are delighted. They charge round the room, setting the globes off in different directions, losing them, finding them and fighting over them. Soon, a host of green and purple globes is hugging the ceiling.

The weather brightens. More women arrive. Women of every description – careworn and youthful, dark-skinned and light, festooned in colour and clad in darkness. There are small children everywhere. The noise level steadily rises.

Suddenly, I see Queen Anne Legs thrusting her way through the crowd. She takes up her usual place with her back to me. 'Welcome,' she says, 'to this celebration of International Women's Day.' She talks at some length about why it's important, and about how the many exhibits round the room show just how talented women are, and what wonderful things they can achieve given the chance. She builds it all to a terrific climax, at which moment a huge cake is brought in and placed on a table beside her. The cake is a delicate shade of mauve and tied with a green ribbon. 'Made by our own students,' says Queen Anne Legs. She takes the knife that is offered and digs into the cake with a flourish. There is applause all round, followed immediately by an immense hubbub.

The day is filled with an ever-shifting montage of women: women drawing, women kneading, women working with intensity over confections of beads and wire, women shaping coherent objects from awkward shards of glass. There are many who simply stand and admire. But some are persuaded to try things for themselves. I see

117

their timidity transformed into incredulity and delight as they make their own first marks on proceedings.

At intervals throughout the day there is music: raucous and insistent, low and plaintive, loud and affirmative. The women leave what they are doing to listen, clap and dance. And everywhere there is the smell of food, a glorious melange of sweetness and spice intercut with frying onions. Food is consumed enthusiastically in large proportions. Spoons and forks are abandoned in favour of fingers. Clothes are spoiled and paper plates dropped.

Towards the end of the afternoon, when the room has started to empty and the air has become stale, two elderly women catch my eye. They make slow progress round the room, examining the items on the walls. As they approach me, I see that neither is glamorous. Both short in stature, one has strands of iron-grey hair pulled away from her face and folded into a pancake on top of her head. She wears spectacles that rule a heavy line across her face. The other is shorter. She has a frank, business-like expression, and vigorous white hair that halts abruptly where it meets her jaw line.

They stand, faces upturned, examining me for some time.

'Would you just look at that,' says the one with white hair at last. 'If I hadnae seen it masel I would not have credited it.'

The pancake one is wearing a close-fitting coat that seems to make her uncomfortable. I can hear her breathing heavily.

'Me neither,' she pants. 'It's an outrage.'

'What do they mean by putting it here?'

'The other stuff's bad enough...'

'...what with the no perspective...'

'...and the muddy colours, painted with a dishcloth dipped in shit...'

'...but this?'

'It's just an outrage.'

They reflect for a moment.

'And what is it she's wearing exactly?' says Pancake Woman.

'It's a string vest,' says her friend.

'It's a sack.'

'I don't think it's a sack. It's a string vest. Maybe a bag.'

'So here we are,' says Pancake Woman bitterly, 'in this year of Our Lord, after decades of arguing against the objectification of women, a statue of a woman with a bag over her head.'

118

'And on International Women's Day.'

'After all the work we've done for women's equality in this town, sitting on committees and working parties night after night...

'Aye. Arguing the case for dignity in the workplace and equality before the law.'

'Calling on every last relative to babysit so you could get to their bloody meetings in the first place.'

'It's not on, Zelda.'

'You're right, Maeve. It's not.'

They look at each other.

'I'm not going to let it pass,' says Zelda.

'What're you going to do?

'Write to the leader of the council.'

'Well, that'll work.'

'So if it doesn't, we'll take...'

They chant together: 'Direct action!'

I discover self-loathing.

It's dark outside. The lights are on in here. The caretaker is stacking the chairs and hoovering up the last of the crumbs. I've seen him often before, this man: thin, slightly stooped, with a few straps of dark hair plastered on to the narrow dome of his skull. He plies the hose of the vacuum cleaner steadily to and fro. As he approaches, the cylinder of the machine follows him erratically across the carpet. Occasionally, he turns and boots it along the ground. When he reaches me, he stops suddenly, straightens up, clicks a switch and drops the tube. It makes a boink as it hits the floor. He steps back, folds his arms and looks at me critically in the silence. It's the first time he has ever done such a thing.

Then he reaches up, and briefly fingers the necklace you gave me.

'Dog tag!' he says to himself.

I can hear the air in his nostrils. His mouth curves unpleasantly.

'Fuckin dog tag. Cunt! Cunt needs showing.'

With some fumbling, he reaches into a pocket in the centre of his overall and begins to draw out the handle of some tool. I assume that it is an implement of his trade, for cleaning or hammering, perhaps.

'I'll show her.'

But in fact, the implement won't come. It's stuck. The caretaker pulls harder. Still no joy.

He works the handle this way and that. 'Show – her – what – it – means – to – be – in – combat – fuckin' – slag.'

He develops a look of ferocious concentration. He hunches his shoulders and drops his head. He redoubles his efforts. The air leaks from him now in small gasps: oof-oof-oof. There are no longer any words.

It is at this point it occurs to me that this is something different from a work-related task, a menial chore. I am a party to something I should not be a party to. I wish desperately to remove myself, but cannot stir. I am fascinated but horrified. Finally, a judder passes through the man's frame. He clutches himself and groans. He stays hunched over for some time, then hastily stuffs the implement back into his pocket. Without glancing back at me, he scuttles out of the room. I realise he hates me.

The feeling is mutual.

We are in some mausoleum of detritus. The caretaker and another man grappled me down the stairs and into the freezing outdoors. I wished to extend my neck and project a well-directed arc of spittle at the caretaker for daring to lay a finger on me, but couldn't. The pair of them heaved me into the back of the small vehicle you used to bring us here. We jolted and twisted our way to this destination. Shadows moved across my vision, grey on grey, but I could make out nothing of our journey. A chill seeped into the vehicle along every metal seam and through every pane of glass. At my base was a grey plastic box that you used to keep me wedged in place.

The speech Queen Anne Legs had given to mark the end of the year had been plain enough. All students had done well and they took with them her every good wish for their future. In addition you would take with you this piece of work which, she regretted, she could no longer accommodate. The time she needed to devote to continually defending me was more than she could cope with in the course of her ordinary duties. She was sure I would find a good, and more amenable, home.

120

And so I stand here, surrounded by iron-walled containers, wondering what you have in mind for me. A thin drizzle starts to fall. To my left I have a partial view of the maw of a container. It is piled high with broken furniture, a lampstand with a buckled shade and a pink plastic animal with its legs locked in a perpetual gallop. To my right is a lop-sided stack of white metal boxes, with doors missing or hanging forlornly from their hinges.

You have your back towards me. The back door of the vehicle is raised and you are busy with the plastic box. When you turn towards me, you have a metal bar, bent at right-angles, in your hand. I cannot read the look in your eyes. Perhaps bitterness, perhaps contempt. The rain dampens your face and is forming glinting beads that are caught in your hair. I long to tell you that nothing matters because my passion for you still burns. But you draw back your arm.

The first blow falls in my belly, shattering my too-solid flesh and opening my carefully contrived innards to the dismal air. I reel at the shock and can barely gather my senses. Your second blow is vicious. You emit a shriek as you deliver it. As I topple backwards, the veil falls from my eyes.

Finally I see what I am worth.

Painting the Waves

by Simon Jackson

The hotel could have been taken direct from an Edward Hopper exterior. It was so nondescript in appearance it seemed a pastiche of impersonality. White stucco walls, Italianate colonnades, neatly manicured, slightly browning turf, identical box-rooms, all clean but with a faint air of neglect. It could be anywhere in the world.

There was nothing luxurious or distinctive but his room was not unbearably tiny or uncomfortable. It suited him fine.

The floor was even, white tiles. All the woodwork was painted grey – desk, chair, wardrobe, bed-base, coffee table and chest of drawers, by the head of the bed. The walls and ceiling were white plaster, largely unstained and with only a few cracks and holes. The plaster was the texture of choppy water.

The handles on the drawers and three light fittings – one over the bed, one on the desk, and a dome in the centre – were the yellow-gold of cheap jewellery.

The bathroom was tiled and held a sink with perpetually dripping taps, an uncomfortably low toilet and a shower which flooded the floor whenever used.

The door was gilded with the number 103. As you entered, the bathroom was on the left, the wardrobe on the right. Five paces brought you level with the bed, another two took you out onto a long, west facing balcony.

The only way in which Trevor had 'made the room his' was in removing the pastel print of water-coloured flowers, framed in gold and grey, which was reproduced above the head of every bed in every room in Hotel Alexander. He hadn't checked. He just knew. It was now leaning against the wall, under the desk.

He arrived at the end of July and seemed prepared for a long stay. He had a trunk and a travelling bag for clothes and personal possessions. The larger part of his luggage was taken up by four large canvases, a bag of paints, jars of linseed oil and turps, brushes, and an easel. He paid for two months in advance. This seemed not too optimistic a length of time considering how he'd responded to treatment. He'd said goodbye to everyone necessary before leaving London.

The only thing Trevor missed was a bath. He was in the habit of long soaks, letting the warmth work through his body and steam into his brain. He adapted. Five hundred yards from his room the sea licked the curls of smooth pebbles. It was here he walked for his daily immersions.

The water was cold enough to refresh, warm enough for fatigue to determine when he left it, rather than chattering teeth or cramp. The Alexander was the only hotel with access to the beach, and the end-of-season guests preferred to lie by the pool on sun loungers than side step the donkey shit on the winding track to the sea. Fishing boats patrolled the shore-line and occasional families picnicked there, brown children splashing naked in the water, grandmothers removing woollen stockings and pulling high black dresses to expose varicose calves to the sun.

Today the sea was calm and deserted, as flat and featureless as a blue rug laid over the sand. Trevor left his clothes in a pile and shuffled over shifting pebbles to the sea. The first few steps into the water were the hardest, where boiling surf conspired with rolling stones to dislodge your footing. The pebbles, pale and dusty on the beach, were sparkling jewels beneath the sea's varnish, each holding its own miniature sun.

He hobbled to waist deep, chest, shoulders, arms raised in the warm air, pulled his goggles over his eyes, and pushed out. He swam three strokes then turned to follow the line of the shore.

After the initial stony slope to chest depth the sea bed became level and sandy with occasional rocky cliffs where weeds and shellfish clung. A hundred yards out the bottom still looked bright, clear, attainable. Even when he could see what lay below him Trevor preferred to swim near the shore. Katherine, his ex-wife, loved to swim out. Face tilted to the horizon, nothing interrupting her view but sea and sky, she would swim until her head was a black dot between shore-line and sky. She liked to immerse herself totally in a new environment, leave the shore as only a memory. When they first married she'd learnt to cook, taken up housework, subscribed to various ideal home magazines. They hadn't swum together much.

He didn't like being out of his depth. Not knowing what was lurking beneath terrified him. Katherine always said it was a boy-thing. The need to measure everything – penis, salary, engine capacity, inches of column space (especially for favourable reviews). How else could you compare and compete?

There was, maybe, something in this. Swimming away from the shore was swimming for the sake of swimming. He felt a certain satisfaction, picking a point down the shore – a clump of trees, a moored fishing boat – and swimming until the goal was reached, floating a while, then returning to the bright marker of towel and shirt on the beach. Each day he tried to swim a little further, see how the coast-line changed, how his strength improved. He was still pretty fit, outwardly.

The sea was calm and deserted. He felt the water thrum between his fingers. Clouds of silver bubbles surrounded his paddling hands, clustered like Apollo's wings about his ankles.

The sun painted a rippled mesh of wave shadows on the pale gold. His own shadow chased him – quivered, rose and fell to the sandy bed's gentle undulations, yet always kept pace with him.

Curled horns of shell grew matchstalk legs and crawled across the bottom. Shoals of transparent fish darted around him, only visible by their leaping shadows.

The brain relaxed and drifted, leaving the body to the ritual of repeated movement. Three puffs of exhalation, breath rushing to escape to surface, the head's tilt, led by dipping arm and shoulder, a bright flash of sunlit coast – inhale and drop as spinning arms continue the cycle, four kicks to each arm's circle.

He reached today's target, an upturned boat, red paint peeling, a gap-toothed hole dark against the sunlit slats. He floated on his back, arching his spine to bring belly then toes up to warm in the sun. Above the beach the mountains squatted, dark, immovable clouds. Wherever you were they seemed to loom over you. Out to sea the loose change of strewn light flashed momently on blue peaks, sank and appeared elsewhere. Further out, a black dot against the ocean blue. Perhaps a sea bird.

He swam back more slowly, observing clustered mussels beneath him, black, bunched finger-tips, sea anemones jostling between them. When he reached his towel the black dot was visible as a head, long black hair tied back in a pony tail. She floated, level with him as he attained the shore. He felt clumsy and awkward, clambering over the stones. He wished she'd leave. She called something which he ignored.

He rubbed his head with the big white and red hotel towel, hiding in its warm, fluffy blizzard. The sun poured down on his shoulders. He emerged into daylight.

"Mr Carson?"

He looked out to see the girl, still floating a little way from the beach.

"Will you paint our little village?"

"Why does it concern you?"

"A famous painter like you could take our whole coast and offer it the world, and we could never even know."

"I've neither interest nor intention of painting your 'little village'."

"You like the sea?"

He turned away from her and began drying his legs. As far as he was concerned the conversation was over.

"Don't be so afraid. Trust her and she'll give you what you want."

All he wanted was peace and quiet and her not sticking her nose in where it wasn't needed. But she was already swimming away, her pony tail floating behind like an oil slick.

He lifted his clothes and stomped up the beach.

Stupid girl. Stupid bloody stupid girl, spoiling his peace, his quiet contemplation, with her nosiness and meaningless aphorisms. When the beach was out of sight he stopped to finish drying. He was steamingly annoyed and angry at himself for being so. It was irritating to be accosted by a total stranger, but nothing he wasn't used to. At one time his photo had been in all the major papers, and there were still occasional retrospective exhibitions. Must have caught him off guard. Artist as thief, stealing her village. And that assumption he was scared of the sea. The track curved back to overlook the shore. He stopped to gaze at the blue but she was gone.

He had not yet visited the village. He saw the clustered roofs from his hotel, and watched the small fleet of brightly coloured fishing boats float back towards it in the evening but until now had no interest in visiting. He had never enjoyed painting people or buildings, but maybe he could find a heart, something to inspire him, point him to the pulse of this land.

As there was no bus service from the Alexander he took a taxi. The driver had been a cabbie in New York for two years. His grasp of the English language covered the names of all New York districts, 'yellow cabby', and 'plenty dollar'. He communicated in a mixture of sign language and broken Anglo-German. He now had two houses in the village. The two lane dirt track they took was flanked by acres of level gravel. To the right, grey cubic skeletons shadowed the sea.

"Here nova highway, nova hotel, nova house. Zwei year plenty people, plenty money."

He cackled gleefully and hooted at the tractor in front to pull over. As the sole taxi owner in the area he was probably right in predicting that some of the 'plenty money' would head his way.

Trevor got out before the main square. A dust-covered bus, which no amount of hooting was going to levitate away, was blocking the road.

"Damn makt," he was informed.

He arranged to be picked up in two hours.

The bus reached the main square at the same moment as him. It was full of women, the younger ones in flowery dresses or slacks and blouses, the older ones dressed in black, most with matching head scarves. He wondered if it was a symbol of age or of mourning, and if the latter, whether it was required by custom or a matter of choice, and would the custom extend to the death of a divorced spouse. He couldn't imagine Katherine wearing black for any longer than was required to watch his remains drop out of sight. Unless it was elegantly cut and in fashion. He wondered if she'd already picked the dress.

There was indeed a market in progress. He wandered through it, hoping the bustle and bright colours would awaken some dormant creative impulse in him. The quality of such affairs had taken a turn for the worse since the days when traders from all over the known world had landed on these shores with Phoenician oils and perfumes, silks from the Middle East, spices from China. Or maybe modern transport had shrunk the known world to a size where nothing seemed exotic any longer. Everything on sale could be found on any main street in London – jeans and T-shirts, dish cloths, soap suds, pans, hammers and pliers, sandals, and lacy, uncomfortable looking lingerie.

126

He left after ten minutes for the shadow of the alleys. Moving above the market, towards the mountains, the air at once seemed cooler. The alleys shrank the further he went from the square until some streets could be almost bridged by outstretched arms. The walls were warped like ballooning sails, white, cold to the touch.

He rested his head against one and closed his eyes. He tried to feel something – anything – an echo of the people who'd lived here, died here – the centuries of footsteps which had echoed off these walls, rushing on urgent errands or just meandering, like him, killing the time, looking for something but not sure what.

Nothing. Maybe it was a bad street. He was about to return to the square and find a bar to await the taxi in when a curved wall ahead caught his eye. He approached and saw it closed off the far side of a small courtyard. It was a plain, circular building, unadorned apart from a single cross on the roof. He ascended steep stairs and entered.

The entrance opened into a corridor, curving left and right along the lines of the outer wall. A pieta sat high on the facing wall, wood-framed and enclosed in glass. To the left were portraits of saints, hands raised, fingers curled in various poses of blessing, as though reaching for chords on the frets of celestial lyres, or making shadow pictures to send down onto the earth, to reassure the faithful and amaze the faithless. To the right was a huge mural of men climbing a long ladder up to angels, perching on clouds. The higher they climbed, the clearer became faint halos around their heads. Yet at every rung were red devils, shamelessly naked, crimson clouds bursting from either side of their mouths, flinging the struggling climbers down to glowing flames below. On the right sat a white bearded saint, contemplating scripture in a high cave in the mountains. Two younger saints pleaded, pointing to the battle, but he ignored them, reading on. Again, the mountains.

Although the painting was old and faded there was something pleasingly contemporary about the devils' grimacing, cartoon faces.

The main doors in front of him were locked, or too stiff for his tentative tugs to release. On either side were ornate golden boxes, raised on pedestals, candles bleeding wax onto the sand within them. He passed the painting of devils and mountains and tried a small wooden door at the end of the corridor. It swung smoothly and silently on well-oiled hinges, revealing a small, dark room.

Everything was made of wood. Twelve wooden chairs in three rows, two on either side of the aisle, faced a small altar holding two wooden candlesticks and a bouquet of white lilies. Their sweet, sickly smell filled the room. Above the altar was a wooden relief of a fisherman, muscles tense as he pulled on a net, the water covering his feet and ankles. A huge halo spread from his head, like a sun sinking into the seas behind him.

A simple pulpit faced not the congregation but the stained glass windows in the east. They were small and let in little light.

Trevor took a seat in a corner opposite the pulpit. There was a calm, relaxing atmosphere in here. Trevor was not religious. As a younger man he'd fiercely derided it in others as blindness, weakness. He'd since seen the support it'd offered dying friends and their relatives. For some the belief that there was something after made letting go so much easier. Peace. It was peaceful in here. A place for quiet contemplation of a personal god, without being dazzled by all the gaudy finery and magic. Mags would have appreciated it. A great painter. Died driving her daughter to school ten years ago. She'd have been 42 this year. The daughter, Tanya, survived with a broken arm and a few cracked ribs.

He'd behaved abysmally at the funeral. She held no truck with religion, while John, her husband, was a quietly devout Catholic. How Tanya was raised had been a long standing issue with them, which Mags had won up to that point. Normal state primary school, no mass before meals or prayers before bed. Trevor'd been angry at the funeral, upset. John had been so fucking... pious. The martyr, accepting God's will with quiet grief and courage. Where was the pain? The anger?

"I know Margaret wasn't a believer, but I feel she's in a better place."

'Margaret'. She'd hated the name. It'd always been 'Mags', or 'Maggie'. And how could a 'better place' be somewhere away from Tanya? She loved the girl. Somewhere away from Trevor.

"If you're talking about a place where angels sit on clouds playing harps all day, the Mags I knew would've shot herself years ago rather than suffer that."

Katherine accused him of having an affair with the deceased on the way home. It was the thing that finally split them up. He hoped it hadn't been so obvious to John.

The door clicked shut as quietly as a mussel closing. A black clad woman walked down the aisle. She didn't see Trevor, covered by shadow and stillness. Her face was hidden by a veil but she walked with the firm tread of a young woman.

She knelt on one knee and bowed her head – a graceful folding of body and neck. From a cloth bag she took fresh lilies, replaced the old ones. Leaving the bag on the floor she stepped behind the altar and pressed her face against the carving, spreading her arms across it.

Trevor felt like a voyeur, intruding into this private grief. He lowered his head as if in prayer. He heard a whisper, a muffled sobbing. Maybe only breathing; the rustle of clothes.

When Mags'd died he felt he'd lost everything. He was at the height of his fame, had exhibitions in New York, Madrid, Paris, London, a beautiful young wife, a baby daughter – everything was attainable. And then, the one thing he really wanted was placed beyond his reach.

In retrospect this 'great love' was only realised by Mags' death. He locked himself in his study and covered a procession of dark canvases, blue meshed, green, red dappled, black shadowed, which were treated with bemusement, then contempt, by the art world.

You couldn't blame Katherine. To all intents and purposes he'd left on the day of the funeral. They didn't sleep together, hardly spoke. She suffered him nearly four months before filing for divorce.

Whether the feelings for Mags had been already there, unrecognised, or were born in the realisation that some things were still beyond his grasp, he didn't know. Would he have ever slept with her again if it had been Katherine who'd died? He doubted it. When he looked again the woman had gone. The fisherman's wooden face shone black with tears.

The bar was on the end of the hotel. It was covered by a wide roof with turquoise girders. One end offered a view of the pool and the sea; the mountains rose above the end where Trevor sat.

Today they were vague with mist, blue ridges, layer upon layer, each one paler than the one before. The outlines of the lower slopes were corduroy with trees, figs and olives, lemons. Higher up the contours were rugged, sharper-edged crags and gullies. They seemed part of the sky, utterly alien to the umber plain which lay before them, corrugated with rows of green shrubs.

The hotel barmen were friendly without being over-familiar. They knew he was a painter – the easel and canvases could tell them this – but were content to wait until such a time as he saw fit to find why he was booked into a two star hotel with no departure date, or why the easel remained folded, the canvases empty.

Leo was tall and stately, slow but purposeful, a touch of grey in his hair. He seemed wise and older than his years, except when Trevor enquired about his daughters, Kali and Gia, both in their early teens. The first time Trevor asked it was a politeness he immediately regretted. Since then he'd started to enjoy Leo's pleasure in telling him that Kali was top of her class in maths, or that Gia could out-swim men twice her age.

Jani was short, red-cheeked and in permanent motion. He couldn't walk to a table, he waltzed, spinning trays on his fingers, or moving glasses from one hand to the other. He flirted outrageously with the German tourists and had something going with the dumpy waitress with improbably blond hair. His friends were camping in the mountains and he wanted a day off to visit them. If the manager agreed, he'd take Trevor and show him the graveyard at their feet, filled with mountaineers who'd died climbing them. The manager was a *malaka* and wouldn't give him the day off though, but if he did...

"Brandy, yes?"

After his drink arrived Trevor was left in silence to watch the mountains fade to black. They didn't fade; the light faded. The mountains solidified, and as the last misty pinks and greys were sucked into their blackness they spread, filling the sky with their opaque weight, leaking their black until the whole sky was rock.

Even with his balcony door wide the room was heavy and claustrophobic. Unable to sleep he lay in the dark, sweating until the sheets were wet. His body was clay, his mortality crushing. He moved to the desk, hunched over the small lamp, pencil gripped in hand, moving in angry jabs and twitches, then longer strokes and waves as he relaxed. Black mounds grew, like hunched shoulders, curved spines of ridges, muscled contours. Slowly shapes came to him.

130

He knew this room well yet had never walked in it. The air was blue and still, like swimming pool water. The windows were huge, bowed out, ceiling high, heavy-curtained. A strip of light dissected the floor, cut a steep white step over the blue-shadowed linen sheets, crumpled over the mound that lay there.

He stood in the doorway. The room swelled to breathing, shallow but slow, ragged at the edges. The rhythm pulsed through him, found his heartbeat, squeezed it to its own deep pulse, subjected him to its dying contractions.

Something sucked him forward but he could not step in and disturb the sediment of pain, grown over slow months of suffering. Nor could he step back, pull himself out of this deep current, although he knew the moment the pulse ceased his own breath ceased with it, and he would remain, disembodied, aching with an irredeemable sense of loss, outside the lifeless, empty room, and would wake, gasping for breath, struggling to break the surface of consciousness.

The sun was shining outside. The shadow of the hotel stretched across low trees and whitewashed wall to bright fields, behind them the misted mountains. He walked to the beach and stripped off.

The water was choppy, ragged peaks breaking diagonally along the coast, interrupting the rhythm of his strokes. Waves rolled over his paddling arms, refusing to let them break surface; he tried breaststroke but the distance between peaks was too great to fit into the pattern of stretch and pull.

Below was murky, stirred by swirling eddies and currents. Wave shadows painted tiger stripes on his extending arms.

He gave up far before his target distance and returned to shore to let sun suck him dry, hot on his back.

Noise awoke him. Distant echoes of clashing metal and cries. Steel flashed. Leather shone dully. People in robes were running into the sea, chased by men with swords and spears. A face hit the sand in front of him. There was no thud, only the background of screams and sea. He saw sand leap from the impact. Dead eyes stared into his own, black hair sticking in tight curls to the wet forehead, blood round the mouth. Trevor tried to move but couldn't. The face slid away, hands leaving valleys in the sand. Another hand clasped his leg. He was one of them, torn from the land to be shaken endlessly by the restless sea.

As quickly as it had appeared it was gone, sucked into the wash of surf. The beach was empty through the heat haze before him. A dream. Too much sun and last night's bad sleep. But the face had been so real.

A hand touched his leg again and he jumped.

"I didn't know if you were awake."

Trevor looked around.

"I didn't mean to alarm you."

"I was dreaming."

"What about?"

Trevor didn't answer. Now that he was fully awake he was annoyed with himself for speaking to her. It was yesterday's girl from the sea, appearing again without warning or invitation. Close up he saw she was much older than he'd thought; crows' feet stretching from the eyes, a creased 'W' joining her eye-brows, an etched triangle linking edges of mouth and nose. Her skin was dark and wide-pored from years of sun and sea and her hair long, black and damp. She wore a blue one-piece.

"This is not pleasant sand for dreaming. There were many battles here, souls thrown to the sea, condemned to be blown always with the ocean winds, to never rest. You can hear their bones rolling in the surf, see their teeth flash as they bite the surface. They howl at night."

Suddenly she laughed. It was a sparkling, charming laugh rolled up from the belly, eyes and white teeth glinting.

"So I'm told."

He couldn't help but like her a little more.

"What else have you been told? You seem to know plenty about me."

"I know you've not eaten seafood worth the oil it's cooked in yet. There's a good fish-bar in the next bay. Follow the path from the hotel on, over the headland and you'll see it. I can meet you there tonight."

"You take a lot for granted."

"Maybe. You should take your shoulders inside. They look like cooked crab. I'm going to swim."

132

She was right. His whole back felt hot. Tight from sun and dried salt.

"What's your name?" he called after her.

"Angelina."

He watched her disappearing, brown into blue, and wet his lips. He tried to guess her age but couldn't. She looked much younger from behind.

Their meeting place was more of a hut than a bar. The only thing visible from the headland path was a green roof and a few tables and chairs, outside, by the sea. On returning to the hotel he realised they'd not arranged a time. He arrived a little after seven. A handsome, curly-haired man who spoke no English greeted him with a flashing grin and served him ouzo. Trevor sat, facing the sea, watching the ice form swirling, white clouds in the clear ouzo.

Brown nets were drying on the rocks to his left. Two boats, green and red, were tied up on the beach. Stretching from the bar was a strand of washing line on which three squid were suspended. They hung, attached by head and two spread tentacles, like huge ragged bats.

The young Adonis brought him a menu and retired to the hut to watch him from a distance. Everything was in Greek. After his second ouzo he started trying to decipher it.

"Do you need a translator?"

"Ah! You've come! Allow me."

He pulled a chair out, tucked it in under her. He'd half expected her to stand him up.

"How's your back?"

"A little warm still. I'm not very good in the heat. I feel like I'm burning up as soon as I lose sight of the sea. No, nothing so active as burning – slowly melting maybe."

"Without the heat you couldn't have such light."

The waiter brought another ouzo and rattled a few sentences at her. He smiled at Trevor, bowed and left.

"What was that about?"

"I told him we'd let him know when we're ready to order. *Yamas.*"

"Cheers."

They were brought fried whitebait and squid with their drinks, and more ouzo appeared. Angelina was good company, interesting and knowledgeable about the history of the area, surprisingly well read about Trevor's achievements and art in general. He found himself talking more than he had in years.

He was feeling recharged and invigorated. He'd taken the first lines of his late night sketches and transferred them onto canvas and the results were promising. Mountains, huge and looming, cloud shapes, heavy, fixed to the ground. It'd been such a long time since he'd felt the need to paint and recently a fear had seized him that he'd be remembered only for his work from the last decade, a few brush strokes in the history of modern art, a painter of potential, unfulfilled. An obituary, unchanged for years, which moved people only to say, 'Carson? I thought he'd died years ago'.

"You don't believe there's anything after death, do you?" she asked.

"You mean God?"

"People call it by different names."

"I don't think God would have been much without us to invent him."

"Neither would death. Tell me about your stab at immortality. How's the painting going?"

When the food arrived he was so deeply involved in describing his plans for the new paintings – a series based on the mountains which ruled this whole area – that he didn't notice a different set of hands were serving them until the sway of a black skirt caught his eye. Following the path of the young woman who left he was filled with a blaze of *déjà vu*. As she dipped to replace the tray on a table near the hut he recognised her as the woman from the chapel in town.

"She owns the place."

"I saw her in the village church yesterday."

Angelina nodded.

"The sea took her husband last week. Her brother brings her fish and helps here but he has his own family and the fish are not so plentiful near the coast. She doesn't want him fishing far out in the deeps. She prays for the return of her husband's body for burial."

Angelina licked her ring finger and drew it across her eyebrow, smoothing the dark lashes into a single black line. "The sea is generous but she gives nothing without taking in return."

134

Before they left the owner came with a strong, coffee liqueur. They drank together. She took Trevor's hand and looked into his eyes. Hers were startling green against black eyelashes and dark skin. Slowly she nodded and stood up.

"She thanks you for coming."

"My pleasure. It was all very nice. Tell her I'll see her again."

"She knows."

He didn't see Angelina for a few days. He kept looking for her on his morning swims. The painting began to grow. It filled one canvas and spread onto another. They were good, better than anything he'd done in years, but something still lacked. They weren't quite the masterpiece he searched for, a final swan song to leave the world. Summer was drawing to an end and he felt time pressing. His nights were haunted by the dream of his mother's room and it left him weak and aching. He couldn't eat the soft cheese, honey and coarse brown rolls they left for his breakfast and the walk to the beach seemed long and dreary.

This morning the sky was grey. The sea was quarrelsome; each broken wave rushing back from the beach dragging tumbling pebbles and sand and holding the next break to a standstill as it paused, spitting and frothing, until it built enough anger to crash down, come roaring up the beach, tearing the shore, and repeat the procedure. Further out waves jarred against each other, hissing, baring white teeth where they met, then joining and racing on.

Getting in was hard. It was impossible to stay upright in the turmoil of undertow and breaking wave and Trevor let himself fall and be towed out by the currents, battered by the waves. At first it seemed a little better, beyond the booming surf, but swimming was uncomfortable and difficult.

The waves which had seemed unimpressive from the shore rose like mountains over his head. Each cliff of water was a different height, sometimes followed by a deep trough, sometimes by a series of smaller peaks. The sea had lost all idea of working from a level plateau and laid itself in uneven slabs making it impossible to judge when to kick or breathe. As soon as one wave had passed, a smaller fin of water would slap his face, fill his mouth with salt.

His strokes took him nowhere. He felt entirely at the whim of the sea. Hanks of seaweed and brown growth tangled in the mess of water and appeared suddenly before him, dark and menacing, and blacker peaks of wave, glimpsed suddenly over foam, seemed shark fins, swift and menacing.

As he dropped into the chasms between waves the shore disappeared, and each time it returned to view it seemed further from him. Angelina stood on the sand, shouting. He swam towards her, panic growing inside. Her mouth was moving but he heard nothing over the sea. He tried to shout but each time he opened his mouth a wave broke over him, taking him down and tumbling him in its surge. In a moment he was lost, rolling under water with no idea which way was sea bed or sky. He broke surface unexpectedly, unsure of where he was facing, but as he gulped in air another wave took him down.

God, what a stupid way to go, yards from the shore, though in which direction he had no idea. His arms and legs thrashed but he seemed no closer to surface. His goggles had gone and all he could see was a mist of deep green, clouds of threshing bubbles as he tumbled over and under.

Something hard tangled against his scalp. As his hand closed over it he came up again. Angelina was gripping his hair. He reached for her and she pushed him under again. When next he came up she was pulling him away from the shore. He shouted at her but a wave curled over him, taking his words and breath.

"Don't fight her! She's too strong!"

They were out, beyond the wave breaks.

"What?"

"You can't fight – trust her! Face the waves!"

She let go of his head and he turned out to sea. Water towered over him, glacial cliffs in a state of permanent collapse, bearing down, but instead of crushing they lifted him, letting him rise over the waves. On the peak he could see all the way to the horizon; a moment of weightlessness when it seemed the water would forget him, leave him floating in air as it rushed away beneath, and then he was down again, swooping into the next chamber, enclosed by walls of water. The fear left him. He was back in control. The surface seemed not to move, skin lying over a huge muscled creature, tendons thrashing beneath, occasional teeth flashing white as they broke this covering, segmented into sharp-edged diamonds, pyramids, all straight edges and angles. Every colour was held, the

136

greens and blues, browns, black, and flashes of deep pink, purple, gold, sucked down from the sky. The noise was no longer terrifying but lulling, like amplified silence, the sound of his blood singing through his ears.

At the next peak he turned to shout to Angelina. She was already climbing onto the beach. He floated, still facing the oncoming towers of water and let them wash him back to the shore until threshing pebbles were bouncing on his calves and he turned and crawled out, wallowing in the surf like a de-tusked walrus.

He was tingling all over as he clambered up the beach. For the first time in weeks he felt fully alive again. It made him sense more deeply how much he was losing.

"Thank you. You saved my life."

She held the plain white towel out to him.

"What's left to save." He smiled sadly. "I'm dying, Angelina," he said.

She nodded.

"Forget the mountains."

He frowned.

"Dreams are like waves. Don't fight them, let them take you."

That night Trevor sat with a bottle of brandy, staring at his paintings. The next morning he changed his room to an east-facing one and spent the next two weeks standing on his balcony, painting. The hotel staff, especially Leo who'd become very fond of him, ensured food and drink were brought to his room though he ordered nothing and rarely ate. Despite this he looked well and glowed with a new strength. He slept deeply at nights and woke feeling strong and refreshed. If he was troubled by dreams, he did not remember them on waking and they didn't disturb his sleep. He swam less often but spent many hours walking along the shore, in deep conversation with Angelina. He ordered more canvases and paints to be brought by taxi from the capital.

On the 28th of September he sent a letter to his agent, Mrs R.S. Montgomery in London. "I realise everything I've tried to paint for ten years has been waves, and these last pieces surpass all my hopes. I'd like you to see them before I go."

A week after the letter he dreamt of the sick room again.

Everything was the same, the blue light, the pulse, the stillness, but this time he let the current take him into the room, draw him towards his mother's bed. Through all her long illness he'd never visited, terrified by his own mortality.

His footsteps echoed as he approached the silent shape.

He expected death to be horrifying, to leave him shaking with terror and futile rage. Instead he felt peaceful. There was none of the sense of decay and ending he'd feared.

"I'm sorry," he whispered.

He could not make out the features of the woman beneath him. Her face was shadowed, and looked younger than he remembered, almost beautiful. He reached out to take her hand.

The curtains to the balcony were blowing. A woman stood over him.

"Mags?"

"Time for your swim, Trevor. The paintings look good."

He rubbed the sleep out of his eyes.

"I should bring them in, but the weather's been so fine, and you need the natural light to really see them."

The sea was still and oily, silently lapping the pebbles, all hollows and curves. A heavy mist hung over it, not lying quite on the surface but resting a few inches above.

She entered silently, slipped the sea onto her like a dress. He took a few steps then plunged. The water rose on either side in two wings, which beat once then gave up and fell back into the sea. She swam straight out and he followed her. The mist soon hid them from the shore. The sun was a red bruise ahead of them.

"Are you ready?" she asked.

Trevor nodded. She smiled and squeezed his hand.

The owner of the fish-bar's husband was found that evening. He still wore his dark jeans and T-shirt. The sea had blurred his handsome features and bloated his body. Fish had eaten much of the flesh from his face and hands but no-one doubted his identity. His soul was laid to rest on the Friday. His wife spent two weeks in prayer, giving thanks for his return.

The same tide brought in the English painter. Death had smoothed the years from his face. He looked younger, contented. He was said to be smiling.

His agent arrived in time for the funeral. It was a quiet affair; the hotel staff, a priest, a few local fishermen to fill in the hole and a woman who ran a fish bar he'd frequented. The agent was told that sea mist had eroded his last paintings so much that only smears of colour and shape remained, but whether they'd been thrown out or taken by one of the staff no-one could tell her.

Of the woman who left with him for his last swim no-one knew her identity or her fate. She seemed to have disappeared as completely as the sea mists.

Tom Christmas

by Christine Frances Collette

Suzannah was flitting around the London gallery, dabbing at pieces of her exhibition, dusting, adjusting, when Tom Christmas spoke to her for the first time. His comical, screwed-up face, bracketed by his big ears, prevented him from appearing threatening, despite his immoderate height and bulk. Suzannah was nevertheless frightened that he would knock against one of her sculptures, or annihilate one of the smaller exhibits, the gnomish figures that she called her Little Men. These brought Suzannah a steady income; she sold them on a market stall every Saturday, although she was careful to keep this fact from the gallery public. Suzannah's life was lived more than ordinarily in separate boxes; the first and primary box was the silent world she inhabited when sculpting. The second was family-sized; her father had been a bus conductor and her mother a school secretary. Suzannah had done well at school, without being brilliant, and it was some surprise, not least to her art teacher, when she won a university place, completed a thesis, and began to sell her sculptures. Academia was the third box; the market was a fourth and the gallery and its customers a fifth. A chunk of money out of each sale paid for one really good dress, coat or shoes, for box five wear. Petite, dark-haired and blue eyed, a combination she owed to her mother's Irish origins, Suzannah looked good in most things, unless she made a really drastic mistake.

Eager to head Tom off before he smashed anything, Suzannah readily engaged in conversation with him, leading him to a corner where bottles of wine awaited the opening. Tom grabbed one of these and it seemed to spring open in his big hands; she found a couple of plastic cups. Tom, she could see, was definitely box five. His shoes, she thought, were hand made; his voice, large like the man, was Eton, or possibly Harrow. Tom proved to be knowledgeable about sculpture and his laudatory remarks about her work were the more acceptable. She found herself accepting a dinner invitation and was glad to leave the gallery and its anxiety behind her for a while.

They ate at a restaurant that Tom might have nicely judged, being just as able to tell background from her voice as she was from

140

his. The venue was Italian, smart, dark, lively. She found he had a bossy attitude towards ordering food and drink but, tired from her day of preparation, was willing to let him go ahead. He told her about himself; merchant banker ('Ah', thought Suzannah, 'right first go') and his unusual name. 'Better get it out of the way first thing,' he said. 'We don't really know where it came from, probably evolved from Christian, but there it was when we are first recorded in the 1300s and the Christmas of the day got his baronetcy.' The meal proceeded pleasantly, Tom took her home in a taxi and correctly did not ask for admittance. She next saw Tom at the gallery opening and he bowed to her, but did not interrupt the business she was genteelly conducting with potential customers and the odd journalist.

After another couple of Tom-directed dinners, Suzannah decided it was her turn, and that she ought to exercise some will-power or she would be swept along, and no doubt ditched when another interest caught Tom's fancy. She had gathered from his conversation that these fancies were wholly absorbing, that he researched whatever subject currently interested him, intelligently and diligently, then filed it away and moved on. She had hit The Contemporary Artist. Suzannah firmly asked him to dinner on her terms, to the local pub where he seemed equally at home as he had been in the smart restaurant. Her small, chaotic flat being near, Suzannah asked Tom home. Inevitably he started to make love to her; because of his bulk and height, there seemed to be Tom everywhere – above, below, beside, under, on top. Suzannah opened magically and effortlessly, like the wine in the gallery, flowed, and found an exquisite sexual release that she had never before known. Tom seemed to think that everything was perfectly normal.

For the next few days, Suzannah thought constantly about Tom. She saw and heard him when he was nowhere near. She found her body melting into an embrace that was purely imaginary. So beset was she by his ever-present image, that it took Suzannah some while to realise that she had not seen the real Tom for several days. Before she had time to develop her sudden panic into pain, Tom telephoned with a proposition. His family home in Kent boasted a separate, and never used, small ballroom, with a pantry and all the usual facilities. This his parents would be glad to loan to Suzannah. She could take her meals with them or cook for herself. She could be as independent as she liked or mix in with the household. Tom would take her down at the weekend for her to decide.

Suzannah liked Tom's parents at once. The father, George, was Tom in body, and the mother, Miranda, Tom in spirit. She had the energy and determination, the concentration. George was vague, a bit weary looking. The ballroom, light, clean and vacant, Suzannah loved. George told her that it was built in the 1880s when the then Lord Christmas had become involved, to his great benefit, in the new business of popular publishing. The ballroom had served until 1916, when the only son, Charles, had been killed on the Somme. George told Suzannah that on some still evenings he fancied he could hear music from the ballroom, an assertion that Miranda roundly denounced as deluded. Suzannah liked to feel that some soft musical presence was watching over the ballroom, a presence undeterred by its use as a hospital during the 1939-45 war and as a barn thereafter.

Having approved her studio, Suzannah returned to town with Tom to pack his car full of her working gear and clothes. They returned to dine with George and Miranda, candlelight and plate and even a butler. She could see that Tom was laughing gently at her, for which she repaid him when he crept into her bedroom, like the young master seducing the servant. In the morning she settled into her studio, ordered what materials she needed, walked into the village to try the shops and the pub, and felt herself blessed. In the following couple of weeks she worked hard and satisfactorily, accompanied Miranda on several morning visits, ate on her own in the week and at the house on weekends. Tom, away on business in New York, neither telephoned nor wrote, but such was Suzannah's content that she hardly noticed. She had to struggle to keep up with Miranda, who had taken her cause to heart and was introducing her to 'useful people'. Miranda had also taken her to the local art gallery/museum and Suzannah had offered to help with the catalogue, or small restoration work.

The whirlwind of Miranda's activity was to finally burst on a dinner party, given in Suzannah's honour, at the end of the week when Tom returned from New York. It would be seen that the Christmases appreciated their new guest and that, despite her voice, she was socially acceptable. Miranda had asked delicately about clothes, and Suzannah had told her of the box five dress policy, which Miranda commended. However, Susannah looked forward

142

more eagerly to seeing Tom – to feeling Tom – than to her party. She was on the look-out on the Friday morning when Tom was due. But when Tom's car drew up, the door opened – the wrong door, the passenger door – and out got a lovely, slim, perfect specimen of young womanhood, her shining hair floating in the breeze, her gestures graceful. Tom joined her and she leant into him, laughing. Suzannah could not move because an elephant was crushing her to the ground and her feet were in a bog. As Tom turned round to greet her, and saw her distress, his own face flushed bright red and then crumpled. He appeared to be in the same bog, though without the elephant. He introduced his friend Sophie. Seeing that Sophie was regarding them both with interest, Suzannah drew on childhood lessons of survival, climbed out of the bog, slipped off the elephant and came forward to shake Sophie's hand and smile. Tom and Sophie went on to the house and Suzannah called after them to excuse herself from lunch, pleading work.

Susannah did not put in an appearance at dinner, which George guessed was due to nerves, but which Miranda rightly attributed to Sophie or, tracing the problem to its root, to Tom. Briefly alone with him, she accused Tom of putting his foot in the smooth running of her Suzannah project. Tom hung his head, truly contrite, somewhat bewildered by the mix of his own feelings. Sophie went to bed early to get some beauty sleep, and also to warm up after dining in an inadequately heated room, wearing a thin dress destined to impress Tom and his father. They had both thought she looked a bit wan, mistaking her chilliness for poor spirits, and she received the attention she had aimed for, if for the wrong reasons. Miranda was sharp with Sophie, as she habitually was with the various girlfriends lightly introduced by Tom and as lightly let drop. Miranda could not understand how a reasonably intelligent woman could fail to see that Tom's interest was perfunctory, nor could she fathom why, warned by herself about the likely temperature of the room, Tom's female guests habitually wore the scantiest of clothing. She herself wore bright woollens and long sleeves, her feet shod in warm boots. She also had a hearty appetite and did not leave the sustaining food pushed to one side of her plate.

Wrestling with his own contrition, Tom went to the kitchen and scooped up the sandwiches that had been left for Suzannah, a bottle of burgundy and one of champagne. Suzannah let him into the warm little pantry. Tom set down the sandwiches and silently opened both bottles. He sat on the table and looked at Suzannah. 'My mother says I've put my big feet in it,' he finally said. Suzanah regarded him gravely. 'You've done nothing wrong,' she said, 'we made no commitments.' 'I'm not sure that's true,' Tom replied, 'Explicit promises, no. I-love-yous, no. But we both offered and received something. I was impolite to bring Sophie with me. I was cowardly and stupid not to think about our relationship, what it meant to me. I'm sorry.' Suzannah thought this was a handsome apology and said so. She was also extremely hungry and yearned for the burgundy. She bit into a sandwich and washed it down, looking at Tom. 'You are, you were, quite free,' she said. 'I don't know if I want to be free,' said Tom. Suzannah ate, sipped, sighed. 'I think I got you mixed up with something out of Mills and Boon,' she said. 'I didn't ask enough, didn't want to know enough about the real you.' She pondered. 'The problem isn't really this Sophie,' she concluded, 'it's that there will always be Sophies. They won't mean anything much to you, but they will to me. I'll become crabby, nasty. It's no good, Tom. We're from different worlds. In all this time it has never occurred to me to get you to meet my mum and dad, yet I've leeched onto yours.' For the first time, Tom was angry. 'You are not a leech,' he said firmly, 'and I am a fool. Sophie and I will return to town in the morning so that nothing happens to spoil your party. You will be wonderful, and I will curse myself for not being there to see you.' He took her in his arms and they hugged and kissed. He walked off back to the house and she watched his figure diminish, darken and disappear. She finished the sandwiches, and took the champagne to bed with her.

In the morning, Suzannah stood under a hot shower to disperse the champagne, drank tea and ate toast, took another, longer, hotter shower for the burgundy, brushed her tongue as well as her teeth. She went to the house to help with last-minute preparations, arranged flowers (at which she was very good) and lunched with Miranda and George, soberly. When it was time, she applied make-up and dressed in her favourite red, swishy dress. Miranda had been doubtful about red, because of Suzannah's blue eyes, but Suzannah had long discovered that while any orange tone was a disaster, crimson reds became her very well. She had brushed back her hair so that its natural curls sprang up around her head, a soft look that emphasised the fine set of her neck. Feeling cold outside in her finery and cold inside, as if she existed outside time, Suzannah went to let the party begin. It was an outstanding success. The guests mixed well, the food was excellent and Suzannah was able to maintain her share in the conversation without difficulty, partly because of the morning visits with Miranda, where she had gleaned the local gossip and picked up an idea of family connections. The better the party went, the more confident Suzannah became, and the more pleased Miranda. George was seen to steal several longing glances towards the quiet morning room, but any escape was forestalled by a quick glance from Miranda, like an optical lasso. When the guests had finally gone, Suzannah and Miranda took a coffee and brandy together. Suzannah stumbled back to her bed and kept Tom firmly where she had put him, away out of her thoughts.

Back to her usual routine in the studio, Suzannah thought it was time to do something to make some money. Her new contacts may be well and good for the future but she needed some present income. It was not too early to think of Christmas goods, and of her market stall, neglected for a few weeks. She decided on some of her Little Men, but in Christmas costume. She made a mould bigger than usual, about three feet high. She retained the floppy hat, her signature on these small, plaster men, but added pom-poms. The body, adjusted to its new size, seemed big. The hands and feet were big. As Suzannah finalized the head, she tweaked the ears, so that they slightly stuck out, seeming to hold up the cap. It suddenly struck her that the mould looked a bit like Tom. When she began to cast from the mould, and then to paint, the resemblance increased. She made ten men and decided that would do, a limited edition. At the end of the week Suzannah said temporary goodbyes and thanks to Miranda and George and went off to reclaim her flat and her market stall.

Suzannah used a local garage as a warehouse for her market stuff. She stored nine of the Men and took the tenth to take orders. Some of the original, smaller Little Men made up a large part of the rest of the stall, with some water-colour postcards and some pen-and-ink sketches. A yell went up of 'Hiya Suzie,' as she set up shop, and there was her favourite fruit-and-veg man, who always looked as if he had just dug potatoes, even when he washed up for the pub, and the leather goods lady, posher than Miranda, and the youngsters on the lampshade stall; the china stall bearing mugs whose transfers had slipped so that the pattern became unintentionally abstract, the Indian sari and scarf stall with its distinctive smell of unbleached cotton. The market was crowded and trade was good. Suzannah took orders for three Christmas Men. She immersed herself in the feel of the market, the sound, the plastic cup of tea that warmed her fingers, the cigarettes she smoked with the veg man. The market was the only place she indulged this vice.

At 6.00pm, tired but elated, she took her stock back to the garage, locked it up, and went to pay her parents a long-overdue visit. Her father, uncritical and eager to see her as always, cried, 'Sue, where have you been?' when he opened the door, smiling and taking her hands, cocooning them in his for warmth. Her mother, more cautious, welcomed Suzannah in with eyebrows just slightly raised. 'It's been a while,' she said, just allowing a hint of a question to be heard. All at once Suzannah, usually reserved, decided on telling them about Tom (the expurgated version), Miranda and George, and the studio. They were both fascinated. 'Our little girl!' exclaimed her father. Her mother wanted to know details of Miranda's tactics, how she had managed the introductions and the party. She wanted to understand the studio, what it meant for Suzannah's work, and whether Suzannah could drop the market stall, which she had always decried. Suzannah told them about the Christmas Men, about the mould, how she had managed the casting. By then her father was getting restless for his television, so Suzannah went out to the shops opposite to get fish and chips for her father, a Chinese take-away for her mother, and a curry for herself. She was used to this round trip – it took a bit of Miranda-style organising; order Chinese first because they took longest; order fish-and-chips second; wait in Indian take-away and pig out on hot gram; collect Indian, fish-and-chips and finally Chinese, all hot. On her return, they watched television, and ate, and Suzannah's father asked her to stay over, as he always did, and she insisted on going back to her flat, as she always did, and he made his customary call to the local taxi firm that he trusted with his precious prize, and gave her, as usual, her fare money. He waved her off. 'Come soon, Sue, come soon!' but it was Suzannah's mother who stood wistfully by the gate, looking at another life drive off, a life she would never have, having given hers to the suburbs, the husband she loved, and the daughter she had bred to leave them behind.

146

Suzannah's life settled into an agreeable routine: work in the studio in the week, with a half day at the museum catalogue, return to the flat and market on Saturday and visit her parents, return to Kent on Sunday evening and eat with Miranda and George. Sometimes Tom was there on the Sunday and that was fine, or nearly fine; Suzannah treated him as the son of her patrons. She had started work on something really complicated and absorbing – statuary that would reflect a woodland location, seeming light and insubstantial, capable of moving in wind or rain, and of reflecting sunlight. In these preparatory stages she was mostly concerned with drawing, and with trying different materials. She realised how much her inspiration owed to her setting at the Christmases and walked in the woods, committing to memory the play of light. She read in the library, learning of the family and local history. The library held a painting of the Charles Christmas who died on the Somme. Smart in his dress uniform, he seemed to smile benignly at her. He was very like Tom. Charles was George's uncle; he had died without issue and George's father had inherited, which was probably good for the family fortunes, because he had been an astute business man. George was blessed with enough of his father's ability to follow where he had led. And of course, he had Miranda.

The Christmas Men that Suzannah made in the evenings, musing on what she had observed and read, sold, and she made another batch of ten. Then one weekday, when drawing a particularly delicate part of her statuary project, Suzannah was surprised by Tom bursting into her studio, carrying a Christmas Man, which he set down on her worktop. Tom looked at Suzannah; he was furious, his eyes mad and the veins in his neck bulging. He tried for speech but it was beyond him. Finally, 'Well?' he said, 'well? What have you got to say? Are you so spiteful?' Suzannah looked from him to the Man and controlled a fit of giggles. 'It wasn't meant,' she said, not pretending to misunderstand. 'It just came out like that. I didn't think anyone would put two-and-two together.' 'Two-and-two!' spluttered Tom. 'Two-and-two! You stand there and talk to me about two-and-two! Do you know these are changing hands at two hundred pounds each?' Suzannah's eyed widened. 'Two hundred pounds!' she said, 'I sold them at twenty-five!' Tom's fury, if possible, grew. 'You sold them! Twenty-five pounds! That's rich. Is it not enough to go through life saddled with the name of Christmas? Do you know, any merchant bank worth the name with whom I trade has one of these in its offices and hides it as I walk in? Can you imagine that? Everywhere you go, go to work, fools fall about laughing?' 'I'm so sorry,' said Suzannah. 'I'm really sorry. It never occurred to me.'

Tom cast himself into a chair, sprawled there, groaned. He looked up at Suzannah and saw the Christmas Man beside her. In spite of himself, his lips began to twitch. 'Okay,' he sighed, 'okay, if it wasn't malicious, I suppose I can get over it about a thousand years from now, before the firm goes bankrupt.' Suzannah had been thinking: 'Wait,' she said, 'don't speak.' She lit one of her Saturday cigarettes. 'Okay,' she said between draws, 'here's what we do. I'm going to cover the mould with resin and give it to you to put in your office. You'll have the mould, you'll know there can be no more copies. And I'll make a bigger one, as if that were the original, decorate if finely, and you can keep it in a display cabinet, have the last laugh. I'll sign it and give you provenance.' Tom looked sceptical for a bit. Then he went to her fridge, got some white wine, scrupulously offered Suzannah a glass and sipped his own. 'It's a deal,' he said. For much of the rest of the week, Tom sat still for Suzannah while she worked feverishly. At last the two Christmas Men were ready, fine and good, the one glowing with auburn resin, the other with gold paint and peacock colours, dressed in materials Suzannah had found in the attic, lace, velvet, delicate shoes. Finally they were ready. Tom and Suzannah were both exhausted, him with sitting still, her with working. She had turned on the radio to help Tom pass the time. As Suzannah threw down her brush, a soft shuffle was playing on Jazz FM; Tom put his arms around her soldiers, massaged her stiff neck, and they slowly began to dance. It was good to feel his arms, good to move freely; the music changed to a rag and they danced on, as if a waltz were playing. Lifting her head from Tom's shoulder, it seemed to Suzannah, just for a second, that the ballroom was full of couples swaying, some tears shed, some laughter, and there in the crowd, distinct against the mist of floating pastel dresses, was Charlie Christmas in his dress uniform, gravely looking at her, questioning. Then Take Five began and the room went back to normal, her sculptures clear again, the chair on which Tom had sat, her brushes. That evening Tom and Suzannah ate with Miranda and George; it was cosy, even the butler familiar now that Suzannah knew him from his village day job of potman in the pub.

At one point, Tom and his mother chatting nineteen to the dozen, George looked at Suzannah and hummed a little waltz song, raising his eyebrows. Suzannah nodded, and smiled. 'What is it?' cried Miranda. 'Nothing,' Suzannah replied, 'just something that came from my Irish background.'

Thinking of backgrounds, Suzannah thought it was time Tom met her parents. She tried to describe them to him. 'My father wanted to call me Susan, after his mother,' she said, 'but my mother wouldn't hear of it. She wanted Siobhan, but Dad refused to call me something he couldn't spell. So they settled on Suzannah. Dad always calls me Sue, Suzie, or Suzie Q, or when I was little, Squib. Mum always calls me Suzannah. They are both interested in me, in my art, in my career. Neither likes the market, especially Mum. If she goes for fruit and veg and sees me, she ignores me. Dad met all sorts when he was a bus conductor, all races, lots of languages, coins from different parts of the world, I had quite a collection. When I was little I used to love to punch a ticket, and he had to put the money in. He let me do it, although money was tight. Mum would have loved to be self-sufficient, cooking and sewing, but in fact is a poor cook and a worse seamstress. She was, however, a very good school secretary. Imagine Miranda with a whole school to run, what bliss.'

Tom was intrigued and excited about paddling in this new stream, and offered to accompany Suzannah on her Saturday market – and parents-visit. There was a bit of a sticky moment at the market when the original Little Men came out of their box, however, they served to show Tom that they originated before Suzannah knew he existed. Tom chatted with the other stall holders and he did not break anything, although he came close a couple of times. When they went on to her parents' house it was, as usual, Dad who opened the door. 'I've heard about you from our Sue,' he said, 'come on Suzie, I thought you'd never get here.' Mum was more formal, asked Tom about the market. Suzannah, seeing that this was an attempt to recruit Tom for the anti-market side, headed her off by introducing Tom to the takeaway run. This he found entrancing, and popped into the off-licence to add wine and brown ale to the hoard. 'How did you know to get brown ale?' asked Suzannah; Tom put his finger to the side of his nose and then told her he had asked the licencee. Seeming to agree with both Mum and Dad at once about the choice of television programme, a difficult task as their tastes were diametrically opposed, Tom passed a pleasant evening. He drove Suzannah home; they both paused but Suzannah did not ask him in. She nearly called him back, but the telephone began to ring; Dad, asking if she got home alright – and the moment passed.

Tom had to spend a week in Switzerland, so Suzannah decided to stay in London and pick up the threads, visit the galleries. In the café at the National Gallery she ran into a young man she had known at university and seen a few times since. Derek was from the same area of London as Suzannah and of similar background, Irish ancestry included; he was now a lawyer. Derek claimed that his London accent was an asset in criminal work; the clients trusted it and the judges pitied it; the opposition did not like to be too hard on him in case it upset the jury. Nothing much upset Derek; he knew himself to be blessed with high intelligence and a quick wit. He was fun to be with, and good-looking in a dark-haired, lean-hipped way. He was not tall, but lithe, his movements quick and deft like his mind. Suzannah always enjoyed herself with Derek, who had made it clear early in their relationship that nothing serious was going on.

'So how goes the up-and-coming lawyer? Clients been nicking the national treasures?' Suzannah asked. 'Budding young artist yourself,' he replied. 'Hi Suze, good to see you.' He got himself tea and they chatted. 'I've been hearing about you,' said Derek. 'Apparently there are some little Christmas gnomes changing hands for a thou.' Suzannah gritted her teeth. 'I sold them for twenty-five pounds,' she told him. 'You never had a grasp of economics,' Derek said. 'Do you remember when I was in *Socialist Worker* and I tried to explain Marxism to you?' Suzannah remembered. She had been more interested in the shape of his mouth and nostrils, and the exact colour of his eyes.

The eyes, bright, laughing, suddenly took on an arrested expression. 'Suze,' he said, 'you're the answer to a prayer. God has put you here in the National Gallery. I have a dinner tomorrow in Chambers; some visiting dignitary and we're all to turn out. Actually I came here to see this latest exhibition, so I'd have something to talk about to the wife and daughters. I have no partner for the dinner.' 'You have no partner? But you always had girls coming out of your ears.' 'Tell the truth, Suze, I'm in a bit of a social desert.' Derek looked not hurt by this, but resigned. 'Even with the blokes, you know, down the pub – if I've got a case the next day, I stick to mineral water. It sets me apart. And if I stop off on the way home, I'm dressed wrong, so I have to go home and change, and it seems like putting on costume, so I don't. I don't mean I never go, it's just become an effort. And I don't get on with the Hooray Henrys in the Chambers. I get on best with my clients. There's some old boys in Chambers I like; in truth, I've sort of become Rumpole. And Rumpole always made me cry. And that's the blokes, mind. With the girls it's worse, being girls. And the posh ones, they expect a bit of rough, and I'm not like that.' He wasn't, Suzannah remembered. He was a kind and attentive lover, but not exciting. Suzannah could imagine Sophie, out for a thrill, looking at her nail varnish, lying back and thinking of England. By now the gallery was closing and they moved on to the crypt at St Martin's, for an early supper. The more they talked, the faster, and the more pronounced their accents. Suzannah found herself telling Derek about Tom. 'So where is this paragon?' he asked. 'In Switzerland.' 'You mean you let him go off? Why don't you pin him down?' 'I'm not sure I want to pin. There's the Sophie problem,' Suzannah explained. 'To be fair, I think you'll always have Sophie problems,' Derek agreed, 'but you'll have to learn not to mind. Meanwhile, come to my dinner.'

Suzannah dressed carefully, donning a dark-blue velvet dress and scraping her hair into an antique comb she had found at the Bermondsey market. Derek called for her, immaculate in evening wear. Suzannah thought that his social problems would not be long-lasting. At the reception she found some people from the Miranda dinner, and these having made other introductions, began to feel less of a stranger and less conspicuous. The dinner and the wines were wonderful. Derek, as always, was abstemious, and drove her home, profuse in his thanks. 'I suppose this Tom bloke being in the picture, you're not interested in anything else?' he asked. 'No,' said Suzannah, 'I'm sort of absorbed.' 'Well, ask me to the wedding,' Derek replied, with a cheerful wave.

A few days later, Suzannah was soaking in a rose-scented bath when Tom indeed entered the picture, crashing through the door and yelling what seemed to be 'Again!' Suzannah eyed him in amazement. She not only smelt like, but resembled a pink rosebud, slim shoulders rising from the steam, slim neck, hair swathed in shampooed furls around her head. She spoilt the image: 'Close the bleeding door,' she yelled back, furious at the draught spoiling her soak. Tom kicked the door shut with his heel and began waving his arms, still shouting 'again!'. 'You've done it again,' he said. 'Do you take pleasure in ruining my career? Is your sole object in life to make mine as difficult as possible ?' 'What do you mean?' asked Suzannah, wondering if any more Men had turned up, or been stolen, or copied. (In fact, some cheap fairy-light copies had been made and were selling well, but neither Suzannah nor Tom knew of this.) 'You and Judge John Deed, that's what I mean. The up-and-coming radical lawyer. Your boyfriend.'

'Derek?' asked Suzannah. 'Whatever his name is. Taking you about and flaunting it everywhere.' 'I went to his Chambers dinner,' said Suzannah. 'What's wrong with that ?' 'Did you think I wouldn't know?' asked Tom, slighting dropping the decibel level. 'My mother was rung by one of her friends to be told that the nice young artist had a nice new boyfriend. I know we've got no commitment.' Then the decibels went up again. 'I suppose he's better in bed than me,' shouted Tom. Suzannah, now equally angry, hissed back: 'Five years ago, when I last slept with him, he was a kind and considerate lover and quite satisfactory, thank you. And he never burst into my bathroom, or blamed me for his own hurt pride. And he never cheated on me when he was sleeping with me.' Tom, who had sat down on the lavatory seat, making it squeak and slew sideways, reared up again. 'That's it. That's it. I knew it. You were Sophie-ing, to get your own back. Well, stick with the Judge; I'm out of here.' 'Fine,' said Suzannah, 'fine. And leave your key, if you had a key and didn't just break the door down.' The door slammed behind Tom, and opened again a chink as the key was thrown through. It fell into the lavatory, Tom having dislodged the seat in his last fury.

Suzannah lay back in the bath and ran more hot water to do some hard thinking. So Tom was jealous. Was that good or bad? Good, in that it indicated deep feeling for her, bad in that it indicated jealousy and fits of irrational anger. Tom had never before used the key to the flat unless she was with him. It had been given for a practical reason, to help with the market arrangements, not as a token of partnership. Or had it, she asked herself. What did she really think about Tom? Was it just sex, or largely just sex? Had she, did she propose a long-term relationship ? Had they ever really been a couple? As she got out of the draught-spoilt bath and wrapped herself in lots of comforting towel, the telephone rang. It was her mother. After the usual preliminaries, the actual reason for the call became apparent. Her mother wanted to know the state of play with Tom. 'Wish I knew, Mum,' said Suzannah, 'wish I knew.'

As neither Tom nor Suzannah wanted to be first to contact the other, there was no further opportunity for explanations. Tom, miserable and angry, snapped at his clients, worrying his chief who had got wind of grumblings of economic discontent. 'It's America, Tom,' he explained. 'If the US of A goes arse about face, what chance we? I know we kept out of the sub-prime market, thank the Lord, but this could be big.' Tom was worried not so much for himself, as for his fiercely independent parents. He had put enough aside in the glory days, in several currencies, in various banks, to survive in reasonable comfort in the long run, or even extravagance in the short term. In fact, he need not have worried about George and Miranda who, always frugal, retained half-full the pots of money that George's father had left them. Tom had been not to Eton, as Suzannah suspected, but to the village school and local grammar school before Cambridge. His excellent first-class degree and family connections were good enough introductions to his first post in a merchant bank and indeed, gave him something of an boy-makes-good edge. However, news of a possible impending economic downturn did nothing to soften his temper. Suzannah meanwhile stayed cool, going back to her studio and what had become comfortable weekend meals with Tom's parents. Miranda noted that Suzannah never froze in the dining room but looked good in her jumpers and boots. Suzannah, herself now in easy enough financial circumstances, insisted on paying rent. Without her knowing, George put this aside for her in a specially created savings account, intending to repay her by buying one of her own works when the time was right. When not absorbed in her ethereal project, Suzannah passed the time by applying for a grant, carefully researching the likes and dislikes of the providing agencies. The museum retained her to put on a special exhibition, paying her a small fee.

Tom and Suzannah spent Christmas with their respective parents. Suzannah's gained rather more profit from this than Tom's, as his acerbity continued to be made felt by grunts and snaps. Suzannah spent an evening at the pub with Derek and filled him in on Tom-events. Derek was rather impressed by the bathroom scene and they debated whether Tom could be accused of trespass. Rather wistfully, Suzannah was forced to give up the idea. Derek himself was making headway with the daughter of his head of Chambers, who had got under his defences due to her gentle eyes and charming deference to his opinions. 'Is her name Hilda?' Suzannah asked. 'Why the hell should she – oh, I get it, Rumpole again. No.' He waited a few seconds and then said: 'Actually, her name is Mathilda.' They both burst into fits of giggles. To celebrate his progress with Mathilda, Derek asked Suzannah to dinner, choosing the Italian restaurant where she and Tom had first dined, thus causing Suzannah to sigh a little until Derek forcibly pointed out to her the difficulty of eating with someone who played rather disgustingly with their food and answered conversational gambits at random. Suzannah apologised and they spent an enjoyable evening thereafter, guessing the occupations of their fellow diners, with more abandon and less accuracy at each course. By the cheese they were quite riotous. Suzanna's mood quickly changed when she got home and found an envelope in Tom's writing. Inside was a note to the effect that, having learnt the Men in his office were now worth upwards of £5,000, he was enclosing a cheque for that amount. Suzannah cut the cheque up into dancing fairy dolls that spelt SLOB, and returned it.

For the following twelve months Tom and Suzannah did not see each other, or rather escaped the regard of the other if their paths crossed. Tom, attempting to achieve some stability in his own sector of what came to be called The Credit Crunch (sounds like a punk band, said his boss), increased his globe-trotting. He had several Sophie-esque flings, but as he remained gloomy and irritable, these did not last, and word got round in his own circle that Tom Christmas was best avoided. He seemed to have personalised the economic doom and gloom when what was needed was some light relief. Suzannah got her grant and her work on the ethereal project benefited as she was able to indulge herself with the materials she used. She had several meals with Derek and, on the eve of his engagement to Mathilda, they slept together. This they both regretted, because each derived therefrom considerable enjoyment. Suzannah was pleased to have male arms around her, pleased to have pleasure, and was sorry that someone so easy to talk to, so civil and yet so sharp, of her own world, was necessarily going out of her life. Derek admitted to himself that his gentle young fiancée lacked

154

Suzannah's salt; but also that, if he had wanted a salty diet on a permanent basis, he would have done something about Suzannah a long time ago. Sitting in his blue-striped boxer shorts at her kitchen table on the morrow, his dark hair fetchingly tangled over his eyes, he questioned Suzannah on the Tom affair. 'There is no affair,' snapped Suzannah. 'Yes there is, you practically live with his parents and you avoid him.' 'Stop the inquisition, I'm not one of your bloody clients.' 'No, thank God. Give me an honest burglar any day rather than a sexy, half-Irish artist suffering from inverted snobbery. And get some clothes on if you don't want to go back to bed.' 'Clothes yourself. And anyway, you can't, not from today, you are now a man spoken for. But Derek, doesn't it bother you, to hitch up with someone out of our world? You were the Marxist.'

'I wasn't a Marxist, I was a Trot. Not that you ever knew the difference. I still am, I haven't changed my opinions. But my opinions, my dear *ignoramous inamorata*, are about the class system, for which I blame the organisation of our society, not individual people who live in it and cannot escape its effects. That is why I don't belong to any party, because I found they all tried to individualise a system, which leads one down a Robespierrian path. I just try to live my life according to my principles. Hence the burglars etc. They are also products of the system, I can attempt to ameliorate its effects on them. By the way, your Tom ('not my Tom') recognises this. It's what merchant bankers do, they study the system and try to make some cracks at some times and heal them up at others, to make the juices of capitalism flow. And even you must have realised that this system now threatens to implode under its own weight, and seen the irony that it's a Labour Party financial genius who has, to mix my metaphors, his finger in the dyke. Sorry, quite a speech.'

'It's okay. Who else can I talk to, who knows me now, and comes from where I come from? It's that as well – it's just more comfortable to be around someone who sounds like me, who knows all the sights and smells of my bit of London, who calls me Suze and is kind to me.'

'Dear Suze, I shall miss you. I do know what you mean, but you don't have to lose your past. You don't have to shut doors in your face, either. Damn, I wanted to take you back to bed, now I daren't, in case I fall in love with you. For Christ sake get dressed, woman.'

155

So Suzannah and Derek parted in fond friendship. As always when bedevilled by personal problems, Suzannah immersed herself in work. Her creation now filled a large part of her studio. It suggested trees in its slim, polished wooden uprights, ending in fans of split bamboo from which glass drops trembled; the floor was rubber, with rock-like bumps and glass rivers. The whole was powered by electricity so that it was in movement. There were several light, imperfectly formed plastic figures, shapes suggesting rather than defining people and animals, that could be added to or subtracted from the scene by the viewer according to taste, so that the viewer in turn became artist. The viewer could also change the colour of the lighting, creating sun, or twilight, autumn or spring. The change in light affected the movement, which was stilled by bright and increased by greyer tones. One exquisite sculpture was fully formed, a young deer made from shiny wood, whose colours danced as the glass drops shook. It was altogether very fluid, very light, massive only in its size, tempting one to enter its space. George loved it and spent much time sitting on a stool which Suzannah had helped him carve, so that he became part of the sculpture. Suzannah told him firmly that he was now part of the exhibition and would regret it when he was installed with it in the London gallery where it was to be displayed, as part of the grant prize.

Suzannah and her parents spent Christmas with Miranda and George. Her father and George got on very well, being, Suzannah realised, of much the same non-judgemental, caring character. Miranda and her mother were equally compatible, although their relationship was given to short, fierce disputes, which both relished. Suzannah suspected Miranda of thinking up fresh subjects of controversy overnight. Tom was in Venezuela and telephoned, speaking to both fathers, on a day when the three women were sales-shopping in the nearest market-town. George's face, on their return, was alight with pleasure at the call. 'Tom phoned, Tom,' he called out as they were getting out of the car, 'just fancy, our boy, out there, and he phoned.'

Suzannah returned to London to prepare her exhibition. Her parents stayed on with George and Miranda, seemingly set on underlining Derek's theory that people overrode class. Suzannah spent most of her time in the gallery. She nipped and tucked, tried different lighting. The champagne came and the first night invitations. Derek and Mathilda were to be guests of honour. Suzannah had met and liked the shy young woman, and found her adoration of Derek touching. She had never adored anyone like that, certainly not Tom. On the eve of the opening, Suzannah was playing with complete darkness for the surround of the exhibit and green light within. She was therefore unaware of the arrival of a large person until Tom tripped over a cable. 'For fuck's sake don't move,' she yelled, as Tom, trying to steady himself, dislodged a tree shape she had spent an hour getting into position. Tom froze, immobilised as much by the beauty that surrounded him as the beauty who shouted at him. Suzannah regarded him gravely, and then changed the lighting to violet, and then soft red. Tom felt his hurt assuaged as he looked and wondered. Sitting back on her heels, Suzannah looked at the spectacle: first, she saw that the tree was better in its new position; second, that big, solid Tom did not spoil her airy sculpture. Rather, he fulfilled it. Suzannah realised that she had made him a setting, that she had worked all this time on framing a void. That, of course, was why George had looked so right sat in its centre. She came slowly towards Tom, who opened wide his arms. She entered his embrace, returning it, holding as much of him as she could. They began to dance, turning, waltzing. Both were crying. As Suzannah's eyes began to clear she saw one of the red-lit plastic figures raise his cap, as Charlie Christmas said goodbye.

Act of Malice

by William Wood

It was difficult not to believe that the old woman behaved with deliberate malice. Her small acts of vandalism were not random: they took place when her daughter's back was turned, when she was on the telephone to the doctor or to social services or opening the door to the district nurse.

Eleanor had moved into her parents' house to care for her father, immobilized by a heart attack and at the mercy of a wife who had no comprehension of his disability. Indeed, for the past five years he had been his wife's carer, administering patiently to the demented old woman's whims. A thankless task, the stress of which had contributed to his own heart condition. And now an act of vindictiveness on her part was soon to contribute to his death.

Had Eleanor been able to predict this she might more easily have borne what seemed for the moment like a life sentence. She moved about the kitchen preparing the evening meal. She had it down to a fine art by now, retrieving the food from the places she had hidden it. The fish she had removed from the fridge and placed in a stone bread bin out of her mother's reach. The vegetables, prepared earlier, she had immersed in a pan and hidden beneath piles of outdoor clothing in the porch. Raspberries picked for dessert were secreted in punnets in the hanging basket of trailing geraniums. Cream and milk were transferred to tins that had held baked beans or lentils.

Such subterfuge was the result of weeks of experience, of interference from the old woman who at any time of the day or night was apt to turn on the oven and burn up anything that looked like food. If something was already cooking for a regular meal, she would steal in and turn it off, or open the oven perhaps to add a packet of sausages, left-over fish or even potatoes and other root vegetables. Fruit she would put in a saucepan, cover with water, bury beneath a bag of sugar and put on the hot plate. Then she would walk away and forget it.

As Eleanor began heating the water on the stove she tried to count the times she had had to scrape the hob clean, wipe down the stove streaked in blackberry juice or apple mush, mop the floor…

"Why do you do it, Mother?" she would ask.

"Someone has to feed us all."

"But it's not even meal time."

"I like to have everything ready."

This evening her mother was dozing, the plaice was beginning to bubble in the oven and Eleanor retrieved the broccoli from beneath the anoraks. She was about to put it on to steam when she heard the familiar panting, and her mother, obese and dirty, heaved herself into the kitchen like an old steam train puffing up a steep gradient.

Eleanor stood between her and the oven to block her passage. The old woman had not yet tried physically to push her daughter aside, but she peered around her at the cooker.

"Haven't you got the vegetables on yet?"

"No, Mother. Broccoli takes ten minutes to steam."

"Half an hour. Anyway, you have to bring the water to the boil."

"I think I know what I am doing. Why don't you and Father have a drink?"

"I don't know what's got into your Father," she said. "He's got so lazy. He won't even get up to pour me a drink."

Every evening Eleanor took a tube of Pringles from the walk-in pantry and gave it to her mother to get her out of the kitchen while she mixed the drinks. A finger of gin topped up with cold tonic water from the fridge and then the extra whoosh of fizz as she dropped in a slice of freshly cut lemon. Making sure her mother could not double back behind her, she carried the drink out to the conservatory where her father sat in his wheelchair.

"You won't get me pushing that thing about," had been his wife's comment when the nurse brought the contraption into the house.

The drinks kept the couple occupied while Eleanor put the finishing touches to the meal. When she served up the locally caught, fleshy fillets of plaice, lightly baked in organic butter, her mother swamped her portion in Heinz tomato ketchup while her father spread a heap of tartare sauce over his. This did not prevent Eleanor from savouring her own helping. The day's watch was almost over. She would clear up, her parents would doze in front of the TV, and put themselves to bed. From about 8pm the evening was hers.

She retreated to her room, phoned or texted a dwindling number of friends, caught up on what remained of her own business. She still received mail and requests for interviews or articles. Her colleagues at the production company still did not understand why, having broken through the infamous glass ceiling, she had resigned.

"Can't hack it," said some of the men. At her leaving party she had almost confirmed their prejudice by saying that she was taking a year out to refresh her creative side; that the managerial burden was eroding her imagination. If only they knew the truth. She had not so much as scripted a thirty second advertisement, let alone worked on a full length programme.

"I will be back," she promised them, declining any presents.

Most nights now she was too tired even to write letters. She might listen to music or to Radio 4, but she usually fell asleep before the end of the ten o'clock news. And so it was tonight, except that she was woken by the shrill scream of the smoke alarm. Opening her bedroom door she smelled something burning at the same time as the increased intensity of the alarm penetrated her ears.

She crammed her feet into a pair of crocs and hurried downstairs in her nightie. Her mother stood, fully dressed, under the kitchen light holding a hunk of cheese in one hand like a child with an ice cream. She was biting into the apex of the triangle with only a slightly guilty look. She seemed unaware of the swirling smoke, of the high pitched alarm and of the blackened stove.

Eleanor, fully awake now, switched off the hot plate and disconnected the alarm.

"What on earth do you think you are doing?"

"Having breakfast. Since no one else is prepared to serve it." This was meant as a reproach to her daughter.

"Mother, it is two in the morning. It is dark. And what the hell have you been cooking?"

"Cooking?" She displayed ignorance, forgetfulness, but Eleanor did not believe this was not an act of deceit.

"What are you making for breakfast?"

"I was cooking some porridge," she said, "before you interrupted me. And now it is all spoilt." Another reproach. She bit again into the lump of cheese in her paw and only now did Eleanor see it was the special Gruyère she had bought for herself. She had carefully wrapped and hidden it at the back of the fridge.

160

Her heart that had just stopped thumping began to hurt in her chest as anger swelled up. She could have slapped the old woman in the face, but clenched her fists, turned her back and looked at the stove, now suitable only as an exhibit for the Turner Prize at the Royal Academy.

Her mother put the remains of the block of cheese on the side board, leaving her bite marks in it. She went over to the pantry and closed and bolted the door.

"I cannot think why that door is always open," she said.

Eleanor bit her lip. "I'm going back to bed and you ought to as well."

For once her mother did as she was told. Eleanor checked on her father, who had slept through the commotion, and went back to her own room. She could not sleep. In the morning there was the kitchen to clean up and the whole soul-destroying routine to endure for another day. She felt unutterably lonely.

There was no time, however, for regret or self pity. Before dawn she heard cries coming from her parents' room. Her father was in severe pain, sitting up in bed trying to call out. Her mother was demanding, "What's wrong with you, Cecil, can't you see I am trying to sleep?" When Eleanor burst in her mother complained, "He won't tell me what is wrong with him." Beneath her irritation, however, was perhaps a vestigial trace of concern.

"He's in pain, Mother." Eleanor wanted to call the ambulance but her father indicated he needed his inhaler. He kept it on the bedside table but had knocked it on the floor and it had rolled under the bed. Eleanor retrieved it once she had grasped the situation. Her father sprayed it into his mouth, gradually the pain subsided and his breathing eased. It was 5.30. Too late to go back to bed again.

"I'll make a pot of tea," Eleanor said.

"Tea!" objected her mother. "At this hour!" But her father said he would like a cup of tea.

As soon as the sun was up the old woman was panting round the house tearing open the curtains and Eleanor set to work on the stove. She set her parents' breakfast out on a tray and went to shower and dress properly. When she came down again the breakfast tray remained untouched but her mother had put lunch out on the kitchen table. She had raided the fridge for more cheeses and spreads, clawing open lids and wrapping off food intended for later in the week. It was still only 9am.

Eleanor was too tired to make a fuss. She gathered the cheeses, the butter, the patés and charcuterie and put them back in what containers and papers she could salvage, walked into the larder and began stacking them in the fridge. There was a click, the electric light went out and behind her she heard and felt the larder door slammed shut and the bolt driven home. She was on her knees in darkness except for the light from the fridge.

"Mother, open the door."

There was no response. She listened. She could hear her mother's footsteps dragging on the brick floor of the kitchen and her receding panting as she went off to meddle elsewhere. Then she heard another sound. Her father's cry of pain and a choking call for help.

Eleanor put her shoulder to the door. It would not budge. It was a solid oak door held by a single iron bolt. She pushed and pushed in desperation, bruising her shoulder, screaming out for her mother, a child locked in as some kind of terrible punishment. Only she was not screaming for herself.

"You stupid bitch..." she sobbed as she sank to the floor. She sat and waited to regain strength and sanity.

Eventually one of the carers arrived. Eleanor heard the doorbell, prayed her mother would let 'the interfering woman' in. When to her immense relief she heard her enter the kitchen the trapped woman called out.

The startled carer, a young Lithuanian, felt rather than saw Eleanor erupt from the dark pantry, brush past her, and rush into her father's room – too late.

162

A Question of Faith

by Cassandra Passarelli

It's as if he'd stepped out of Turnham Green and into the Bible's onionskin. Perhaps the Book of Ezekiel or Haggai, into Babylonia or Assyria and these men are Daniel or Jeremiah. They pray in Syriac, chant in Aramaic, speak Arabic to one and other; as though an abyss of two millennia divides them from him. He steals glances beneath his lids but, with their steel wool beards, granite faces and knotty feet, they're too remote. Whereas I'm familiar; European, soft and fleshy. He wants to know my story.

When mass is over, we'll carry dishes of olive oil, red oregano, *labneh*, goats' cheese, apricot jam and flat bread to Abraham's Tent and he'll sit beside me, as if by chance.

And ask.

We're used to talking; to each other, our souls and God. We're descendants of a long dynasty of philosophical debaters; Isaac of Antioch, Rabbula, Shem`un Quqoyo the potter, Ya`qub of Edessa. Masters of poetry who composed our liturgy of *madroshé* and *sogitho* – dialogues between the Virgin Mary and Gabriel, Mary and the wise men or Cain and Abel. Conversation broadens the spirit.

He'll place my accent at once. Ask questions. And be flummoxed by my answers. That I've been a monk for two decades. That I did a masters in history, was a wine-maker in Oxford and, later, a political advisor in Westminster – making me a man of his world. He'll wonder why a Syriac Orthodox monastery should be flourishing in a Muslim country, forgetting we're a stone's throw from Christianity's seedbed. He'll ask about the brothers' origins, about the black saint after whom our monastery, Deir Mar Musa, is named. And of our relationship with the Bedouin.

He won't ask:

Why did you become a monk?

It would be an admission of scepticism; nudging me further from him and nearer to the anachronistic brethren, cross-legged, with long beards and Semitic profiles that surround us. One honest question might lead to others. What you don't raise in conversation reveals as much as what you do.

Mark, Matthew or Peter... (Biblical names have grown fashionable though Christianity less so.) Let's call him Peter. Peter will drink chamomile and, after lunch, wander up the steps to Al-Hayak, along the riverbed to the goatherd's house and past the cave retreats. For an hour or two he'll consider the life of an ascetic. If his admiration is aroused he'll reflect that this perhaps is the answer he's been looking for. If he's the wry sort, he'll dismiss us out of hand. No head-burying in sand dunes for him. Peter's a man of the real world, needed at the bank oblique media consultancy. Either way, he'll stand on the terrace, captivated by the desert, before bidding me goodbye and returning to West London where I'll become one of a myriad memories that settle into vague longing or subside into anecdote.

Conversion, like conversation, is complicated. What you can't describe is the most important part. Mine began when I fell sick in a hostel in Damascus. Something bad I ate, perhaps *falafel,* I don't remember. Confined to a dorm with its view of the mosque and sprawl of old city I had time to reflect, a luxury I rarely indulged myself. I was exhausted by three months on the road and still going for the sake of it; a bad habit. Well into my thirties, I'd structured life around dodging responsibility; never staying in a job or with a woman more than a year. Perhaps, I considered, my illness wasn't prompted by food poisoning, but something more serious. Triggered by a poorly assembled life. By guilt over my autistic brother, and father who'd spent a quarter century caring for him. By Loretta, my girlfriend of late, desperate for children. An accretion of shame for all those I'd let down. Peter would relate; the details vary, but men of our generation suffer similar angst.

Three days later, when I felt stronger, I left Souk Saruja after breakfast and hopped on a *service* at Abasyn Garage heading north to Homs. Through a small slice of window I watched ugly city blocks blur into suburban high rises and rock, then sand. The roadside was strewn with unfinished buildings, twisted steel rebar clawing at the sky like barbed legs of upturned roaches. Metaphors for my life story; of projects thrown up and abandoned. Snowy peaks fringed the roadside. On the hard shoulder stood carts of pomegranate and oranges. Vendors waved wet fish at oncoming traffic.

I got down at the turn-off to Nebek. The town's façades were more stylish, its cars newer than in Damascus. Its less potholed streets were full of affluent returnees from Saudi or France. I stopped to eat *shawarma* and date *mamouls*. The smiling shopkeeper reckoned Deir Mar Musa was twenty kilometres away and suggested a taxi. I started walking around midday. Undulating sand and rocks spread out before me, the sculpted hills sparged with litter. Sunshine glittered brilliantly, but the air had bite; I pulled my scarf up and my hat down, leaving just a slit for my eyes. Few cars passed. It took three hours to reach a mine and the fork in the road. I could carry on along tarmac or follow the shadow of a path the miner gesticulated towards, over the Qualoun mountains. Snow fell as I began to climb.

I grew anxious. More than I've ever been: breath came short, my armpits itched. Something held me to the path. Hard to say what – a bullish stubbornness or the first inklings of embryonic faith. I put one rounded peak, then another, between myself and the mine. I'd understood just two words of the miner's Arabic: 'hill' and 'house'. As sharp wind cut through my flimsy clothes I came to the conclusion this walk was an allegory of faith. I supposed there was a monastery somewhere ahead. I had it on the word of the Korean girl in the dorm who'd told me of the place, on the smiles of a portly shopkeeper and garbled directions of a miner keen to get out of the cold. I imagined perishing, freezing to death limb by limb; easy with fingers already numb. With less than an hour of sunlight left, even if I didn't twist my ankle or break a bone, I'd never survive night.

As I came in sight of two lonely houses I hit on another idea that lifted my spirits; pilgrimage. Something (God?) told me the house the miner had mentioned was the lower of the only two to be seen and I headed toward it eagerly. A pick-up was parked beside a pen filled with two dozen long-haired goats. Painted on the shed wall were a cross and an arrow pointing downhill. There was no sign of the goatherd, bar footprints along the dry riverbed, which I followed. Though the cleft brimmed with shadows I was protected from the wind and the shale was easier on my feet.

Spotting the old monastery nestled in the crags was the closest I've come to an epiphany; my shoulders shook, tears burned my cheeks. I fell to my knees and mouthed thanks. Hacked in the sixth century by a thief-turned-Christian, Saint Moses the Ethiopian, Deir Mar Musa al-Habashi looks like a fortress. Hewn of the same ochre rock as the mountain, it follows the cliff's curve. For nine centuries monks lived here till it was abandoned a hundred years ago. An

Italian Jesuit, Father Paolo, stumbled upon the ruins in the seventies and dreamt of building a bridge to Islam through unreserved hospitality. He constructed some cells, a hen house and, with a growing strength of brothers and volunteers, a new monastery on the other side of a chasm spanned by a steel bridge. They ran a cable over the reservoir's cracked mud to the crags to send food to those on retreat.

That day, as I drew close, I hesitated over how to get in. Noticing a small fissure in the rock, I ducked into the cavity. It widened to a terrace overlooking yellow flats that erupted in stark mountains on the horizon. I dropped my bag and stood, awestruck. After some time, the voice of a young Syrian woman interrupted my thoughts. Leaving my rucksack and boots outside, I stooped to follow her through another doorway, beneath a hanging rug, into the most beautiful church I've seen. Frescos of red devils, bearded priests, fishermen and their catch covered its walls. In its alcoves stood darkened Orthodox icons, alongside vivid Bedouin oils and pressed flowers. Candles burned beside two silver-bound Bibles resting on lecterns on the floor. The stockinged congregation and barefoot monks sat on carpets, skins and cushions, cross-legged or leaning against columns, Arabic Bibles and Psalm books beside them. Some read the Gospel, others meditated.

One read the story of Jacob robbing Esau's inheritance. A tall bearded man with a resonant voice, Father Paolo, started to talk. I had no Arabic back then but I gathered he spoke of the troubles in Gaza. Switching to English he explained that, as in the reading, people fight over land because it represents a mother's love, which everyone seeks. Then they all chanted in unison:

Kiria elesion, kiria elesion, kiria elesion.
Yara borham, yara borham, yara borham.
Kiria elesion, kiria elesion, kiria elesion...

The mass concluded with the monks taking down stringed lutes, a drum and a tambourine and playing.

Outside, trays laden with food were being carried up the wooden steps to Abraham's tent. We sat down along two mats stretched out on the floor laden with bowls of *labneh*, olives, and oil accompanied by rounds of flat bread warmed on wood stoves. Two large kettles of

166

tea simmered. Once I'd dulled the sharp edge of my hunger, I began to listen to those around me, speaking in Italian, French, Arabic and English.

As well as half-a-dozen monks, there was a rosy-cheeked Czech who told me he spent his days building guest rooms, a Slovak new age traveller who'd just completed a week of retreat, a plump Russian practitioner of alternative medicine and an Italian environmentalist piloting an eco-project. A Lebanese journalist was talking to Father Paolo about the waning numbers of Christians in the Middle East. Instead of being far from the world, I was at its centre. As we finished our meal, I looked up and found Paolo's eyes on me. He asked me my name and if I'd stay.

'If you do, you can help translate my annual letter, Benjamin.'

Acutely aware of myself and those about me, it was a day unlike any other. My clean cell delighted me, so different from the dorm in Damascus. Sweet air and clear skies made me giddy. The brothers' gentleness touched me. Joy is not a word I use lightly, but there's no other. After the service the following morning, I left. My things were in Damascus; I had a ticket home in a fortnight; I needed perspective. These were the excuses I made to myself.

The moment my head touched the pillow at Hotel Al-Saada my fever returned. I spent several days unaware of anything. The concierge, Khalid, called a doctor, who administered drugs. It wasn't a doctor I needed, it was an angel. When I began to think clearly I was fairly sure of where I'd find it. I experienced a powerful sense of expectation, something I'd not felt since I was child. I wrote emails to Loretta and my parents explaining I'd stay at the monastery some time; by examining my soul, I reasoned they'd be free to take stock of their own.

When I returned, the monks greeted me with unsurprised affection.

I helped Father Paolo translate letters and set up his website. Peeled carrots and chopped onions. Washed stacks of dishes that stretched out along the kitchen counter and swept out dormitories. Taught myself to greet the steady flow of guests and answer their questions. Without compassion, Father Paolo reminds us, we're no better than animals. Some days it's tough; Italian tourists snap photos during a service or Spanish students grumble their cells are cold. People bring their expectations with them; the unhappy are met with discomfort; those seeking God find Him. Our task is to welcome them all. Father Paolo puts his hand on my shoulder and murmurs: 'Humility, Benjamin, humility.'

My original fears of stagnation were dispelled early. Our predecessors were rigorous scholars. Mar Musa monks are the first real intellectuals I've known. They debate on a daily basis. Not one speaks less than four languages. They discuss sciences and arts in astonishing depth and have a fierce grasp of history. The stone steps to the library, dug into the mountain, are well-worn. While many books are philosophical in nature, the literary collection would put many public libraries to shame.

But the biggest revelation is compassion. Before, affection had seemed like weakness. My relationships with others was based on what I could gain. My friends needed to be entertaining, my lovers satisfying, my parents understanding. Now, God is revealed in everyone, and I seek nothing more.

He's there, somewhere, in the string of travellers who visit us. And deeply buried in the psychotic Armenian refugee who tries my patience. With a little effort, He can be discerned in homely Sola, an aspiring nun, who mothers us, like it or not. He's firmly rooted in the stern, wiry Abouna Boutros, with his flip-side of impish humour. Writ all over the saintly earnest Abu Jihad. Positively flowing from kind Sister Houda with her quiet brand of wisdom. And ever-present in the eccentric, bombastic Father Paolo and his grand absurd vision that, against all odds, we are realising.

Ascetics are an endangered species; our need of each other is great. I wake each morning before dawn with forgotten enthusiasm. I have no regrets; those I left behind are better off. Miracles happen; I see them every day. Life brims. With care, gnarled trees yield olives in the desert. Sustained on dry grass, goats give us *labneh* and cheese. Tended by Boutros, our gardens flourish; we enjoy greens, tomatoes, cucumbers and herbs. Visitors bring gifts of chocolate, coffee and books. They help us build rooms for visitors, protect our fragile habitat, preserve ancient tombs. Strangers come to Deir Mar Musa and find His spirit here, working its magic in the desert. Prodigal sons, like me, return. Even Peter has come, all the way from Turnham Green.

Peter has finished his walk. He's been standing for some time on the terrace, contemplating the sifting dunes, peppered with Bedouin tents, that melt into mountains and sky. He doesn't notice me, hanging sheets to dry. He lifts his gaze from the horizon, where the sun is sinking, only when a large Italian family fill the yard with their voices. They gave him a lift here this morning and had agreed to take him back to Nebek.

'Ready?' the tanned father smiles at Peter.

'No... I... actually, I've changed my mind. I'm going to stay a little longer. But thanks for the offer.'

The tired mother signs her comment in the guest book and they wave goodbye.

Peter turns to me as though he's seen me for the first time. His face is softer, his eyes bright. For a while he watches me work; lifting, wringing, unwinding, shaking out, hanging.

His question comes, clear and dry as desert air:

'So... why did you become a monk?'

The Coolest Kid

by Peter Caunt

The trundle of the skateboard wheels slowed as he checked me out.

I looked him in the eye, "So who's the coolest kid on the block?"

The young boarder scraped to a halt and stared. He was on an old Santa Cruz. His style was smooth, but his clothes were simple and neat.

I repeated my question. "Which one of these is the coolest kid on the block?"

The question seemed to throw him. He looked me up and down trying to assess what I was after.

"I'm the coolest."

No he wasn't. I'd been hanging around the Malls for long enough to recognise a drone at twenty paces. I did some deep breathing and waited. The campaign had taken a lot of preparatory work. This was the last stage, but my body was starting to pay the price.

I stared back to give him the message that I knew he was lying. He stamped on the edge of his board and neatly caught it in one hand. I ignored him and looked around for a better option.

"What's in it for me?"

"That depends how grateful the coolest kid is after I've spoken to him."

The complexity of my reply took a while to filter through his pot-soaked synapses. I brushed away imaginary spots of dirt from my sleeve and turned my head towards the other skaters.

"Max," he pointed, "Over there in the Duff hoodie."

I looked to my right.

"You'll tell him it was me?"

I gave a reassuring smile and walked away.

"The first graph shows the progress of sales throughout the year. This should be viewed in relation to the expenditure on TV advertising and youth magazines."

There was a general murmur of disapproval around the table as the set of overlaid graphs built up.

170

"Revenue has shown a similar decline despite the price restructuring put in place last January."

The next slides showed the lack of impact on a number of markets and the predictions for the following year.

"As you can all see, there is a need for a reassessment of the market approach."

"Hi Max." I extended my palms in an open gesture.

Max gave me the same expression that I had received earlier. He looked at my casual suit and turned up his lip. We had debated dress code, but come down in favour of giving a sense of paternal authority. Dress too street and the kids would have laughed. Dress too formally and they would have thought I was the police.

Max stood taller than the rest. His clothes were no more expensive than others around him, but he filled them out much better. He moved with an assured ease and his board was scuffed. Most of the damage looked recent. While most of the rest resembled a herd of sheep, Max strutted on his board, prancing through his moves like a gazelle taking its first steps.

"I understand you're the coolest kid on the block."

Max ignored me, pulled a smooth 180 and came back. I repeated my comment.

"Sez who?"

I pointed at the kid I had been talking to, then waved my hand in an arc. "Just about everyone I've talked to."

Max just shrugged.

"I'm looking for someone with brains, not like the rest of these drones. Someone who wants to get to the top."

Max was a child of his generation. Any easy route was the one to take; and the easier the better.

"So?"

This was the tricky part. The company psychologists had walked me through the approaches, but out on the street I had to work on instinct.

"Let's just say that I have something you want. Something that everyone will want, but I need to talk to the top guy."

He looked me in the eye and shook his head slightly, saying "Duh!", as if I was some moron, who didn't understand that he was top dog.

"I need the coolest kid in the district. A smart kid like you will see the advantages to yourself of introducing me to him."

I could see his shoulders drop, "Piss off." He put the earphones back in place and was about to turn his player back on.

I thrust the leaflet into his hand.

He was on the point of screwing it up, but I could see that the greed would be my way in.

"This is what we're selling. Introduce me to the coolest kid in the district and you get one of these half price."

He turned the leaflet over. "I've got one."

"Not like this you haven't. It does much more than play mp3's"

He screwed up the leaflet and tossed it aside.

"Okay, but I'll find the coolest kid in the district and give him one of these. And everyone will know you turned me down. Well, what have you got to lose?" I took out another of the leaflets.

I could see him weighing up his options, then he grabbed the leaflet from my hand.

"He's Bones. He hangs around the Wellington Mall from eleven every day."

"So what's he look like?"

He looked at me. "He's Bones and he's cool!" Then he skated off.

I suppose it was enough to find him. As I walked off, I added Max to my list.

"Traditional methods do not seem to be reaching our targeted demographic. These kids are the MTV plus generation. Their attention span is no longer fifteen minutes. Years of education have left them with an almost zero ability to concentrate. Reading a magazine is too much effort for them and on the television they cannot differentiate between programmes and adverts."

"In many ways their culture has reverted to a more primitive form. They still rely on parents or state cash handouts, but have no respect for either. For this primitive form of target, we need a primitive form of attack."

It was nearly twelve before I made it to the Wellington Mall. There were nearly a dozen boarders dotted about, engaged in a variety of displays. I shouldn't have worried. Bones stood out. Not just the heavily moussed hair; he held his head high. His moves were fast and graceful. He was certainly further up the food chain than Max. More of a cheetah than a gazelle. His clothes were of a different class. He cared a lot about his appearance but not so much that he didn't mind displaying the scars of high speed impacts. What impressed most was that he stood on a Heroin short deck. And from the look of it, he was on Bones bearings. I guess that's where he got his name. I watched as he did a kick flip 180, then a very fast backside flip. He seemed like someone used to pushing the envelope. I looked down at my suit and decided that it was not appropriate, so I left it to the following day.

My wardrobe wasn't up to this encounter, so I made a visit to the high street. Careful combination of fake designer and casual for me, and a few items from our marketing department that should suit Bones.

He was late. It was half eleven when I spotted him walking casually out of one of the stores, the alarm blaring. No one was interested in him, someone else had stepped too near to the exit, clearly holding a piece off the rack. I recognised the guy who had set off the alarms from the Mall the previous day.

"I just wanted to see what it looked like in the light."

The store guard stared, but he had obviously not been making any attempt to leave. All they could do was take the item off him and send him on his way. Meanwhile Bones walked clean away. Simple but effective, a nice scam. I knew I had my man. I would have liked to move up the food chain to the best in the town, but time was short. I watched Bones pull the tags from the sweatshirts – he had obviously done this many times before – and hand one over to his accomplice.

As he skated past I grinned, "Nice move Bones."

He turned and skated past me again, looking disdainful. I took out the sweatshirt and held it in front of me.

Bones screeched to a halt, "Are you taking the piss?"

"Nice move. I admire people with guts."

Bones was obviously not sure if I meant his acquisition in the Mall or his prowess on the board. Before he could decide, I handed him the sweatshirt.

"For the coolest dude around."

"Who says?"

"Everyone I've met."

"You the bill?"

"Do I look like the police?" I spread my arms.

"Hard to tell these days. Narks, nonces, pigs all dress the same."

I caught my breath, "Look, I just want to reward those that deserve it."

Bones looked at the sweatshirt. "What's that?" He pointed at the bottom left hand corner.

"That's the logo for the new player we're giving away."

Bones looked me in the eyes, "Penrose tiling?"

Yes it was. We had wanted some neat five-fold symmetry. We never thought anyone would recognise an obscure piece of geometry.

"We're giving it away, but only to the coolest people. It's pre-programmed to keep up to date with the newest music but it does much more. Look, I could explain, but best if you just try it out." I handed him the player.

My legs ached and wanted to take the rest of my body home, not that there was much there any more. I did the deep breathing again. Bones hesitated. He had good instincts, but who in his generation could resist a freebie? In the few moments while he decided, the fatigue kicked off memories of my own son. He would be the same age as Bones, but I had not seen him for over two years. The last present I had given him was a skateboard. His mother had not approved.

Bones glanced down and I realised I was playing with the redundant wedding ring.

I don't know if he realised what it meant. He was an intelligent kid; but he took the player anyway. He rolled it around in his hand, discarded the sweatshirt to one of his henchmen then skated off.

Moments later he grabbed back the sweatshirt, swapping it for the one he was wearing. The others crowded round to see what I had given him, but he pushed them away. Now it was all a matter of time.

I sat on a bench in the Mall, watching Bones and his gang. Perhaps in better times Bones would have made it off the street. I watched them for a while until I could get my mind clear of the idea of giving my ex a ring.

"This demographic used to be dominated by the cult of personality. Now this has been devalued by the constant stream of C-list celebrities and members of the public receiving fleeting elevation in status through reality shows."

The projector flicked through example slides.

"This demographic no longer has any heroes. The old ones have discredited and are not even derided; they are just forgotten. What we have left is a simple group dynamic, but in every group there is still an alpha male."

It was nearly a week later that Max finally approached me. I had been hanging round for several days. Maybe Bones was a bit slower than I thought.

"You told me I could get one of these half-price." He thrust the crumpled leaflet into my face.

"What's the hurry?" I knew exactly what the hurry was. Bones was using his unit, and therefore everyone else wanted one.

"Look, why don't I go one better?" I reached into my bag. "Why don't I give you one for free? Just tell anyone that wants one to be here in the Mall the day after tomorrow."

Max took the unit then turned. "Why don't you let me have a few of the units and I could deal for you?"

Max was more intelligent than I thought. Using some of the brighter kids as dealers could be incorporated later and save on costs.

"Just the one Max. Perhaps later you could help out."

He skated away muttering, pulling off a fakey reverse 180, yelling, "Sucker."

I didn't care. I needed to get to the rest of Max's contemporaries on my list before I gave the go-ahead for the launch.

"Distribution will be by word of mouth. Initial units will be given out free to the dominant individuals, then sold at a cut rate to the rest. The increase in demand has been modelled on the organic growth of a virus. The data fits well with the pilot study we ran."

A graph of the comparison of expected and actual data flashed up.

"The operation of the units has been designed by our psychologists to provide an almost addictive supply of multimedia, updated automatically on a regular basis."

More graphs showed a rapid increase in sales for national release. Others showed the corresponding increase in profits projected forward for the next five years. Then finally, one showing the comparison of the much lower projected sales from a conventional campaign. Murmurs of approval could be heard around the room.

The launch in the Wellington Mall went better than expected. We sold out within an hour and had to set up again the next day when new stocks arrived.

Two days later the first of the units stopped functioning. A clear message on the screen directed the user back to the Mall to purchase a topup to reactivate it. The crowd was much larger than I had expected. We had timed out too many of the units in one go.

By the time the police arrived, all the stalls in the Mall had been trashed. I'd pulled the staff back to safety at the first sign of trouble, but the stock of units had to be left. Sets of gangs were standing off against each other as they picked up any of the units, even ones that were smashed beyond repair. In the midst of it I saw Bones and his gang. He was still wearing the sweatshirt I'd given him in the Mall a week ago, but he seemed to be trying to get his gang to leave. Then it all happened very quickly. Someone made a grab for the unit round Bones's neck and I saw him fall as the crowds retreated from the riot police charge.

When the Mall had been cleared, I picked my way through the broken stalls and ambulances to assess the damage. Then I saw Bones being attended by a paramedic. He looked pretty battered, but then I saw the large blood stain on his chest.

"Do you know this kid? Are you a relative?"

I bent down, "Just a friend. How is he?"

The paramedic shook his head.

Bones opened his eyes and saw me. He still had the unit in his hand.

Then he slumped, and the paramedic moved on to the next victim.

The presentation was complete. Then came the inevitable question.

I had prepared carefully.

176

"The riot in Wellington Mall had been unfortunate, but we were completely cleared of any responsibility."

In answer to the likelihood of this being repeated nationally, "We have used the Wellington Mall incident to model the dynamics of a national launch. This enables us to optimise the timing out of the units. Death rates in any riots will be considerably less than in the pilot, but not zero."

"Taking the worst and best scenarios," another graph appeared, "the expected death rates are between one in a hundred thousand and one in a million of the users in any year. This gives us, on average, projected fatalities of ten per year in the UK. Using the current government generated figures for the calculated cost of a human life, the lawyers have estimated that the expected compensation payouts for these incidents would consume less than ten percent of the profit in the worst case."

Heads began to nod around the room. I relaxed for the first time in six months. All the pioneering work had been done in the seventies by the motor industry. Attributing a cost to human life so that business did not overextend itself on safety. It had been controversial at the time, but was now part of mainstream economics.

The CEO smiled as he approached, then took my hand; the vote had been unanimous. I knew it would be. I had already picked the team to do the national launch; the factory had been tooled up to begin production. We needed to work fast before the competition got wind of the campaign. It meant working round the clock. What else would I do? This was all I had left in my life now anyway.

Within three weeks members of the team would be pushing the units out onto the street; within six weeks everyone in the target demographic would be in possession of one of the units; within eight weeks they would be clamouring for more.

Sobek Refutes the Plover Theory

by R A Martens

Oliver Al-Sobek loved going to the dentist. It made him chuckle to feel their fingers tremble, particularly over his back teeth. It was one of Oliver's few joys in a life which had not, so far, been at all as advertised.

"Right, Mr Al-Sobek. If you could just move your tongue a little to the left... Thank you. I'm rather winging it here, as you can imagine, but I've come to the conclusion that given your surfeit of teeth, the universal numbering system will be more appropriate than Palmer notation. Let's begin." The man peered in from the side, and tapped a tooth at the back of Oliver's upper right jaw with the end of a shiny scraper. "One..."

It had become increasingly hard, for various reasons, for Oliver to find a dentist lately, but now here he was with James Sturgeon, BDS. This fine fellow, with his brightly-polished brass plaque and his tray of spectacularly shiny instruments, with his sweetly-fragranced waiting room air, this fellow had seemed almost keen to take him on. Good for him.

Oliver's last dentist (for one visit only), the delightful Alice Jones, had fallen foul of Oliver's irrepressible puckishness. He couldn't have known she was pregnant. Having never met her before, he had reasonably assumed she was simply plump.

The joke he played on Ms Jones was one he had first discovered when still in short trousers. His jaws already two or three feet long, he had, for a little joke, snapped them half shut – around, but most definitely not upon, the head of Mr Nigel Brakes, BDS. Mr Brakes had scraped his head on a tooth trying to whip it out of the way.

"I'm sorry, it was a joke," the young Oliver had said as a nurse applied pressure to the copiously bleeding head wound. "If you had stayed still, you would have been fine." The truth was also, he later admitted to himself, that his jaw muscles were designed for snapping shut, not halfway shut, and he didn't have as much fine motor control as he would have liked.

Mr Brakes had soiled himself, to the eternal shame of Oliver's mother and father. They had given him a terrible row when they got home. Then they had given him ice-cream and awkward, nervous cuddles when he cried about how he would never fit in. They had been awfully easy to manipulate, bless them. Perhaps, after that rather awkward post-natal introduction in the hospital, they should never have taken him home. But they were good people, and respectful of incarnate gods, so they did. And they had named him Oliver, rather than the Arabic name they had in mind, in order to give him a better chance of fitting in. Bless them again.

In fact, Oliver didn't need to go to the dentist at all. He grew, a few times a year, new healthy teeth which pushed out the old, and allowed for no decay. He was all incisor, no molar grinding surface on which bacteria could settle and dig. There was no call for dentists, none at all. However, he did love to feel them tremble. Trembling was something he'd been led to expect rather a lot of, and it had proved to be in very short supply, so he would take it where he could get it.

A few years after the episode with Mr Brakes, having reached majority and begun to attend dental appointments sans parental accompaniment, Oliver had found himself, dispirited and glum, repeating the joke for a little light relief (he was working in a call centre, we mustn't be too harsh).

On discovering that his joke admirably fulfilled the purpose of lifting his spirits even further than mere trembling, he continued. Through a slew of dentists (they tended not to be keen on second appointments), right up until the time his favourite joke had sent Alice Jones into premature labour. He had narrowly avoided an expensive lawsuit by promising celestial blessings upon the baby's head (he would owe Ra for this for some time to come), and had sworn off the prank for good.

He should not, however, have blamed himself. Oliver's 'mischief' was simply a reflex, of course, a genetic imperative, if you will (although, being the product of a virgin birth, which caused no end of awkwardness between his mother and father, he didn't really possess genes as we know them). Having reached late puberty, the blossoming of his human hormones had fully engaged his crocodilian bite reflex. It was actually amazing that with a mammal head inside his mouth, he was able to stop short of digestion. He simply, truly could not help himself. But Oliver blamed himself as though he was free of biological drives.

"And now move your tongue over to the right," said James Sturgeon, as he peered in front of the upright walking pole that held Oliver's jaw open to look at the front teeth. "Twenty-two, loosening, twenty-three..." Oliver had submitted to this indignity figuring he could easily break the pole if he so wished, with his masseter muscles like elephants' buttocks. But he found on testing it a little, that if he pressed down, the pointed end of the pole gouged painfully into the soft floor of his mouth. It was clear that the force required to break the pole would cause him great damage. So he sat silently, and submitted to the inspection, as he imagined James Sturgeon on hearty, serious Lakeland walks with his pole and his hearty, serious family.

There had been a long time of knocking on doors and begging before he had found James Sturgeon. Oliver was already well known in the Royal College of Surgeons Dental Faculty and the British Dental Association, even prior to the Alice Jones incident, and had been discussed at meetings of both. Being a god, he found it very easy to eavesdrop. He had rather enjoyed the notoriety, but following Alice Jones, he had been blackballed. It was impossible to find a dentist that didn't refuse him service on just hearing his name. And maybe that was for the best. But then the awful pain in his gum had started.

It occurred to Oliver that he hadn't had a full inspection since he was a teenager. No-one knew what was going on at the back of his mouth, as his little feints were always irresistible the moment they got there, and the rather sour atmosphere that followed was never conducive to completing the exam. And now of course, the mysterious, uncharted reaches of the back of his mouth were where the pain was. What if something had been festering away for years unnoticed? His teeth might be fairly invulnerable, but incarnation did bring with it the whole squalid drag of entropy, and his meat was as fragile as the next man's. What if it was the big C?

The dentist interrupted his doomsday reverie: "I wanted to ask, while I have you here, what is it that drives you to so torment dentists, Mr Al-Sobek? Why do you insist on alienating every one of us that tries to help you?" He continued to tap away at teeth as he went, calling out their numbers and conditions to the hygienist sitting to Oliver's left, who was marking them on a makeshift chart the dentist had drawn up that morning.

"Ichs i ai aicha," said Oliver, unable to close his mouth. But his answer (a fatalistic but undeniable "it's in my nature") did not seem to be required.

"We work hard, you know. We care deeply, we study hard, and every one hates us, even though our concerted mission is the ending of pain. That's a complicated thing in a tiny area filled with pointless nerve endings, you know. It's like a cosmic joke, that teeth have nerves. They're not necessary at all. We're figures of fear and loathing however many funny posters we put on our ceiling."

Oliver looked up. James Sturgeon was clearly not your average dentist, his ceiling sporting a mean caricature of George Bush.

"We have the highest suicide rate of any profession. And now, Mr Al-Sobek, we have you. Many of my colleagues have not returned to work since you visited them.

He tapped a tooth at the bottom of Oliver's jaw to the left. "Oops! Just came off in my hand, guv'nor! To be honest, I was rather hoping you'd shed one while you were here. May I keep it?" He slipped the tooth into his breast pocket without waiting for approval. "My little boy will be thrilled."

"We're about the same age. Do you remember this from your school days?" James Sturgeon pointed at a yellowing poster on the wall, of a crocodile with a bird settled on its cartoon teeth. "You can thank this poster and my sentimental old heart that you're here. I sought this poster out, paid a fortune for it because I remembered it as a child, the impression it had on me. This gentle, friendly crocodile living in harmony with delicate little birds. In some way, Mr Al-Sobek, I wanted to be that little bird, and now here we are. Call it the fulfilment of a childhood dream.

"Why can't you be more like our friend over there? If you are going to avail yourself of dental surgeons rather than our feathered friends the plovers, ought you not at the very least do us the same courtesy of leaving us unmolested to go about our helpful business?"

Oliver remembered fruitless hours spent lying on his belly in the garden with his mouth wide open, waiting for friendly birds to settle, and tried to say to James Sturgeon: "I think you'll find that theory is widely disputed." Due to the pole, this could only be articulated as: "I hig ooh hi, a heey igh igly ichooid."

Without asking for clarification, James Sturgeon, a practised interpreter, said: "I know this story is widely disputed, but it is yet to be entirely discredited, and I prefer to believe it is true. I suspect your problem is that you're afraid, that's usually where aggression comes from, isn't that true, Tina?"

The young girl in a white coat smiled like a magician's assistant, showing her perfect teeth (an occupational perk), then went back to humming along to the radio. Oliver comprehended that this was the act they had developed. The dentist would make a comment, sometimes a gag, and his pretty, gnomic hygienist would provide a rimshot, a budum-tish, with her smile. Who knew whether she enjoyed or merely tolerated this man? He was certainly wearing a little thin on Oliver.

The dentist was still counting and dictating as he went along: "...sixty-eight, sixty-nine..." and tapping each tooth with the blunt and heavy end of his picking instrument. Suddenly, there was a rocket of shimmering pain through Oliver's right jaw, the whole side of his face. He yelped, and reflexively tried to close his mouth, then let out a deeper, more guttural bellow of pain as the walking pole gouged his soft mouth parts.

"Ah, sore, eh?" Oliver tried to growl at this offensive understatement, a noise for which his anatomy was ill-equipped. James Sturgeon cooed sympathetically. "Aww, oh dear, that's not so good, is it?" Oliver wanted to tell him that maybe people hated dentists because their bedside manner was commensurate with the 'surgeon' part of their title. That was to say, terrible. But Oliver couldn't say anything. Wet pooled in his eyes, and his translucent sideways-moving eyelids cleared it like futuristic windscreen wipers.

"We'll need to get some x-rays here I think, Tina." James Sturgeon turned on his swively stool to reach for something behind him.

Oliver waved his stubby arms to indicate that he wished the pole to be removed with some urgency. James Sturgeon acquiesced, and gently, with forearms braced against the front of top and bottom jaws, widened the reach of Oliver's snout to let it fall. As he apologised for its bloodied end, Oliver lunged and bit off his hand.

Tina looked on and screamed as James calmly, full of adrenalin and deep in shock, cast about for something to get her to make a tourniquet with. Oliver looked sheepishly at the blood pumping from the man's wrist and wondered whether he did have a tumour, and if so who on earth would remove it, now?

182

The Market

by Morag Edward

The dockside market is separated from the city by high spiked walls but the ornate gates are rusted open. A stone sea-beast is curled atop each pillar, all claws and gull-shit. They hold carved stone human heads in their jaws. Henrietta is carried between the pillars on the wave of unwashed people, unable to prevent them from brushing against her. It is the noise that signals her arrival; gulls, horns; voices in here rough and guttural. She manages to glance behind her towards civilization but she's not the sort of person to allow dire warnings to affect her excursion. She walks on, head held high, adrenalin surging from fear of this place and the thrill of exotic goods shipped in from all over the world just waiting for her. The tips of masts and furled sails bob above the market horizon and she smiles at the thought of their cargo. It is almost enough to override the disgust for the vermin around her.

Mountains of clocks and old books are stacked into walls. Henrietta sees her distorted reflections in cracked mirrors within antique gilded frames. Dead animal eyes stare out of carcasses admiring her perfect skin and the smoothness of her latest fur. Eyes are watching her from beneath the stalls too; feral eyes in starved child faces, small scabby hands darting out to grab at scraps and dropped treasures. Henrietta's delicate shoes click across wet cobbles and something soaks through the fabric, damp against her toes. Sticky little fingers reach out as she passes between huge pillars of oriental silks. Tiny blackened fingernails nip her ankles as she stands still to buy jewellery cut out of the newly-discovered graves of Egypt. She averts her gaze from bowls of gold fillings and wedding rings. Fish monsters are piled on crates filled with ice. Meat is hacked from anonymous lumps then roasted in ovens or revolved at grills or added to highly spiced stews. Customers place their orders then gulp down dribbling mouthfuls from chipped bowls. Henrietta shudders, and strokes her silky fur wrap for comfort. She shouldn't have to see things like this. She smoothes back her perfect hair and hopes everyone is watching her as she passes by.

There is meat all around her in this area, dead and alive. Behind the counters butcher boys are violent in their work. They seem to have no squeamishness, no manners, no concept of her status when they stare at her. There is nothing familiar about these men; they are young but exotic and alien. She feels repulsed yet wants their attention to linger. The looks in their eyes thrill her more than those from the fawning men back in her world. By the food stall's old ovens, one boy has used another's best knife and so they begin the blood flicking ritual to teach the offender a lesson in proper kitchen etiquette. Henrietta is caught in the crossfire; blood splatters on her face, her coat and her hair. She shrieks outrage and revulsion to the butcher in charge, a huge man who resembles a ship's doctor in his blood-striped apron. She demands apologies, retribution and extensive compensation. She is making too loud a fuss. Old customers feign deafness and quietly leave. The drops of blood trickle darkly down her pale face. She's close to hysterics as she grabs at the nearest guilty boy, who kicks back hard. The butcher-chef, veins now throbbing visibly in his face, is not a happy or forgiving man. He knows her sort can't be ignored.

"Oven!" He bellows the command and the boy shrinks back, a little less defiant than before.

"That'll teach him," snigger the others, "teach him not to get caught next time!"

An old man grabs Henrietta by the elbow. "This'll make you feel better lady, see the boy toasted nicely and you won't mind the mess so much."

Henrietta stares at him in disgust. The man's laughter sprays green spittle onto the front of her coat. "Best punishment for apprentices lady, shove them in the oven till they've learned theirselves a lesson and let 'em out when they've stopped complaining. Don't look shocked; they don't cook 'em, just scare them a bit. Never did the rest of us any harm." He waves his scarred hands as proof.

Because of the audience, the oven is turned up high for dramatic effect as the boy is shoved in. The door slams and there is screaming from inside. Steam gusts out past men who have seen it all before. Only when the screaming stops does the butcher-chef heave open the oven door. There is a sigh of disappointment from the onlookers at the brevity of the punishment. The boy is dragged out by the foot and he thuds onto the cobbles. Butcher-chef, suddenly looking grim, checks the apprentice boy's eyes. The boy's eyelids slide off at a

184

touch, like well-cooked flakes of fish, revealing opaque white eyes, still steaming. Henrietta opens her mouth to scream, but there is a movement, a flicker and everything pauses for a heartbeat. Henrietta turns to fetch the authorities; desperate to leave this place immediately. The patrolling dock police ignore her screams. She looks back and sees a woman slumped, a woman wearing a fur coat like hers. As the men drag the body into the meat preparation area she sees clearly now that the body is her own. The neck has been neatly slit open, just the centre to open the trachea without painting the walls red. She thinks: maybe she felt a scratch as she turned to scream. She remembers the knife in the butcher's hand and the flick of his wrist, but then she'd run, and she is here. Henrietta staggers in shock, unable to find her way out of this damned place. She staggers across the cobbles, hair still perfect and jewellery still glinting, but this time no-one is admiring her because now no-one can see her. Exhausted, she roams in her stained fur, invisible except to drunken sailors and the ghost of a well-cooked kitchen-boy.

Izzy

by Andrea Tang

'*The Snow Princess*' she writes with a fine brush at the top of the paper. She sits back in her chair and admires the cold beauty of her painting: a pale blue-skinned lady draped in an ice-blue gown, surrounded by falling snow.

She is reminded that she has company in her small box room at the psychiatric ward.

"You've been through a stressful event, Alisa," a middle-aged man with square spectacles and a stiff tie says as he checks his clipboard of notes in his hands. "I've heard you mentioning a name several times: 'Izzy'. Who is 'Izzy', Alisa?"

She places the brush into a plastic cup of stained water holding other painting brushes. Her aqueous blue eyes glance up at her psychiatric doctor. He is sitting in a chair facing her, patiently waiting for her response.

"I never liked the snow, Doctor," she says quietly.

She lowers her eyes.

"There was an unusually long spell of snow fall over three days. One of the longest-running periods of snow we've ever seen. The snow piled up around my house, roads were carpeted. I was confined to the house.

"I woke up in the snow one afternoon outside my house. I was lying flat on my back on the white stuff. Snowflakes were falling and melting onto my face. I didn't remember how I got there. I picked myself up and returned into the house.

"I was warming by the fireplace in my living room when I noticed a piece of paper lying on my coffee table. I didn't remember leaving myself any notes. It couldn't have been anyone else. I live on my own. The note had uneven writing on it. Didn't recognize it. Only one word was written there: 'Izzy'."

"Did this unnerve you?" the doctor asks.

"Thought it was odd for a moment, but then I dismissed it. Scrunched it up into a ball and threw it in the bin. Just a piece of rubbish.

"The snow was still falling heavily the next day. The electricity was cut at midday. I used the daylight while I could to do some painting. That's my occupation and hobby, Doctor."

Alisa gestures to her recently completed *Snow Princess* painting on the table behind her. "I sat by the window with my drawing stand and brushes. Watching the icy conditions outside made me glad to be indoors. I put brush to paper. As I painted, I became drowsy. It was like a heavy blanket was being pulled over my eyes. I blinked once, twice, three times. Then I succumbed to the temptation of sleep.

"I awoke in a foreign land, a white land of snow. A forest of icing-topped trees beckoned to me from ahead. Each descending snowflake added to the breathtaking beauty of the place. It filled me with wonder, a feeling I had never experienced at the sight of snow before, a liberating and uplifting feeling. With a gloved hand I bent down and picked up a handful of powdery snow. I allowed the snow to shower down from my grip like the sand in an overturned hourglass. I observed the misty 'smoke' coming out of my mouth as I breathed out into the cold air. Pretending to be a great dragon, I stomped around leaving deep footprints in the snow with my green wellies. I stopped as I heard the soft crunch of other feet from behind. Two large adult hands reached down to mine from either side of me. I took hold of them happily and, together, the three of us went to explore the icing-topped forest ahead. Me, Mother and Father. Somewhere in the distance between the trees, I spotted the smooth and clear surface of a frozen body of water.

"I awoke again, back in a chair. Snow still filled my vision, but I was looking at it through a glass pane, from behind my window. I glanced down at my hands. They weren't small and I wasn't wearing gloves. I must've been dreaming. I lifted my head and looked to my painting sheet beside me. I remembered only having painted about three lines on it just before falling asleep. There was a complete painting on it now. A simple picture of three smiling stick people walking through snow, apparently a family of three: two parents and a little girl in between them holding hands. And there were dots all around the family: falling snow. The painting appeared to have been done by the hand of a child."

"You'd somehow painted a scene from your dream whilst you were asleep?" the doctor asks with intrigue.

"She did," Alisa replies calmly. She shifts in her chair and crosses her legs to make herself more comfortable. "Not me."

"After pondering and staring at the child's painting for some minutes, I tore it off the board and set it aside. I left painting for the rest of the day.

"Night descended. Darkness seeped into every corner of the house. The power was still off. There was a temporary break in the snow fall outside during the early evening, but the white stuff still thickly carpeted the land. I used a battery-charged torch to find my way to bed. The chilly air provoked goosebumps on my skin as I crawled into bed. I pulled the blanket tightly around my neck and curled into a ball. The darkness behind my eyelids was no different from that beyond them.

"I was in another bedroom when I opened my eyes. A child's bedroom. Soft dolls sat along a shelf opposite me. The walls around were of a pale blue hue and a faint floral scent wafted into my nose. A dressing table with a white-framed oval mirror decorated the corner of the bedroom. The reflection of a young girl with long, dark blonde hair faced me as I sat up in bed and looked into the mirror. She must've been about eight years of age. A yawn escaped from my mouth and I rubbed my eyes. Then the bedroom door opened and a petite lady entered with gentle feet. She had blonde hair tied into a bun, and a bright smile. She spoke to me.

"Good morning, Sweetie."

She drew the curtains at the window apart, allowing morning light to flood into the room. A young girl's voice came out of my throat.

"Mummy," I said to the lady, "I had a strange dream."

"What about, Sweetie?"

"I dreamt I was a grown up and painting pictures," I found myself saying, "but I was living in a dark house on my own. And I didn't like the snow."

'Mummy' sat down beside me on my bed. She looked me in the eye.

"Well that doesn't sound like you at all, Isabelle darling," she chuckled. "You love to play in the snow."

"It felt really real, Mummy."

I paused for a second. A thought that should've been familiar to me but instead created an unsettling fear crept into my mind. "I don't want to be lonely, Mummy. Will I have to be one day?"

"No, darling, you don't ever have to be alone," Mummy said with a reassuring smile.

"Besides, Daddy and Mummy will always be there for you," a male voice added.

A man with neat, dark brown hair came into my bedroom and joined me and Mummy on my bed.

"Promise, Daddy?" I asked.

"Yes, we promise, Princess," he cheerfully replied. "We wouldn't leave you alone. Hey, look outside, it's snowing!"

It was falling thick and heavy outside. The ground was already covered in white and tall trees from woods nearby were caked with white 'icing'. An excitement rose inside of me.

"Can we go play in the snow?" I asked Mummy and Daddy eagerly.

They both smiled in approval.

"Alright, little Snow Princess," Daddy laughed.

"Get properly dressed and we'll go out together," Mummy said as both she and Daddy left my room.

I jumped out of bed. I went straight to a wardrobe and dug out a pair of green wellie boots, a thick coat and a scarf. I felt such excitement at the prospect of going out to play in that wonderful white stuff.

My eyelids fluttered open. It was still dark and I was still in bed. But then I realized I was lying on top of my blanket. Something else was wrapped around my body though. I reached for the torch I had left on the bedside table. In its light I saw that I was dressed in a thick coat, scarf and boots in bed. I was perturbed.

"You got dressed in your sleep?" the doctor interrupts.

Alisa shakes her head.

"It wasn't me, Doctor," Alisa replies, slightly annoyed.

"It was 6:30am when I woke to find myself in additional winter wear. I didn't attempt to go back to sleep after removing them. My dreams involving the little girl seemed to be affecting me. I went to look out my bedroom window. Snow had started falling again. It filled me with a stronger sense of dread now than it had before. I felt like it was burying my soul.

"The following morning, as I went to throw an empty milk carton into the bin, my eyes fell upon the scrunched up ball of paper I'd thrown in two days ago. Instinctively I fished it out and opened it up again. The uneven writing of 'Izzy' on the crumpled paper was a child's handwriting. Then it hit me. Could 'Izzy' be 'Isabelle' from my dreams? I rushed to my work room. By the drawing board I found the painting I had done in my sleep the day before. The picture of the smiling family of three surrounded by snow seemed to take on a life of its own and suddenly I was afraid to touch it, like it was a cursed object. I focused on the little stick girl in between her taller stick parents on the picture. Then I looked at 'Izzy' written on the crumpled note still in my hand.

"As I fiddled with the lock of a mystery in my thoughts, a dark wave of lethargic heaviness descended upon my eyelids again. Sleep embraced me. In the twilight between reality and dreams, I recall a sense of travelling backwards against forward-moving water currents, like I was being pulled in an unnatural opposition to a natural direction.

"And then I was back there in the snow again, wandering among the icing-capped woodland trees, alone. I listened to my green wellie boots compressing the snow beneath them with every step. The snow-pressing sound made me smile with glee. I held out a gloved hand and collected some of the falling snowflakes. Precious tiny white tears from heaven. There was a clearing in the trees ahead. I made for it. The sight of a vast frozen lake greeted my curious eyes. An explorer's instinct coaxed me into going closer to the icy surface. I imagined I was on the verge of discovering a fantastical ice kingdom. I kneeled by the edge of the mirroring ice and peered down at my reflection. Another long, dark blonde haired, eight-year-old girl stared up at me, wearing the same excited grin on her rosy face as mine. My twin trapped within the ice mirror touched my gloved hand where mine touched hers. I rose to my feet and looked out over

190

the vast area of ice. I wondered if I could walk on it, it looked hard enough. Tentatively, I placed one boot on the ice. It held solid. Then I placed my other boot on it. Again it seemed hard as rock. Daringly, I slowly slid my boots along the ice. Inch by inch, then foot by foot, until I had reached a long distance from the snowy land. I stopped and looked back at the white woods in the distance. Standing there on clear ice, I felt like a princess of the ice. I held out my arms for balance and twirled myself around like an ice skater. I spun myself in faster circles on one boot. I heard a crack. Then another. And another. I looked down to my feet. Lines were branching out from under my boots along the ice. Panic caught in my throat. I cried out for Mummy and Daddy. The ice dipped slightly under my feet. A short, sharp scream escaped my mouth. Then I spotted Mummy and Daddy running onto the snowy shore. Terror gripped their faces as they saw me out here on the icy surface of the lake, far out of reach.

"Mummy, Daddy! Help!" I shouted at the top of my lungs.

"Isabelle! Get off the ice!" screamed Daddy.

"I can't!" I was tearful now. "Please help me!"

The cracks deepened and spread suddenly. The ice beneath me sank down. Another sharp scream of terror escaped my mouth, in unison with the screams of my parents from the shore. I trembled on the unsteady ice and hot tears streamed down my feverish cheeks. I saw Daddy put a foot onto the ice, but there was a snapping noise and he recoiled. They did nothing except stand and look on at me terrified.

"Don't leave me here!" I cried.

A louder cracking filled my ears. Fragile ice gave way under my feet. I fell. From nipping dry cold to sudden stabbing, freezing cold. I sunk, blinded and muffled, a thousand needle-like icicles jabbed into my frail young body.

"I was gasping and shivering uncontrollably. I held myself tighter. My eyes flew open. I realised then I was curled into a ball in a chair by my drawing board, in my work room. I attempted to return myself to a calmer state, but I was shaking vigorously for a good couple of minutes. I had goosebumps all over. I felt so cold. My body settled eventually and I managed to sit up in my chair. My heart skipped a beat when I looked to my drawing board. Something new awaited me on it: another child's painting. This time it depicted a sad-looking little girl in the centre of many crack lines on the far right hand side of the sheet, and on the far left hand side were her parents standing out of reach from her. I touched the image of the little weeping stick girl with tear drops falling from her eyes. I don't know how I was so sure then, but I knew at that moment that Isabelle had never emerged alive from the ice."

"So you believe 'Isabelle' is a victim of hypothermia then?" the doctor asks. He touches his chin thoughtfully.

"Not 'is', 'was'," Alisa corrects. "But that isn't the end of her story."

The doctor raises an eyebrow in puzzlement. Alisa's gaze falls to the polished white floor beneath her feet.

"Doctor, I think sometimes the dead can get second chances at life. Can you imagine the kind of fear and desperation a child would experience as she plunged to a tragic end under ice? Izzy's parents could not save her. She was left out there on the ice. Her parents didn't keep their promise. They left her alone. Izzy was yearning to be saved."

"Snow was falling gently when I went to the window. Even though I was indoors, I couldn't shake the coldness from my body and had pulled on a coat. Deep feelings of sadness and pity were numbing me as I continued to look back at the new painting of the weeping girl standing beyond help in the middle of cracking ice. Then I observed something outside through the window. Through the falling snow, I thought I saw a figure standing on a small frozen pond nearby. Panic gripped me instantly at the sight and an uncontrolled chill spread through my entire body. Didn't that person out there realise how dangerous it was to be walking on ice? I rushed to the door and pushed my feet into a pair of boots. I was out the door in seconds and running toward the frozen pond. As I got closer to it, the person standing on its ice became clearer in my vision. It was a young girl. A young girl with long, dark blonde hair and rosy cheeks. Izzy. Fleeting rational thought told me that I could not possibly be really seeing a girl from my dreams. But there she was, perilously dancing on the ice right before my eyes.

"Izzy! Get off the ice now!" I screamed at her.

The girl stopped twirling and looked straight at me, an innocent curiosity in her wide eyes.

192

"I've seen you before…" Izzy's light voice rang. "You were in my dream..."

"Don't move, Izzy! I'll come and get you!" I shouted.

I took a cautious step onto the ice. Though it did not break under my first step, I sensed it was fragile. I had to get to Izzy though. Another step. Both feet were on the pond ice now. I carefully progressed toward Izzy, one step at a time. Faint cracks sprouted from around my feet when I was half way to her. I looked up to the girl and saw that cracks had appeared underneath her feet too. She looked at me fearfully. The snowflakes landing on her eyelashes were melting into tears that streamed down her rosy cheeks.

"I'm scared," she spoke breathlessly.

"Don't worry, Izzy, I'm coming for you," I tried to reassure her.

The fault lines in the ice spread further as I reached nearer to Izzy, like a ticking time bomb. Finally, I was an arm's length from her. So close. I reached out a hand to her.

"Take my hand!" I instructed.

She looked down at my outstretched hand uncertainly.

"Where's Mummy and Daddy?" she suddenly asked.

I paused for a moment, not sure how to answer.

"*I'm* here for you now, Izzy," I told her gently, "and I promise I won't leave you alone."

A trusting smile emerged on Izzy's rosy face. She lifted her small gloved hand and reached for mine. Centimetres separated us. The ice cracked threateningly beneath us. I willed my arm to stretch further to reach Izzy's hand. Our fingers touched. The cracks underneath me and Izzy branched into each other. With a push forward I grasped the whole of Izzy's small hand. I held onto it tight, determined never to let go. Izzy's hand squeezed mine back with all the need and trust of a dependent child. I pulled the small girl into my protective embrace. For a frozen moment, our eyes connected, our faces locked, our bodies bonded together. We were foreign and familiar, strangers and family to one another at the same time. We were two parts of one. The ice gave way under us. Together we went down into the cold."

"You were the only one in the water when the ambulance came and rescued you, Alisa," the doctor states. "And locals near the pond reported seeing only you walking out onto the ice. There was no little girl."

Alisa remains silent. The doctor thinks she looks tired. He leans forward toward her.

"Alisa, I'm not suggesting that you're intentionally making up your story about this girl you call Izzy. You obviously have been experiencing very vivid dreams."

Alisa seems to ignore the psychiatric doctor's words. She turns back to her earlier *Snow Princess* painting on the table behind her. The doctor watches his patient neatly fold the picture in half, pick up a pen and start writing on the blank back of the paper. He sees her write in curly letters:

To: Izzy

From: Alisa.

She inspects her curly writing. Satisfied that it is neat enough, she picks up the folded painting and holds it out to the doctor.

"Would you pass this to Isabelle when she arrives?" Alisa requests politely.

A puzzled look forms on the doctor's face, but he takes the folded picture and places it on his clipboard.

"Sometimes we first move backwards before we can move forwards in life," Alisa comments. "Old wounds to heal, promises to keep."

The doctor carefully observes Alisa's expressions.

"So have you seen Izzy since falling through the ice?" he inquires.

"She's always close by."

"So where is she now?"

"She'll be along soon, I'm sure. She's a little shy sometimes."

The doctor observes Alisa's head drooping then, as if she is going to sleep.

"Alisa?" he asks in an attempt to gain her attention.

Alisa's eyes close.

"Alisa?" the doctor calls once more, slightly perplexed.

Her eyes open again, a wide and curious look in them. She uncrosses her legs and presses them together instead. She brings her

194

hands up and rubs her arms. Her mouth opens. The light pitch of a young girl's voice emanates from her throat.

"I'm cold," she says softly to a surprised doctor.

Her gaze falls to the doctor's clipboard on his lap. She sees the folded picture with curly writing on it. Her face lights up.

"Is that for me?" she asks with hopeful excitement, pointing at the folded paper.

The doctor stares at the woman speaking with the innocent voice of a young girl in front of him. He manages to offer a kind smile and lifts the folded painting to her.

"Yes. Yes I do believe this is for you."

Lucky Links

by Dianne Stadhams

Link 1

To be or not to be … man it was sure not a snap decision to be a celebrity. It just sorta happened – fame was flung and postcards printed. Camera clicks … my enigmatic smile … my perfect jaw line … my glistening orthodontics … a skin to die for … a torso toned and triggered. Guess that makes this dude an icon … in water and on land?

The game begins.

Decisions … decisions will have to be taken. Mine and yours.

Backwards or forwards? Linear or profile? Who first? What's best? When's right?

I've heard it all in the last few months and then some. Facts and fantasies of the guide as she shepherds the visitors along beside my vantage spot, their eyes agog.

"Do you know his descendents can be traced back 200 million years?"

Dudes the resemblance is not uncertain at any time.

"Did you know his family have been worshipped?"

Fear and respect inspire legends.

"Can you guess his vital statistics?"

The banal assumes elevated status.

The golfers are more pragmatic. "Does he return the golf balls?"

Beware, oh my voyeurs. Myths are rooted in fact. Wisdom has it that my family are guardians of knowledge. Remember to respect that wisdom lest it swallow you whole. Artists have immortalised my family as symbols of sunrise and fertility. My ancestors grabbed the foolish and ate the guilty without a trial.

Because that's what we crocodiles do … and have always done … for the last 200 million years … and are likely to keep doing unless you dumb tourists kill off the planet! And just for the record – I'm called Atta Gatta, I'm four metres long, weigh 100 kilograms, and my best time on land is 17 kilometres an hour. Although I am prepared to admit the chance of my running for any longer than five minutes is extremely unlikely. Celebrity dudes like me prefer to pose. Especially as these marketing-savvy, politically-correct, flora and fauna conscious kebabs on two-legs at the golf course have constructed a palatial lake as my home away from home. "Water hazard or what!" those golfers say as if it was an original joke.

Want to get into the water and say it direct?

Golfers and crocodiles have more in common than you might think. Focus is our motto, timing our creed. A golfer locates the target and fixes his gaze, all the while assessing distance, ground covered and potential obstacles to the flight of that ball. Crocodiles target their location and gaze upon their fix … obstacles can be opportunities. A water hazard to a golfer is but a portent to an Atta Gatta.

Golfers and crocodiles admire strength – the golfers to swing and hit their object of desire, crocodiles to grab theirs and run. And though our tools of the trade, so to speak, are different (golfers use clubs and crocs have teeth), we both know that we have to be precise, measured and accurate, to score. Both of us play against ourselves to win.

Concentrate – one wrong move and it's splash – but not a birdie!

The girl hid in the bushes beside the water hazard, watching for rogue golf balls. Brave of the kid. She couldn't have been more than six years old. Tooth-pick scrappy – limbs with no flesh, tangled curls, big eyes with bigger questions. She carried a chicken with long golden feathers. Tucked under her scrawny shoulder, its staccato-air head pecking a 180 degree trail as she walked. Miserable offering – hardly an hors d'oeuvre! The chicken took one look at my magnificent fangs and screeched chicken-shit prayers.

Hey feather-brain, the gods are off duty.

The kid didn't offer me the bird. She stroked its crested crown and gently massaged its trembling wattle. She lifted its wing and nudged its head under before folding the wing over. A sort of bird brain chicken that lost its head but saved its beak. I liked that. Showed respect ... even if I wasn't going to get a chicken wing bite ... so to speak.

The girl rocked the chicken. It went silent. So did she. But her eyes stayed fixed on mine. I blinked. Let her know I was watching ... and waiting. She blinked back. The chicken kept swinging.
Check, honey, your move.

Crocodile chess is not a game for an amateur. Human brains may be larger and more complex. But we crocs have patience evolved over mega-time ... DNA coded ... watch and wait ... humans become careless. Dangle a limb over the side of a boat to cool in the water. Take your eye of the ball. Forget to check behind you.
Patience is the patron saint of reptiles.

The girl moves closer. The chicken remains silent. I blink – fast.
My move.
She winks – slowly.
Her move.
I leave the starter block. The jaws are tight. I roll twice in the water. Marinated chick-kid equals check-mate!
Crocodile tears you call them. Me I put them down to indigestion. Feathers and femurs are an eclectic starter. What's that adage? A bird in the bush is worth two ... *Chomp, chomp. Game over?*

"Knock, knock."
"Who's there?" asks a golfer.
"Chicken," says one.
"Chicken who?" says the other.
The golfer who lost his ball is convinced it's not in the water. He heads towards the bushes.
New game started.
"Chick-en the bushes," says the golfer. They laugh.
Pawn to king dude.
A celebrity croc won't look a gift horse in the mouth.
Take-away to rook.
Food parcel to check mate. Main course coming up.
Checkmate ... a hole in one you might say!

198

A month later the game begins … again.

Blink … blink … celebrity steps.

Media mayhem … crowds coo approval … the current trophy girlfriend of the celebrity golfer pirouettes … a clapping chorus … twinkle toes on show … stiletto action … summer shoes …

"How was it for you?" the television presenter starts.

"Long story," the golfer begins with a smile.

"Not for the crocodile it wasn't," says the presenter.

"The earth moved … for us both," says the golfer.

The ghost of a laugh.

Shoes are to die for.

"I got lucky … no apology," nods the golfer.

"Golf really is your lifeline."

"It pays for the souvenirs," the golfer says, smiling at the heels.

"A nine iron used?" says the presenter.

"Not a conscious choice. It was the club I had in my hand. I hit the croc right between the eyes – six or seven times. Ugly experience," explained the golfer.

"What a reminder!" says the presenter looking at the shoes.

"My woman wears my trophy – the best pair of crocodile skin shoes this side of the water hazard," the golfer replies.

Walk tall honey … your shoes move my spirit … crocodile fashion.

Snap … the trophy stumbles … her foot buckles … the heel cracks…

Crocodile tears. Poseur fears.

The challenges remain for crocodiles and golfers. Will I, Atta Gatta shoes, re-incarnated, keep walking? Will he choose new prey? Will he hunt for beast or beauty?

~~~

Link 2

"We make the goodest of good flip-flops[1] sir. Best in village, the bestest of all villages in this area," Urday's boss said to the European visitors. "Time to see best factory."

The foreigners nodded. One checked his watch. The boss pointed to Urday. The boy stepped forward and spoke parrot-perfect English, hand-crossed with a large smile.

"We make good flip-flops from dead tyres," Urday recited.

"Dead?" said one of the men.

"No can use no more," explained Urday's boss. "Tyre no good to car, truck, tractor. No groove left. Too dangerous keep on car. Take tyre off car. Put dead tyre in dump at end of village. Cart dead tyre to here factory. Him wash tyre. Them cut tyre into bits. Me work on bits – punch holes for straps."

"Ah, sustainable development," said another of the men, "Recycling!"

"No, wrong," said the boss. "We no use bicycles. Tyre from bicycle too skinny – no good. Break easy."

"I think we're talking at cross purposes," said one of the visitors to another. "Same thing – dead tyres to cheap sandals equals recycling. Fairtrade footwear we can all agree?"

"Good sound bite," said another of the foreigners and smiled. All the visitors nodded and smiled. The factory boss, the deputy boss and the floor manager boss smiled too.

Urday smiled. If the foreigners were happy, his bosses would be happy. He was fine. *Lucky day – still got my job!*

"What is this boy's name?" asked one of the visitors.

"Urday," whispered the floor manager boss to the deputy boss who spoke to the factory boss.

"Urday," said the boss to the foreigners.

"Urday," said the foreigners to the boy.

---

[1] Flip-flops are a very basic type of footwear — essentially a thin rubber sole with two simple straps running in a Y from the sides of the foot to the join between the big toe and next toe. Wikipedia 2009

The factory boss spoke to the deputy boss who turned to the floor manager boss and whispered an order to the boy.

"Urday," shouted Urday, smiling at them again.

Why did the foreign men want to know his name? Was his boss going to be angry that he had spoken directly to the men?

"How old is Urday?" asked one of the men.

"Sixteen," whispered the floor manager boss to the deputy boss who spoke to the factory boss.

"Sixteen," said the boss to the white men.

"Sixteen?" said one of the men.

"Sixteen!" said another, "Do pigs fly?"

Is the white man mad? Pigs fly?

"He's very small for his age," added the boss to the white men.

"We have a very strong policy on child labour," said another of the foreigners. "Please ask the boy to tell us directly how old he is."

The boss spoke to his deputy, but not in English. The deputy boss spoke to his factory manager, but not in English or the language used by the boss to his deputy. Finally the factory manager called out to the boy in yet another tongue.

Urday breathed deeply and spoke clearly in his best English. "Sixteen," he said proudly, "all healthy."

Everyone smiled at each other.

Why did the white men want to know how many sisters he had?

Urday smiled at everyone.

Would they ask about his brothers?

There were six of them if you only counted the live ones. Ten if you included the ones in the cemetery.

"Please ask Urday how may hours he works each day?" asked a foreigner.

The floor manager boss frowned. He turned to his deputy and translated. His deputy turned to the factory boss and spoke in another dialect.

"Eight," said Urday, puzzled.

Why am I asked how long I spend away from the factory each day?

Urday did not smile any more.

Do they think I am lazy working sixteen hours?

201

What will happen to my family if I lose my job, Urday wondered.

These questions were not on the script that the boss had made him learn.

The foreign buyers began again.

Strange questions!

Why do they want to know how many days that I don't come to the factory?

What do I say are my favourite days? All days are the same – work, work, work!

What is this game?

The foreigners beckoned Urday as they spoke amongst themselves. The factory boss did not look pleased. He shouted to Urday to remember the rules.

Like I'd forget! I need this job.

" It's a fair trade set up alright," one of the visitors said.

"The boy says himself he's sixteen years old, healthy, works eight hours a day and has two days off," said another.

"And we're here – seen the factory. It's light. There's clean air. Food is provided," said another.

Urday stood silent and politely stared at the ground.

The foreigners had it all wrong!

"This is a good place to take the pictures, with him – Urday – you think?" said one of the men.

"Potential face for the publicity campaign back home?" another asked.

The factory manager took Urday to the side while the foreigners met with the factory boss and his deputy.

"Will you tell the big boss man that them foreigners got the wrong information?" asked Urday.

"You want your job, boy?" replied the manager.

Urday went silent. The bosses and the foreigners talked and talked. Urday stayed silent. He was confused. Finally the big boss man clapped his hands together and everyone cheered.

The foreigners shook hands with all the bosses.

"Time is money – precious," said one.

"We need to head off to the golf course," said another.

"Ah fair trade and good golf – perfect day," said the boss.

All the foreigners laughed. The factory boss escorted them to his Mercedes. All the workers waved farewell. Just like the rehearsal!

Urday was devastated.

"What went wrong?" he asked the floor manager. The man shook his head but said nothing. He pointed towards the door.

Unlucky day – there goes my job.

Urday walked out of the office, across the yard, out the gate and down the hill, turning right at the bottom. He walked under the corrugated tin lean-to and sat on the ground. His punch lay beside the rubber straps just as he had left them.

"How go?" asked one of the other boys.

"Maybe no good," said Urday, "The men from Europe not buy."

"Same old, same old, happens every year," said another boy. "Big pretend game. Them bosses don't want to show foreigners our real factory, real workers."

"You think they will buy big order?" asked Urday.

Hey, they ask questions about family?"

"Yes, " said Urday. "But they take out no flip-flops."

"The boss sweet talk after. They buy. Big time. Me get paid. You get paid," explained the boy. "Boss and buyers go play golf?"

Urday nodded.

"Good sign."

"What you learn?" asked another boy.

"Strange stuff," said Urday, "Mystery talk. Foreigners think pigs fly. And foreign money is called time."

"Weird, hey Urday? You got to wonder about those other places."

"The teacher show books with pigs standing on the ground," said Urday.

"Sure," said the boy," But there are no pigs in our village. So what does that teacher really know?"

"Last year them foreigners said that money can buy anything where they come from," said a boy.

"All that money-time, flying pigs," said Urday. "Why do they visit here to buy dead tyre shoes to wear?"

All the boy workers agreed that away from home must be a strange place to go.

"I want to be a tourist when I grow up," said Urday, "Eat and drink all day. Travel the world, play, have fun, see flying pigs."

"You going to wear flip-flops?" they laughed.

"Fingers crossed," agreed Urday, "my flip-flops will fly."

~~~

Link 3

I hate birthdays.

In my family a birthday is a misnomer for a 'dead-darling' day. Whatever happens to other people on their birthdays doesn't work for us. We get a kind of upside down, inside out, back to front, reverse celebration. In my family when it's your time to have a birthday you lie down with cloves of garlic nailed to the bed, a fetish around your ankle and fingers crossed not to sleep … until it's all over … one way or the other.

"Garlic on the bed head? What next – elephant dung under the pillow?" my pa mocked on the eve of his 45th. He ordered my ma to remove the protection. My pa didn't wake up. "He's dead darling," said my ma.

And not just my pa. My uncle died on his birthday – bitten by a snake. My first aunt got out of bed, ate her birthday breakfast with an up-yours-darling smile … and fell sideways off the chair. They said she was dead before she hit the floor. The celebrations were cancelled. My ma said we could use my aunt's birthday cake for the funeral. But it took 60 hours from birthday party to burial pit. The cake got weevils. Nobody ate it. Ma fed the remains, weevils and all, to the hens. Their chicks were born with extra length feathers and super-wart wattles.

I could keep going as fifteen of my close family have departed this world on those bad days, their dead-darling days. My theory is that our family are mutants... with a genetic trigger alarmed for birthdays!

But this story is not about my family history and its genetic dysfunction. It's about the big question – luck. A girl or a boy – who is the luckier? When a girl is born the old men in the village say to the father "Better luck next time!" My ma says to the fathers, "You are a lucky one. A daughter will be there to hold your hand when you die."

And so it starts with my sister's sixth birthday. Her best present was a pet chicken with long golden feathers... and a red wattle with so many purple warts it was impossible to agree on the total. It was one supreme-ugly bird but she loved it on sight. Personally I would have denied ownership of something so hideous. But I digress – a birthday present is a gift after all.

Party games like *Snap* and *I Spy* take on a whole new meaning when your sister gets eaten by a crocodile. The crocodile that lived in the water hazard on the nearby golf course got lucky with the chicken (a boy) and my sister (a girl … obviously). We don't know if it was a boy or a girl crocodile. It seemed to me that the crocodile scored top points with a double whammy birthday deal.

Eat one, get one free.

Nobody ate anything that day or at her departed-day ceremony. I guess there is no advantage in being a girl or a boy with a crocodile around.

I watched the grab and gobble fiasco from up in the tree behind the bushes next to the water hazard. It was my first day of wearing the hijab. I was twelve years, three months and six days old.

"Today is your first-fortune day," my ma had said when she gave it to me to wear. "You are now a woman."

"Welcome," ma's friends said.

Welcome? Worry is more like it! What if there is a connection between first-fortune and dead-darling days?

In DBH (days before hijab) I could climb a tree before my sister could count to ten. I always beat Urday. Urday says it's luck. But that's just Urday acting like he isn't bothered. Or trying to act chilled. Because Urday and me both know I am the better tree climber ... and runner ... and jumper-over-fences. Probably I am better than Urday at everything from school to sport. Which has to be more than luck as Urday is eight months, four days and fifty-eight minutes older than me. He is also three hands-stretched-open taller. Urday and me have been friends since my ma and his rendezvoused beside the river with the other women in the village to wash clothes. Us turbo-charged, grubby kids went too. Fences and trees were our first challenges. The boys were fast but clumsy with bravado. The girls cautiously tottered in a bid for freedom. It was not luckier to be a boy or a girl on the move as your ma always caught you before it got really interesting. But Urday and me learnt that if you waited for a brother or sister to head off first, there was a degree of half luck as your ma chased a sibling before she got round to you.

And so I worked out that girls could create their own luck, whatever those old men said. But DWH (days with hijab) changed the odds. Tree climbing, running and jumping all took longer. And that's after you work out what you can see and where to run and jump – blinkered by a hijab!

When Urday turned up at my house wearing a hoodie my ma was unhappy.
  "A hoodie," she said.
  "Latest – like it?" Urday said to my ma.
  "No," said my ma. "What is wrong with what your father wears?"
  She might be a woman but she's definitely not subtle.
  "Time for change," said Urday.
  "Change does not bring luck," argues my ma.
  "Maybe ..." says Urday.
  Yeah, whatever, like they're ever going to agree.
  "Today is a day to take care and give thanks for our blessings. Today I have one daughter with six years of life behind her, and thanks be to Allah, six and sixty ahead."
  "Happy birthday, little one," smiles Urday.
  My sister shows him her present.

206

"Am I invited for a chicken dinner?" he asks her. She shrieks and places the chicken under her arm. We all laugh. My sister knows Urday is joking.

"Today my other daughter is also blessed. Today she starts to wear her hijab," my ma announces proudly.

Urday looks at me and winks when he knows my ma is not looking. That wink is a challenge. He knows my luck has changed. The handicap has been granted.

"Hijabs can not run as fast as hoodies," he says.

My sister starts to run. Urday and I chase her. The game has started.

"That's hoodie hoodoo," I shout.

My ma calls in alarm, "Hijabs behave like women. Women walk."

So what about hoodies ma? Do they have boundaries?

In DBH I might have been able to scramble down the tree and run faster to beat Urday to the crocodile. But that day I learnt that a hijab is not less lucky than a hoodie. For Urday got to the reptile before me. He ripped off his hoodie. He crept forward and threw it over to blind the beast. Confused, the croc paused and then tossed it off. I threw Urday my hijab. He lunged at the beast and lassoed the jaws with the sleeves of his hoodie and bound them as tightly as he could. The crocodile lashed its tail, trying to smack Urday sideways. But he was quick like a flea and hung onto the tail – this way and that way. I screamed. Urday hollered. Golfers – white foreign men – appeared, startled by the commotion.

"Bloody hell," said one of them.

"Mobile, give me the mobile phone," screamed another.

A third golfer ran towards Urday and the crocodile with his golf club. He smashed it down on the beast's head. Stunned, the crocodile froze for a moment.

"Geez … it's got a bit of flesh in its teeth," shrieked a fourth golfer.

That's my sister you're talking about.

One man threw a golf club at Urday. He caught it. Between them they pulverized the croc's brain. The beast shuddered and stopped moving. What a scene – blood and brains splattered everywhere – on the ground, the golf clubs, the hoodie and my hijab.

They saved Urday but not my sister and her chicken. I told Urday later that the best luck a hoodie or a hijab could have was a golf club. Especially on a dead-darling day!

"You two were damn brave," said one of the golfers.

"Or bloody mad," said another, "Weren't you scared?"

Urday stared ... and said nothing. I looked at Urday and then studied the ground.

Foreigners can be just as scary as crocodiles.

"Hey, isn't that the kid from the factory?"

"Don't know," replied one of the men, "Hard to tell. These kids all look the same."

"Urday," began the other. "Hey kid, is your name Urday?"

Urday looked at the man. The golfer repeated Urday's name, wildly flinging his hands between the two of them. Urday put him out of his misery and nodded. The men walked towards us. They hugged Urday, saying his name over and over. They turned towards me. Urday jumped in front of me, preventing them from touching. Ma would have been proud. I felt lucky that their unclean hands had not defiled me. What penance I would have had to pay – a first-fortune day with my honour questioned?

"Hey Urday, you and your friend play golf?"

As if ... you have to pay to play that game.

"You've got a great swing Urday," one said. "You're a natural – calm and strong."

"We should recommend the kid for the publicity campaign," said a golfer.

"He'd get paid a shed load more than making those flip-flops."

The men outlined their ideas to Urday in theatrical pidgin-English. I asked Urday why he didn't tell them he had won second prize in English for the school. He told me he would lose his job if he spoke English to foreign visitors.

"Stay silent," he said in our village language. "Be strong."

My ma says the strength of women is on their lips and in their ears.

"Flip-flops fly?" asked Urday.

"It's your lucky day mate," said the golfer.

So maybe the boy in the hoodie got lucky. But it was my hijab they use to wrap the souvenir – crocodile skin.

~~~

Link 4

There are worse stains than carrot juice splattered across a beige, raw silk blouson. Double strength cappuccino cascading down a white linen shirt is one.

When Marguerite and Sidney collided in the organic café on the corner of Main Street, the owner of the neighbouring dry cleaners knew his prayer for the day had been answered.

"Oh God, I'm so sorry," he said.

"It was soooo my fault," she said.

"For the floor art," said the manager, presenting wet cloths and complimentary refills.

Marguerite silently mourned. Was the stained jacket an omen?

"Impressionism gone wrong," scowled a waitress arriving with paper towels, a bucket and mop.

Tepid toe squelch prompted Sidney to drop some of the paper towels to his splattered feet.

"Are those shoes what I think they are?" he asked.

"Long story," Marguerite replied.

"Not for the crocodile it wasn't!"

"Would you believe the skins came courtesy of an ex ... who killed the crocodile ... that tried to eat him ... on a golf course ... in Africa?"

Sidney raised his eyebrows. "You with him?"

"No," she said, "I don't do travel ... no time... out of luck."

"Boyfriend ever consider the croc might have been hungry?"

"Reptiles and you do deep and meaningful?" she asked.

"I can see why you dropped the boyfriend."

"At least the skin wasn't wasted."

"I prefer flip-flops ... especially these gourmet enhanced ones," he said.

And so the meeting began. It was to be a joint project between two organisations from different ends of the spectrum. He crusaded. She campaigned. They both cared. He raised funds for a non-governmental organisation. It supported sustainable development that linked poor communities to global markets. She managed advertising strategies for FMG^2 retailers. They both worked too long, played too little and loved even less. It was a collision of collective enthusiasm for profit meets process. With all the frisson-sparked collaboration between polar-opposite consciences!

"Who have you chosen as the face for the advertisements?" she asked.

"His name is Urday," he said.

"Background?"

"He's sixteen."

"Photogenic?"

"Aren't they all at that age?"

"Depends – cherub or toe-rag? Angel or demon?"

"Not my area. I just want him to have a future."

"Speak any English?"

"Not really," he said, "but they worked with translators to make sure they got the truth."

"Whose version?"

"The version for our vision," he said.

"Ouch – sounds like a strap line," she laughed.

"I try hard. Our organisation's done lots of advertising campaigns for fair-trade products," he replied. "Urday works for a local entrepreneur. Makes designer flip-flops from re-cycled tyres."

"Sounds like an oxymoron," she said.

"You make me feel like one!" he replied. "Well okay, they're flip-flops. Made from old rubber. The local women hand paint the footwear. Designers in the West flog the finished product for inflated prices. Shorthand – they're designer flip-flops."

"That what you call those?" she said, surveying his footwear complete with sticky coffee-daubs.

They smiled at each other.

He warmed … a lot.

She melted … a little.

---

^{2} Fast moving consumer goods

"Urday's entrepreneur got started through a micro-finance project," he began.

"Your organisation fund it?"

"We channelled the money. Seed funding was a corporate donation from a multi-national."

"Who made their money how?" she asked.

"The parent company has lots of tentacles. Mainly known for its involvement with petro-chemicals."

"Just gets better," she said. "Any recent scandals?"

"You mean like oil spills, environmental stuff ups?" he asked.

"Wider than that – worker exploitation, women's rights in the workforce, child labour issues, health and safety? Environmental scandals are only one small concern in the package."

"Not to our knowledge."

"We'll still have to down-play that petro-chemical aspect," she said.

"The company say they're giving something back," he said.

"That has to stand up against a charge of grabbing the cake first, offering crumbs later," she replied.

"At least the company's at the table. Dialogue and action offer hope."

"You always dine with the devil?" she asked.

"That's good from someone with crocodile feet!"

She blushed ... a little.

He bristled ... a lot.

"We believe the boy Urday is healthy, works in light and well ventilated conditions; gets a fair wage for fair work," Sidney said.

"Who carried out the ethical checks?" Marguerite asked.

"Independent regulators," he said. "Using a quantifiable matrix on sustainable social economics. Ticks in the all the right boxes."

"When were the checks carried out?"

"The regulators went at the same time as the buyers," he explained.

"Tax efficient?"

"Hey I'm supposed to be the cynic," he replied.

"Did I say do-gooders had to be naïve?"

He smiled ... to himself.

She smiled ... to herself.

They looked at each other and smiled ... a lot.

"Okay so we have the face for the fair trade campaign. Your organisation is satisfied that Urday is bone fide. I'm sure we can mount a major promotion within the budget to fit the target markets. But ..."

"I knew there'd be a but," he said.

"But I think it would be better to have two faces. Male and female. Fits both genders. Promotes equality ... in addition to the primary objectives," she said.

"Shouldn't be a problem. I'm sure Urday has a sister or cousin or female friend that's photogenic."

"What about trans-cultural? To make it appeal to our politically correct sensitivities?" she said.

"Like you mean he wears a hoodie and she's in a hijab?"

"Not bad thinking," she said, "Might be a possibility. I'll need to do some market research on the possible impacts – positive and negative."

"How long will it take to finalise the campaign plan?" he asked.

"I should have a presentation ready with mock-up visuals and graphics within ten days," she said. "Shall we co-ordinate our diaries to see when both organisations can schedule a joint meeting? Your office or mine?"

"We do fair trade coffee," he winked.

"Lucky me," she replied.

When the date and presentation agenda were agreed, Sidney said, "You will use a local photographer?"

"Yes, of course," she said. "Our agency holds a data bank. It shouldn't be a problem to locate a suitable candidate. It also gives the photographer more access to western markets for his images."

"We could always travel there together – for the photo shoot. Might help if you saw the product first-hand?" he said.

She tensed.

Oh no ... this was way too much ... how to play this one?

He was puzzled.

Why had she changed? Perhaps the not-so-subtle innuendo was way too explicit?

212

He noticed how she gripped her hands – the knuckles were white.

She saw him notice.

They sat in silence.

"You know whether our boy Urday can customize those flip-flops?" she asked.

"Dare I ask why?"

"I hear crocodile trim is all the rage this season," she said.

"Isn't this where we started?" he asked. "You like flying close to the edge?"

"You've made the link!" she said.

"Sorry, I'm lost."

"Flying. Can't do the flying stuff with you," she said.

"Chicken!" he replied. "I'm perfectly safe to travel with … seriously, I am. This banter's just a game … mostly. The work is for real … not a problem."

"It is a real problem. Not flirting. Flying, I mean. I'm scared of flying."

"True?"

"Read the books, taken the pills, said the prayers," she said.

"And?" he asked.

"And … nothing works," she replied.

"You know fear and sexuality are linked?"

"That's the worst chat-up line I've ever heard," she said. "Do you know that vomit and vertigo link with no way José?"

"A compromise? If you can't go to Urday, maybe he can come to us?"

He offered a solution … at least.

She reflected on it … at length.

They nodded in harmony … at last.

"Luck can link a dream to reality," he said.

"Maybe," she smiled. "So what are my chances of getting another carrot juice undiluted with cappuccino?"

Earlyworks Press

Putting writers on the road to success

Earlyworks Press produces three or more anthologies a year, based on the Open Competitions on the website. All the competitions offer cash prizes and publication opportunities – but exactly how many anthologies we publish, and whether we publish ten or twenty or more authors from each competition – depends entirely on how many of the shortlist we consider of publishable quality, so appearance in an Earlyworks Press anthology really is a feather in the cap (or points on the CV) of the author. The anthologies are promoted online and at literary events and libraries around the country, giving winning writers a chance to profit from their success.

If you would like to sample more prize-winners, please visit the **Publications Page** on the website. We usually have some discounted or secondhand books available as well as new ones so if you are a reader hungry for new stories and poetry, or a writer researching the market, you don't have to spend a fortune to find out what a winning story or poem looks like.

If you would like to see your work in one of our anthologies, then visit the **Competitions Page** and sign up for our e-newsletter, or send an SAE to the address below for details of our club, events and competitions.

Earlyworks Press
Creative Media Centre
45 Robertson Street
Hastings
Sussex TN34 1HL
UK

www.earlyworkspress.co.uk

Publishing Poetry, Literary & Genre Fiction